THE VAMPIRE'S SALVATION

THE ELITE: BOOK 3

STACY RUSH

Copyright © 2024 Stacy Rush.

All rights reserved. No part of this book may be reproduced, stored, or transmitted by any means—whether auditory, graphic, mechanical, or electronic—without written permission of both publisher and author, except in the case of brief excerpts used in critical articles and reviews. Unauthorized reproduction of any part of this work is illegal and is punishable by law.

ISBN: 979-8-89419-244-4 (sc)
ISBN: 979-8-89419-245-1 (hc)
ISBN: 979-8-89419-246-8 (e)

Because of the dynamic nature of the Internet, any web addresses or links contained in this book may have changed since publication and may no longer be valid. The views expressed in this work are solely those of the author and do not necessarily reflect the views of the publisher, and the publisher hereby disclaims any responsibility for them.

One Galleria Blvd., Suite 1900, Metairie, LA 70001
(504) 702-6708

PROLOGUE

TAVEN

I have lived the last three hundred years as a vampire, trying to find my way in the world, with the card that life has dealt me. As a boy, my father would beat me senseless and I always vowed that I would never turn out like him, but some days I wonder if I did just that. Not that I have gone around beating people up, but deep down I have this constant urge to inflict pain.

I was turned at the age of thirty, by a female vamp who fancied herself in love with me. At the time, I didn't know she was a vampire, and to be honest, I was so entranced with her beauty, I had not noticed anything out of the ordinary with her. Mary-Beth was her name, but everybody called her Beth. We spent every day, for a whole two weeks with each other and not once did I feel the need to inflict any kind of pain. I thought she was my future, the one who would keep the demon at bay, but it was not to be. It happened the night that she finally decided to give herself to me. I like to believe that it was an accident that happened in the throes of ecstasy, but I could never find out the truth, because upon awakening, Beth was gone, never to be seen again. I struggled with my new life and with the disappearance of the one person that held it back, my urges came back, stronger than ever.

Over a century ago, I found an outlet to this sickness that I have. I stumbled upon a club one evening, while out drinking with some friends. It was dark and tantalizing, the perfect combination for my own desires. My friends weren't impressed with the scene and left shortly after our arrival, but I stayed, transfixed on the couple who were performing out on the floor.

In that day and age, there really wasn't a name for it, but it was frowned upon and so it was done in secret. People didn't understand the true meaning behind the acts, and at first, I didn't know either. Don't get me wrong, I am not one to take it to the extreme like others do, but the life does fascinate me. I began finding women that were masochists, so I could sate the cravings that I had from time to time, but they all wanted to take it further and be my submissive, my slave. I wasn't looking for that kind of commitment and so I would move on from them.

It's been almost a full century now, that I left that lifestyle behind and became an Elite. I had run into an older vampire, Miguel, who told me that he was a protector of the innocent and that he needed to train more men to take on more territories. He wanted to try and balance out the good and evil of the world and once he informed me of what it entailed, I was happy to have him take me under his wing and train me as well.

I was with Miguel for a full year before going off on my own. He was a very private guy, still is, never telling me his story on how he came to be. I lost contact with him a few years later. Not knowing if he was dead or alive, I began his teachings with others, Raven being my first student. We started to grow in numbers, some moved on to form their own groups and some stayed with me, these men are my true brothers, I would die for each one of them.

Now a new obstacle lies before me. One with long blonde hair and eyes, the color of the deep blue ocean. Liz is a petite little thing, maybe five feet two inches in height to my seven feet. I am told that

I am a big mother fucker, which helps tremendously when trying to intimidate people, except for Liz. She is a feisty one and stands her ground every time.

I was awestruck the first time I laid eyes on her, walking down the aisle at Jax and Cassie's wedding, causing me to fumble a little beside Duncan. It wasn't until she got to the end and turned to take her place, that a light breeze swept by and with it, the scent of sweet, warm apples drifted over to me. I knew right then what she was, and my heart stopped, but for a moment, before beating again. At the same time, it scared the shit out of me. She looked like the type of woman who is shy and also well reserved. I just kept thinking how it would be between the two of us and in the end, I thought it best to just leave her be. I didn't want to dirty her with my insatiable habits.

She is now living at the Compound with her two little boys for the time being, until we are able to finish off Mika. He is the head of the Hunters, a group who has vowed to take out vampires because they do not understand who we are. They have just heard the stories and that is a good enough excuse to do it. Liz was targeted a while back and was even shot the night of the wedding and so she is here under our protection.

It continues to get harder to stay away from her and to be perfectly honest, I don't want to. I just know that for her benefit, I need to. Whenever I think of my golden- haired beauty, the song 'Demons' plays over and over in my head. Yeah, the song describes my situation perfectly. The chorus of *"When you feel my heat, Look into my eyes, It's where my demons hide…"* and so on. It's like a broken record, playing constantly. How in the world can fate do this to me? Does it not care for Liz's well-being? How do I stay away from the one woman that I want most in this world?

ONE

LIZ

It's been months now that my boys and I have been here at the Compound, waiting until the day that the Elite are finally able to take out Mika and his group of men who are determined to get rid of the Elite. I wish it would happen soon, I have already had to give up my rental house, because there is no sense in paying rent for a place that I'm not living in. Then there is the factor of my two boys, Jack and Nate. I can see that they love being around the guys, which are good role models for them, but there is just something that keeps nagging me about the whole Elite. I can't put my finger on it, but there are times when things seem so hushed, that it gives me room to pause and wonder what secret is being kept within the very walls that my boys and I reside in.

Jack is ten and is at the age where he feels like he is old enough to train so he can become a warrior just like the others and Nate, he is seven and is the most impressionable boy I know. Being so trusting and innocent, he is susceptible to being hurt once we leave here. I am between a rock and a hard place. Do I stay and risk my boys being heartbroken after forming a strong bond with these men or do I go and hope that we will be safe, that Mika has forgotten all about us?

As much as I would like to say that my concerns are only about my boys, I need to confess that there is one other concern. Taven. The longer that we stay here, the more time I spend with the head of the Elite's and with my track record with men, I don't know if it's a good thing or a bad thing. I mean, Taven is a great guy and very gracious towards me and my boys, but I don't know what his feelings are for me. He is hot one day and cold the next. It's like he is a Bipolar Sex God! His seven-foot-tall height with a massive, muscular chest, yes, I have seen him in training, which usually sends me to my room to ease the build-up of pressure that the sight of him causes each time. He used to have thick light brown hair with natural golden highlights that hung a little past his shoulders but was always in a ponytail at his nape. He's cut it since I first met him, though, and now he wears it short. His eyes are a little shade lighter than my own, but still reminds me of the ocean.

We have become good friends these past few months and most of the time, on his good days, he is very attentive with me. I wish I could learn more about him, about his past, but he remains bottled up when I try asking him, which makes me wonder if he is hiding something. I understand that people have their own skeletons that they like to keep hidden, but after my last boyfriend, I had decided that from then on, I would need to know everything about the guy that I have coming into my children's lives.

My husband, the boys' father, was killed by a drunk driver when Nate was just a toddler and the only guy figure that he has ever had in his life is my ex-boyfriend, Dean. I met him a year after my husband's death and a few months later, we moved in with him. He was actually a pretty good guy, at first. The first year, he would always take me and the boys out places and spend a lot of time being a great role model for them, but then something changed in the second year and things started to go downhill. He was an accountant and usually never worked late hours except for during tax season, but he started coming home later and later smelling like alcohol and a few times like perfume. We began arguing more, which eventually turned into Dean throwing things around the house. He never once laid a hand on me and the boys though and I thank God for that.

The last straw was when he had a few friends stop over after the boys were in bed and instead of playing cards like they usually did, they decided to turn their attention on me. Poking and prodding me, grabbing my ass and breasts, and Dean did nothing but sit there and laugh. He then snatched me around the waist and sat me on his lap, telling me to stay there while they played cards. One of his friends pulled out a syringe and proceeded to inject himself with some kind of drug. I excused myself to go to the restroom and Dean let me go, but when I returned, he was shooting up himself.

I remember locking myself in the bedroom for the duration of the night. He had come knocking at the door informing me that his friends wanted to try a piece of me, causing me to cringe and pray that they would leave. The next morning after Dean left for work, I called into my own work at the local paper, letting them know that I was taking a sick day. I then hurried and packed up mine and my boys' things and moved out before he came home from work. That was almost two years ago, and I have never heard from him since.

There is a knock at my door, and I know right away that it's Taven on the other side. It's an occurrence that happens every morning during the week at this time. Ever since the threat, he has taken it upon himself to drive me to and from work every day. It is the only way that they will allow me out of the Compound until the threat is eliminated. I call out for Taven to come in as I am putting the last touches of my make-up on.

"Good morning, are you about ready?" He asks as he looks me up and down, his eyes landing on mine through the mirror.

"Yep, just about. I will need to run to the kitchen on our way out and grab one of Max's muffins for breakfast."

"No need, I stopped on the way myself." He holds up the blueberry muffin and gives me the smile that always makes me want to drop my pants for him.

"Thank you, but you don't always need to do everything for me." I chide.

"I was walking by the kitchen anyway and I know your routine. It really isn't a big deal. Besides, I like doing things for you."

"Well, thank you, I appreciate it very much." Looks like it's going to be one of his good days, I think to myself.

We walk to his SUV, and he opens the door for me. I climb in and he reaches across me as he clicks the seatbelt into place. He knows how I always forget to buckle up, so this is yet another thing that he does for me. Our eyes meet for a brief moment as he pulls away and I swear there is something there, as if he is struggling with something, then it's gone, and he is closing my door.

Taven pulls up to my work and turns to me, "I was thinking. How would you and the boys like to go for Pizza tonight? You know, get out of the Compound for a bit."

"That would be wonderful, but only if you let me pay for it. You do so much for us already, it's the least that I can do!"

"You do know that I can eat a large pizza all by myself, right?" He chuckles.

"Yes, I do. I have seen you in action. I don't know how you keep your body looking so good with as much as you eat!" I can feel my face flush after I realize what I just said. Taven looks at me with what looks like hunger in his eyes, but quickly loses the look and smirks at me.

"So, you think I have a good-looking body, do you?"

"You know perfectly well that you do, and I would be blind not to notice. No need to get a big head over it!" He gives a hearty laugh and then I realize again, what I had just said, "God, you are such a pervert sometimes!" I can't help to join in and laugh as I shake my head.

"I love messing with you and seeing you blush! Go, get out of here before you are late for work." He urges me.

"What are they going to do, spank me?" I cock a brow at him. The look of hunger comes back to his eyes.

"I would if I was your boss." He says it so matter of fact, that I can't tell if he is joking or not.

"Well, I guess I am lucky that you aren't my boss." I joke and lean in to kiss his cheek, "Thank you Taven, for everything you do for me." I quickly jump out and hurry into the building.

My thoughts are filled with Taven all day while at work. Every time my thoughts shift to him, I would mess up on what I was working on and have to start again. "Get your head in the game, Liz!" I chastise to myself multiple times. Before I know it, it's five o'clock and time to head out.

Taven is waiting for me in the usual spot, but this time, the boys are with him, excitement etched on their faces, "What's with all the smiles?" I turn in my seat and smile myself.

"Taven is taking us bowling!" Nate cheers.

"I thought it was just pizza?" I turn towards Taven.

"I figured the boys could let off some steam while we are out. The bowling alley has pizza. You can pay for the pizza and the bowling will be my treat." He winks at the stern look I give him.

"You just had to find a way around me paying for tonight, didn't you?" I grin.

"Hey, I am the man and I asked you guys out, so I should be paying for all of it."

"Whatever, I am done arguing with you over it. If it means that much to you, then you can pay for it. Happy now?" I chuckle.

"Extremely. You should know Liz; I always get my way when I want something."

"Do you now? Well, we will have to see about that." I challenge him.

"Oh? Do you have something in mind?"

"Not particularly, but I am sure something will come up in the future." I smile smugly at him as he pulls into the parking spot.

To everyone else, we look like a nice happy family walking in, especially when Taven has his hand on my lower back, leading me in, but I am here trying to sort out all of these feelings that this man next to me has me feeling, and there is nothing happy about that.

TAVEN

As I lead Liz and the boys into the bowling alley, I rest my hand on her lower back, not really sure why, but I do. Part of her shirt has slipped up and my finger can feel the smoothness of her creamy skin beneath it. My thoughts go to a darker place, where she is in my room, naked and at my mercy. I feel my arousal and curse to myself. Once we are in the building, I excuse myself to the restroom. Looking at myself in the mirror, I can see the blue in my eyes has changed to a darker shade and looks as if it there are dark clouds swirling within them.

The door to the bathroom swings open and Jack walks in. I turn the water on quick and wash my hands while I smile at him.

"Mom wanted me to check and see if you were okay. You have been gone for ten minutes." He informs me.

"Yep, I'm fine. Had to take a call while I was in here is all." I hate to lie, but I can't believe I zoned out for ten whole minutes, damn. We walk out together, and my eyes meet Liz's blue ones.

"Everything all right?" She asks.

"Yes, everything is fine. I got a call while I was in there, so I took it quick."

"Sheesh Mom, what if he needed to poop? Let a man poop in peace!" This coming from Nate and it makes us all chuckle.

"You are right. I shouldn't ask a man what he's been doing in the bathroom. Where are my manners?" Liz hugs Nate from behind.

Smacking my hands together, "Alright, who is ready for some pizza and bowling?" Cheers go up all around and we head over to get our shoes and bowling balls.

The boys fall asleep on the way home, so we have to wake Jack up, but I carry Nate into the Compound for Liz. I take him to the room that he shares with Jack and lay him on his bed. After Liz takes off his shoes and tucks him in, we walk out together.

"Thank you again for tonight, Taven. The boys and I needed it."

"Of course. I always enjoy hanging out with the three of you." I grin. We walk to her room next door, and she bids me good night. I go to leave and then swing back around, "Liz."

"Hmm?"

"I was thinking about watching a movie in the rec room, would you like to join me?"

"Sure, sounds like just the thing to relax after today. Just let me change into some comfy clothes and I will meet you down there."

"Great, I'll grab some popcorn." I leave her standing in her doorway. I feel like a schoolboy asking a girl out on a date! What's wrong with me?

While waiting for the popcorn to finish popping, Liz walks into the kitchen. She has changed in stretchy yoga pants and a tight-fitting tank top. Nothing special, I've seen Cassie and Jill in less than that and never thought twice about it, but seeing Liz dressed this way, makes me turn in towards the counter, so she doesn't see the evidence of what it does to me.

"Hey, just wanted to let you know that Kai, Stone, Jagger and Axel are in the middle of some tournament on the gaming system, so no tv for us." She pouts.

"That's okay, I have a big screen in my room. We can watch it there, if you want." I don't want to make her think that I'm trying to get her alone, so I leave it up to her to decide.

"When did you get a tv? I didn't see one in there the night you were puking your brains out." She smirks at me as I frown at the memory of her being there when I drank too much at Duncan's Bachelor party a few months ago.

"Yeah, well I get tired of trying to watch a movie when everyone is around, so I just installed it about two weeks ago."

"I didn't realize you like watching tv much."

"I don't, but I like watching movies when there are good ones out. It relaxes me after a stressful day."

"Are you saying that my boys and I stress you out?" She giggles.

Chuckling, I answer, "No, but it has been a stressful week, and this is the first night that I have had time to be able to unwind."

"Are you sure you want company then? I don't want to interrupt your alone time."

"Did you forget that I asked you to join me? You don't stress me out, Liz. In fact, I very much enjoy having you around."

"You say that now," she laughs, "but wait a few more months and you will be ready to hand me over to Mika!" She laughs.

"Please don't ever say that. He will never get his hands on you! Not while I'm around."

She places her hand on my arm, "Hey, it was a joke. I know you will protect me. Is there something wrong?" She asks softly.

"Sorry. No, I'm fine. It just really pisses me off how that piece of shit keeps escaping us! I hate that you and the boys have to live cooped up here at the Compound. It's not a life anybody should have to live." I say sorrowfully.

"You live here." She states.

"Yes, but that is by choice. I chose this life. Besides, I can come and go. You have to have a guard on you at all times."

"I'm not complaining. I love his company and he isn't too bad to look at, pretty easy on the eyes if I may say so myself!" She winks at me, and it actually makes me blush.

"Let's go, popcorn is getting cold." I smile.

I had also brought in a couch when I had my tv installed in my room, so that is where we are sitting. Since I have the popcorn on my lap, Liz sits beside me curled up, while my arm drapes on the back of the couch behind her head. Liz chooses a thriller that neither one of us has seen and so here we sit, munching on popcorn and relaxing.

Halfway through the movie, Liz falls asleep against me, and I hate to wake her up, so I leave her there until the end of the movie. Okay, I like having her body snuggled up to mine while she sleeps. Once the credits start rolling, I slowly move out from under her, being careful not to wake her. I decide that I'll let her sleep in my bed and I would take the couch. I don't want to carry her to her room in case we run into someone and have to answer twenty questions.

As I pick her up and start carrying her, she wakes up and yawns, "Is the movie over already? I am sorry I fell asleep on you." She frowns.

"It's okay. It's not every day I get to have a woman fall asleep, snuggled against me." I chuckle, "I figured you could just sleep here in my bed, and I would take the couch."

"Your bed is big enough for the two of us." Her voice almost a whisper as she states it.

"I am trying to be a gentleman, Liz." I look down at her, "I don't know if I would be able to hold that status if we were to share the same bed."

"Then don't. I never said that I needed a gentleman." Her words come out seductively and that is all it takes.

My mouth claims hers as I bend over to lay her on the bed, my body hovering over hers. Her lips are as soft as I have always imagined them to be. She opens them up and my tongue delves into her mouth to find hers. I lower myself more and she wraps her arms and legs around me, causing my arousal to rub against her sex. I hear her moan, persuading me to go further. I start to grind my hardness into her while I rub a hand up and down one of her thighs. I feel the heat through her leggings and know that she wants me just as bad as I want her.

I need to try and stay in control. The last thing I want to do is scare her, but it's been a damn long time since I have been with a woman, and knowing that Liz is my mate, that what is happening between us is right, still doesn't mean that I can let my demon out to play.

"You need to tell me to stop if I go too far, sweetheart." I tell her as I trace kisses down her neck. What I wouldn't give to be able to sink my fangs into her soft neck and taste her.

"You have a long way to go before you hear that word come out of my mouth." She moans.

I lift her tank top up and kiss along her bra line before sucking her nipple through the material. As she arches her back, I slip my hand underneath and unhook her bra. I pull her tank up higher and she lifts her arms for me to pull it off. I do so, and her bra is the next to go. I massage her breasts before I latch on to one nipple, sucking it hard, earning me a gasp from her lips. I move to the other one and do the same as she arches her back again. I slide my hand down to the waist band of her yoga pants and slip it in, finding her wet with desire. My fingers slide back and forth through her folds before I dip one inside of her. Damn she is tight. I am going to need to work her good before she will be ready for my cock.

"I need to taste you." I say to her, and I pull my hand out and then pull her pants and thong down and then off.

"Yes, please!" She groans.

I gaze at her naked form for a moment, appreciating the beauty of every curve. Grabbing her legs, I pull her until her ass is at the edge of the bed. I kneel down and hook her legs over my shoulders, opening her up for me. I watch as I thrust a finger back into her, pumping it and getting her juices flowing. I slide another in before leaning in to take her clit with my mouth, circling my tongue around it and giving it a suck when needed. I move down and lick her folds as my fingers are working their magic and my other hand has now replaced my mouth on her clit. She is keeping the tempo as she fucks my fingers. I hear her breathing change and I know she is about ready to come, so I thrust harder into her and take her over the edge. When she is finally over her orgasm, I pull my fingers out and taste the sweet nectar dripping from them, then move to her pussy and lap up any remaining cum with my tongue.

I stand up and look at her as I remove my shirt and then my jeans and boots. She watches me under hooded eyes until I pull my boxer briefs down and her eyes widen at the sight of my cock. I can't help but smile at her expression.

"Are you sure that thing is going to fit?" she asks worriedly.

"Just relax sweetheart, it will fit, I promise. If you want me to stop, tell me now, because I don't know if I will be able to once I am inside of you."

"No, I want you. I have wanted you for a long time and I am done waiting." She informs me.

Hearing her words sends shivers through my body. The thought of her wanting me makes me even harder. Will she still want me when she learns that I am a vampire? I am surprised that she hasn't figured it out yet. Maybe I should wait until she knows the truth. That would be the respectful thing to do, but I have come to far now. I can only pray that she forgives me when I tell her and with those thoughts, I slowly enter her with my tip. Stretching her inch by inch, I pull out just to slide right back into her. I can see that she is a little uncomfortable.

"Do you need me to stop? Is it too uncomfortable for you?"

"It is a little uncomfortable, but it isn't so bad. It will go away once you are all the way in."

"God, but you are so fucking tight! I will try and hurry."

I keep at the pace I have been going and start rubbing her sensitive nub to help her relax and in no time, I am planted deeply within her. I pull out some and thrust back in, slowly picking up the tempo each time I do. She begins to move her hips in rhythm with my own and soon I am thrusting into her hard and fast. I lift both of her legs and go deeper yet. The desire in her eyes as she gazes at me, tells me everything I need to know. She wants this just as much as I do as she moans and thrashes her head back and forth while I take her higher. I feel my balls pull up and know that I'm about ready to come, so I slow down and hold it off. I pinch her clit, knowing how sensitive she is to my touch, and her orgasm explodes. She screams my name and I slam my mouth over hers to muffle the sound as I begin to fuck her fast and hard until my hot cum explodes into her. Fuck! I have never come this hard before. It is never ending. Just when I think I am done, my cock jerks again with new spurts.

Finally, once we have both come down from the high of our orgasms, I pull out of her and go to the bathroom to get a wet cloth. I come back and clean her up myself before cleaning myself. Tossing the cloth into the nearby hamper, I pick her up, bring down the covers and place her in the middle of the bed. I lay down behind her and I fall fast asleep, my fated mate safe and sound in my arms.

TWO

LIZ

I awake in the early hours, still wrapped in Taven's arms. What am I doing? I shouldn't be here. I can't be doing this. I snuggle deeper into his embrace, and he squeezes me tighter. I feel safe here, no one can get me while Taven is near. Cassie and Jill both claim that once you have one of these men, they will cherish and protect you always. Will it be like that with Taven? Should I throw caution to the wind and just be here, be with him? Does he even want me? Ugh, stop over analyzing everything Liz. I close my eyes and fall asleep again, only to wake up at the crack of dawn, alone in bed.

I sneak back to my own room to shower and change, thanking God that it's the weekend, because I am so sore from last night's activities. I go in search of Taven and find him sitting at the desk in his office. I knock softly, "Can I come in?"

"Of course, my door is always open for you." He smiles at me. I step in and shut the door behind me.

"You were up early this morning. You could have woken me."

"Yeah, I couldn't sleep, and I didn't want to wake you."

I step behind him, wrapping my arms around his neck and lean down to kiss his neck, "You can always wake me, and I can help you fall back to sleep."

He removes my arm from around his neck with a nervous chuckle, "Like I said, I didn't want to wake you."

Well, if that isn't a blow off, then I don't know what is, "I am sorry that I disturbed you. I will let you get back to work." I hurry off out of the room, hearing him call my name, but I continue on. How could I be so stupid? The girls were wrong. Maybe they got the only two good ones in the group, I don't know, but if Taven's actions prove anything, it only proves that I am just a roll in the hay for him.

I keep myself locked in my room all day, only opening the door for my boys. Cassie comes by to see if I am feeling well, but I won't allow her entrance. Taven comes by once, wanting to talk, but I shoo him away as well. I am too embarrassed by this morning's conversation with him that I can't face him. I am thinking that after everything that has happened, it's time I move the boys and I out, so I begin to look through the rental ads in the paper, circling the ones that I will be calling on first thing Monday morning.

After eating all three meals in my room today, I decide to take another shower and try venturing out. I am going stir crazy here all by myself, besides, I am sure Taven is busy with Elite work anyway, so my chances of running into him are slim.

I turn the shower off, wrap a towel around me and head to my room for my clothes. I jump to the sound of my name being spoken. I whip around and there is Taven sitting on my bed.

"You scared the shit out of me! I don't remember inviting you in, by the way." I say sarcastically.

"I assumed you didn't want to see me, so there was no point in asking to come in." he states.

I turn back towards my dresser and start looking for something to wear, because looking at him is too painful. We shouldn't have crossed that line last night, because now we can't get our friendship back. While continuing my search, I talk to him without looking, "I know what you are going to say Taven. You're going to tell me that last night was a mistake and that it can never happen again, blah… blah… blah."

He is standing behind me now, caging me in to the dresser, I can feel his arousal pressed against my back, he responds in a low baritone voice, "Last night was a mistake, but not how you are thinking. I don't regret any minute spent with you, only that I wish we had waited until I was able to talk to you about a few things. Oh, and yes, we will most certainly be doing that again!"

I whip around on him, "I am so tired of your bipolar tendencies! One day you are being yourself and then the next day, it's like you try to avoid me! I don't need these games in my life Taven. You made it perfectly clear to me this morning that you didn't want me touching you, so you win, and I am leaving hopefully sometime this week!"

"Liz, you took it the wrong way this morning. I tried calling you back to explain, but you just kept going. I couldn't have you touching me or else I was going to take you right there across my desk. The same reason why I didn't wake you this morning, I left so I wouldn't wake you and take you over and over. You were still too sore and raw from last night. Liz, last night was the best night of my life and I don't regret any of it!"

"Are you sure? I only ask, because I refuse to stay somewhere if I am not wanted."

"You are very much wanted, but I would really like to talk to you about a few aspects of my life before we go any further. You may have a better understanding of my "Bipolar" ways."

"Okay, why don't you start now? The boys are off playing, and we are alone."

"It's not as easy as you think it is." He states as he looks down at the floor.

I walk over to him and encircle his waist with my arms and hug him, "You know that you can tell me anything, right? I would never judge you, Taven."

He returns my hug with one of his own and kisses the top of my head. He pulls slightly away and lifts my chin, so he can look me in the eyes, "I am truly sorry for making you think that I was refusing your touch this morning. The thing is, I have wanted you since I first saw you walking down the aisle at Jax and Cassie's wedding; you are all I think about. There are days that I am so happy to have you in my life, even if it has only been in friendship, but then there are days that I feel I should stay away from you. Days that I feel like you deserve a better man than me. I have dark thoughts, Liz. Thoughts that would scare most women and that is the last thing I ever want to do to you."

His words go straight to my heart and melts it. How can anything that he does, scare me away, I think to myself? Then I think, why would he think it would scare me away if it isn't as bad as I think it would be? Everybody has their own closet full of skeletons. What if his is overflowing? It doesn't matter to me. I will hear him out and then decide for myself if it is too much.

I take hold of his hand and lead him over to the bed to sit down beside me and then I turn to him, "Tell me, Taven. Tell me all of your deep dark secrets."

He looks at me before he scoots himself back to lean against the headboard and then motions me to join him. I don't hesitate as I crawl over and snuggle up against him, laying my head on his chest. He starts by telling me a little about his childhood and about how his father would beat him over the littlest thing. How he would hear the noises from his parent's bedroom, his father ordering his mother around and then her cries. His mother would have puffy eyes the next day and walk around like it hurt to take a single step.

"I vowed that I would never be like him, would never raise my hand over anger towards the people that I love," he says solemnly, and goes on, "and my wife would only know pleasure behind our closed door."

My body quivers at the thought of the pleasure that he would bring behind that closed door.

"Unfortunately, my upbringing had more of an effect on me than I thought it would. Not so much the anger part, but more of the, I am not sure how to describe it, but it's more like a sadistic part of me. Not a bad sadistic, it is just cravings that I get."

I start to become confused at this point, so I look up at him and what I see is a little alarming. His blue eyes have turned a darker shade and it looks as if his irises are swirling, almost like storm clouds. After a moment, he blinks, and they are back to the blue that I love.

"May I ask, what kind of craving is it that you get?" My heart begins to beat a little faster. Whether it is due to fascination, I am not sure, but he has my full attention as I wait for him to answer my question.

He looks down at me, "Let's just say that I have certain tastes and expectations when I am with a woman behind closed doors." His eyes are fixed on me as he waits for my response.

"And what are these tastes and expectations that you are talking about?" I think back to last night, but I can't think of anything that I would find out of the ordinary when being with someone.

He gazes at me a moment and then moves to stand up, "It's better if I show you. Come with me."

He offers me his hand and I slide mine into it. He then leads me out of the room and towards the rec room where my boys and a few of the newer recruits are playing video games. Taven calls out to Stone and asks if he can keep an eye on the boys for a while and Stone agrees. He then takes me out and has me get into the SUV.

"Where are we going?" I'm confused as to what he wants to show me and where it is at.

"We are running over to the new Compound quick. What I need to show you is there, at my house."

I get a little tingly at the thought of being with him in his house and nobody else being around. The new compound area is about a mile or so on the outskirts of Augusta and in a very remote area. Since it's a Saturday evening, the building crew are gone, and it will be deserted. Moving day is this coming Wednesday, and they are hoping to be completely in by next weekend.

"Oh, I didn't know you had moved anything from your room over to the new place yet."

"I haven't. What I am going to show you is all new. It is my hope that it will get used every once in a while." He glances at me nervously and then goes back to watching the road.

I am now starting to get a little nervous, not knowing what he is about to show me. His hands are clenched tight over the steering wheel, and I can see a little tick in his jaw. He appears to be nervous as well, which does nothing to help calm my nerves.

I place my hand on his thigh, "Hey, it's going to be okay, just loosen up a little, because you are starting to make me nervous." I let out a slight giggle.

"I'm sorry," he blows out a breath, "it's just that I have never told anybody about this, let alone shown anybody what I am about to show you. I want you in my life Liz, you mean more to me than you know, so I'm kind of nervous. I don't know how you will react."

"I am more open-minded than most people, Taven. Even though I am a little nervous about why this is making you so anxious. You are who you are, and I like having you in my life. I highly doubt whatever this thing is, is going to scare me away. Just relax." I smile over at him, and I see some of the tension leave his body.

We pull up to the new Compound and I am amazed at the surroundings. I was here a few months ago for Duncan and Jill's wedding and I thought it beautiful then, but now, it looks like a fairytale kingdom and its village hid amongst the forest. I gawk openly at the scenery before me and don't realize my mouth is hanging open until I hear a chuckle come from Taven and I close it quickly.

"This is beyond beautiful Taven! It's hard to believe that a bunch of big, bad Elite Warriors created this place."

"Well, we did for the most part, but Cassie and Jill helped a lot as well, especially with the décor." He drives past the Compound itself and continues on towards the houses by the lake, stopping in front of a greenish-gray colored, two story home. "This is my house. Jill insisted that I build one for myself, so I did, but I will probably mostly stay at the Compound. I can't see myself living in this house by myself."

He hops out quick and comes over to my side and opens the door as I unbuckle my seatbelt. Taking my hand, he helps me step down and out of the vehicle. Keeping his hand in mine, he leads me up the steps and into his house, where again, I gawk open-mouthed at the sight before me.

"Wow, this is beautiful!" I turn to him and smile.

"Thanks. I was a little worried when I gave the reins over to the women, but they listened to the type of style that I liked and did a fantastic job. Even I was amazed when I first saw it."

He gave me a tour of the whole first level and the family room below, before taking me upstairs to the second floor. There were three bedrooms with their own bathrooms and the Master suite, which included a big walk-in closet and a massive bathroom with a jacuzzi and all. He stopped in front of a closed door and turns to look down at me.

"This room is the only one that I designed myself. You are the first one and the only one to see it finished." I can see he is nervous, so I squeeze his hand.

"I can tell that this room means a lot to you, so thank you for sharing it with me." I smile, even though I am nervous as fuck as to what he is about to show me.

He rummages in the pocket of his jeans and pulls out a single key, attached to a simple keychain. It looks like the keychain is an initial, but I can't make it out. He unlocks the door and steps aside, motioning for me to enter. I look up at him, take a deep breath, and step inside the room. It is dark and has no windows, all I see are outlines of whatever it is that he has in here. Taven flips the light switch, and the room is illuminated. As my eyes adjust, I take in everything that occupies the room. I suck in a lung full of air and freeze.

TAVEN

I watch Liz's reaction as she takes in my secret room. The main focal point is the king-size bed with a black iron frame. It has metal rings drilled into the frame in different areas for attaching cuffs and whatnot, chains and rope also hang from some areas. To the right, there is a big wooden X with wrist and ankle cuffs, and a head rest attached for a little more comfort. On the other side of the room, there is what's called a bondage horse or bench, as some call it, with padding and cuffs on all four sides. Hanging from the ceiling next to it, is a swing. I start to picture Liz strapped inside of it and my cock grows with arousal.

There are also eye loops screwed into the ceiling to string rope through. She is taking it all in. I wait patiently for her to say something, but she doesn't utter a peep. Instead, she steps in further and opens a floor to ceiling cabinet that holds everything from different whips, floggers, crops and paddles. Some sadists use harsher kinds, but I keep mine basic. I'm not into it hard core like some.

Liz next moves to a dresser that holds all of my blindfolds, vibrators, and anal toys, all of different shape and sizes. She goes to turn around and notices the wall with all the different kinds of handcuffs, wrist, ankle and neck cuffs hanging from their hooks. She visibly shivers as she runs her hands down some of them. I am not sure how to take her response and it seems as if I have been holding my breath since she first laid eyes upon my room.

When I designed this room, Liz was who I had in mind the whole time. Picturing her and only her, strapped down and submitting herself to me was all I could think about. Will she embrace this life of mine and let me dominate her in the bedroom, or will she run from it, from me?

I walk over and stand behind her, my voice a low baritone next to her ear, "Now that you know one of my darkest secrets, does it scare you?"

Continuing to stare at the wall of cuffs, she responds, "I don't know. I have never experienced any of this personally, only seen it in movies." Her voice a little above a whisper.

"I will confess that I made this room with you in mind. Hoping that someday you would let me show you all the pleasures that you deserve. This isn't a room to torture, at least not in the bad sense. It is a good torture. You would feel so much pleasure, that it will be torturous and make you want to come, especially when I make you hold your orgasm in until I am ready for you to come. I won't lie to you, there will be some pain, but again, it's a pleasurable pain. That I can promise."

I bring my arms around her waist and nuzzle her neck, "I have a very important question to ask you, sweetheart."

"What is it?" Her body shivers within my embrace.

"Will you submit to me in the bedroom when the need arises? No questions when I tell you to come to this room?"

I begin to scent her arousal, which in turn, hardens my dick even more and I press it against her lower back. I hear a little moan escape her lips and I press my own against her neck, kissing her softly.

"Will you be gentle? This is all new to me."

"I will be as gentle as you need me to be, but I promise, you will beg me for more."

I spin her around to face me and stare into her beautiful blue eyes, "I want you, Liz. If this isn't something you can do, then you need to tell me. I will work through it, but I won't let you go. I want to share this darkness with you and hope that you are the light that will keep the demon at bay. In fact, I know you are. You just need to trust me and communicate your feelings. No harm will ever come to you when you are in my care... ever!"

"I do trust you, Taven. Actually, I trust you so much, that it scares the hell out of me."

"There is nothing to be afraid of, sweetheart." I kiss her forehead and run the pad of my thumb over her soft cheek, "So, again, will you submit to me?"

After what seemed to be long, agonizing minutes, but is only a few seconds, she answers, "Yes, Taven. I submit to you."

A huge weight lifts off my shoulders, and I slam my mouth over hers, demanding that she open up for me. I grab her ass, lifting her up, and she wraps her legs around my waist as I carry her to the bed. I lay her down and break the kiss, "Ready for your first lesson?"

"I'm nervous." She states as she bites her lower lip.

"Don't be. What I am going to do to you is vanilla compared to everything else. You won't even need a safe word for this, which we will get to another time. I just need to be inside of you right now!"

I strip her down to her bra and panties and then take off my own shirt. I move her to the middle of the bed and tie only her wrists to each bed post. I leave her for a moment and come back with a blindfold, which I slip over her eyes.

She gasps as I slip the cups of her bra down so her tits are hanging out and I dip down, nipping first one and then the other. She is a sight to behold, the way she is laid out for my taking. Next, I use my tongue to play with her belly button, before moving down to her waiting sex. As I align my face with her crotch, I revel in the scent of the sweet nectar that has her panties wet. I shove my face into the cradle of her thighs and take a deep breath before running my tongue over the area. Oh yeah, she is so wet!

I slide her panties down slowly, keeping my eyes trained on that glorious pussy of hers, until I get them off and toss them on the floor. I kiss my way back up her legs, taking hold of her thighs once I reach the top, and opening her up as far as I can.

I start from the bottom and run my tongue up and through the gentle folds, ending with a suck to her clit, the taste of warm baked apples on my tongue from her essence. I repeat the action as she moans in pleasure. On the last swipe, I nip her clit, causing her to cry out.

"Oh, my God, do that again!" She cries.

With a smile on my face, I suck on her nub and nip it once more, making her hips jerk. I insert a finger and then a second one into her opening as I torture her clit. Her breathing quickens and at last, she is coming all over my fingers. When her orgasm is through, I remove my fingers, licking each one clean and kneel between her legs. I remove my hand from one of her thighs long enough to open my pants and slide both my jeans and boxers down until my hard cock pops out. I place the tip at her entrance, and in one long stroke, I slowly enter her.

"Oh...!" She squeals.

Once I am all the way in, I stop and give her my first demand, "I don't want you coming until I tell you to do so, and I do not want to hear a peep come from that luscious mouth of yours. Do you understand me?"

"Yes."

"When we are in this room, you will refer to me as Sir. Got that?"

"Yes, Sir!"

"If you come before I tell you to, there will be consequences. If you make a sound, there will be consequences. Do you understand me?"

"Yes, Sir."

"Good. Now, hold on tight, love!" With me holding her legs wide open, I watch as I begin slamming into her with my cock. The sight of it makes my dick even harder. I look up at her to make sure I am not hurting her. Her lips are sealed tight as she tries to not make a sound. I continue thrusting into her until I know she is on the brink of orgasm, and then I pull all the way out. I hear a faint sound of displeasure come from her and I pinch her clit hard, and it makes her jerk.

"I said not a sound!"

I thrust back into her and start all over again, pulling out just as she is about to come. I do it three more times before I let go of one of her legs and lean in to take a nipple into my mouth. As I grind my cock into her dripping pussy, I start to feel my balls ache and I know I am close. I feel her walls around my cock tighten up and know that the desire that is consuming her body is about to spill over.

"I want you to come all over my cock. Do it now!"

On my command, her orgasm explodes and my own follows, filling her up with load upon load of my cum. I slump over her as the last of my orgasm fills her, keeping my weight off her. I then claim her lips passionately for a few moments before I take the blindfold off. Blinking her eyes, she looks at me under hooded lids and smiles, before closing her eyes and falling fast asleep.

I untie her wrists and pull her into my arms, but I don't fall asleep. My thoughts are filled with the woman in my arms and how happy she has made me by accepting this part of me. One down, one more to go. Will she be as accepting of my last secret as she was to this one? How do I tell her that she has submitted herself to a vampire?

About an hour later, my phone is buzzing, and I regret having to leave Liz's warmth to go answer it. She wakes up when I move my arm from beneath her.

"Go back to sleep, sweets. I need to take this call." I say as I look at my phone and see that it's Kole calling me.

"Hey buddy, what's up?"

"I thought you would want to know that Mika is back at his personal residence. The video from this morning shows him going into his house and I haven't seen him leave again."

"Yeah, thanks for letting me know. I'll be back in about thirty minutes."

"Okay. I'll text you if anything else happen before you are back."

"Thanks." I hang up and look down at Liz. She has that "just been fucked look" and I feel myself becoming hard again.

"How are you doing? I didn't hurt you or anything, did I?"

"I feel amazing." She smiles up at me, "Is that how it is all the time?"

"I'd like to say it's better, but you will have to experience it yourself to determine that." I put my shirt back on and Liz starts to get up. I clear my throat, "I didn't say you could move yet."

She looks at me confused.

"When you submitted to me, you turned every aspect of yourself over to me. While we are in this room, you don't do anything without my permission."

She starts to giggle until she sees the serious look that I give her, "I'm sorry."

"You are sorry, what?"

"I'm sorry, Sir."

"It's okay, you are still in training. I'll let it slip for now." I smile as I climb into bed next to her. I look at her naked form and then reach up and pinch her nipple. She squeaks and so I do it again to the other one.

"I want you to know that you have made me the happiest man by submitting to me. Just know that the submission is only while we are in this room. I want you to be yourself, outside of these walls, but while we are within, I am your Master. Your body is mine for the taking and to do as I please with it. At least within your guidelines. What I am saying is that, if I pinch your nipples like this," I do it again, "I don't want to hear a peep out of you. You need to learn to control that part of you."

"I am sorry, Sir."

She looks down at her hands and I grab her hair, not too rough, pulling her face up to mine, "You are forgiven." I take her lips for a quick kiss and then release her. "As much as I would love nothing more than to gaze upon your delectable nakedness, I need you to get dressed. I am needed back at Headquarters.

Once she is dressed, I grab her hand and leave the room, locking it behind us, and we head back to the normalcy of our daily lives.

THREE

LIZ

Taven kisses me quick at the front door and we go our separate ways. I stop to see if Jack and Nate are still in the rec room, and they are, along with Jill, Cassie and their children. Jill and Duncan had her their twin boys two months ago, the night of Thanksgiving. Cassie and Jax followed two weeks later with the birth of their second child, Jace. Three new boys who will be growing up and most likely following in their father's footsteps. The new generation of Elite Warriors. The way Jillian, Cassie and Jax's oldest, acts, I wouldn't be surprised if she joins as well! All four children have found a place in my heart.

I walk in to see what everybody is up to, and they all smile at me.

"Where have you and Taven been all this time?" Jill asks smugly.

"He took me over to see the new Compound and his house." I feel the color rush to my cheeks.

"I bet he took you to see his house. What did you think of it? Most importantly, what did you think of his bedroom?" Jill and Cassie both burst into laughter.

"What the hell?" I look to my two boys, but they are busy gaming with their headsets on.

"Oh, come on, we can smell the sex all over you!" Cassie taps her nose with her finger.

"You can't hide stuff from us." Jill states in a fit of laughter.

"What do you mean? You can smell it on me? How?"

The women look at each other as if they had just revealed something that they shouldn't have.

"Okay, out with it! One of you are going to tell me what's going on!"

"It's nothing really… you just wreak of sex is all."

"Why don't I believe you?"

"Believe what you want. How else would we know, dork?" Cassie rolls her eyes at me.

"Well, I guess I better go take a shower before I run into anybody else!" They laugh again as I turn to leave.

"We will be in your room in twenty minutes for a little girl talk!" Jill warns me.

"Not happening!" I call over my shoulder.

After my quick shower, I sit in my room and contemplate on what happened today. I wasn't lying when I told Taven that I had only seen that kind of stuff in movies, but I left out that I read a lot of Romance novels with it in them. Reading about it has always gotten me hot and bothered, but I have never experienced it with anyone. That is one of the reasons why I agreed to submit. I am curious about it all and it stirred the desire in me just looking at it all. To submit to Taven is easy, I would do anything for that guy.

There is a knock on my door, and I swing it open, ready to tell the girls that there will be no talk of my sex life, but it is Taven who is standing on the other side.

"Oh hey!" I smile.

"Hey yourself. Were you expecting company?" He cocks an eyebrow at me.

"Jill and Cassie said they were coming, because they wanted to have a little girl talk, after they smelled you on me. I was about to tell them to go away, but it was you."

"Oh, I see." He gives me his sexy smile. I am assuming it's because they could smell the sex.

"Yeah, so I came back here to shower. I still don't understand how they were able to smell it on me. I couldn't even smell it."

"Mm, I should have come sooner, then I could have joined you in the shower."

"Sorry, Charlie. Next time I'll text you when I'm about to take one. Come in."

"I better not." He chuckles, "It's all I can do not to take you in this hallway right this second! Besides, I have some Elite business to take care of, but I wanted to stop by and see how you were doing."

"Oh, I'm good. I'm more than good." I look at him and flush as he takes me in from head to toe.

"That, you are, Liz. No regrets on your end?"

I step towards him and look down the hall both ways before bringing his head down and whispering, "Not a one. I'm actually looking forward to our next session!" I smile seductively at him. I look down and see my words have the desired effect that I was hoping for. When I look up, I notice that his eyes have taken on the stormy look that I had seen earlier.

"Do you know that your eyes change when you are aroused?" I put my hand over my mouth to hide the smug smile.

"It's what you do to me, baby."

I reach up and slap a quick kiss on his lips, "You better go. I wouldn't want to be the one to keep you from doing your job!" I smile and step back, shutting the door on him.

"You are a little vixen. Do you know that?" I hear through the door. "You will pay for this next time I see you!" I can hear his laughter as he walks away.

I am just getting ready to go get the boys ready for bed, when a text notification comes through on my cell. I don't recognize the phone number, but I read the text anyway.

Hey Liz, it's me Dean. How are you doing?

I tell him that I have nothing to say to him and that he needs to not text me again, but another text comes through.

I just want to talk to you. Can we meet sometime?

I say that I have no reason to meet with him and that I don't want to talk. I kind of feel bad, because I am usually not like this and we did have a great relationship that first year, but I cannot turn my head on the last night we were together. That was not the Dean that I had fallen in love with. That Dean was gone.

I go in and block his number on my phone, so he can't send me any more texts. Then I turn and go in search of my kids.

Monday is a good day at work for me. Taven had snuck into my room last night and stayed with me all night. He was my alarm clock this morning, waking me up by making love to me. We even had a quick make out session as he was dropping me off for work this morning.

About quarter to five he sends me a text that he is running a few minutes behind. I jokingly text back that it was fine, but that he had better hope I don't find a new man while I'm waiting for him.

I find it a little ironic that as I sit and wait for him, I am approached from behind, by a voice from my past.

"Hello Liz."

I whip around to find Dean standing only inches away from me. He looks horrible. Like a shell of the man that he used to be. I frown as I stand up.

"What do you want Dean? I told you that I have nothing to say to you!"

"I know, but I really needed to see you."

"Why? You can't possible have anything to say that I want to hear."

"You are looking good. Although you always did look good."

"Just leave me alone, Dean. Go back to whatever drug house that you live in!"

"I'm clean baby, I swear!"

"Yeah, it really looks like it." I scoff.

I see that I have angered him, "What do you know? You have this nice job; you are looking fantastic… this is what you did to me!" His voice raises to a higher pitch.

"I didn't do anything to you. You did it to yourself! I left, because you started using and cheating and God knows what else!" I'm letting my anger get the best of me.

He seems to calm down a little bit, "Hey, I didn't come here to fight with you. I was hoping you would do me a favor and lend me some cash to tide me over until I can find another job."

"Are you fucking serious? I am not giving you any money, now leave me alone and don't contact me again!"

He grabs me by both of my arms and shakes me, "You will give me money if you know what is good for you! You wouldn't want me to send my friends over, now, would you? They have been wanting a piece of your ass since we were together." He sneers at me.

"I highly suggest that you remove your hands from my woman, and step far away from her." The voice was very familiar to me, and I was so thankful to hear it.

"Who the fuck are you, to be telling me what to do! Liz is my ex, and I will talk to her if I want to!"

"I couldn't care less what she used to be to you. She is mine now and I don't do well with people man handling her! Now, I will tell you one last time... take your fucking hands off of my woman!"

Dean looks to me and then back to Taven, "You haven't heard the last from me." He whispers and shoves me over to Taven.

"Take the damn whore! She is all used up anyway!" He takes off quick and Taven goes to go after him, but I hold him back.

"No, don't. He isn't worth it." I can't get my body to stop shaking.

"Who was that?" he asks, still angry.

"My ex live-in boyfriend, Dean." I went on to tell him the whole story of our relationship and then told him about him texting me two nights before.

"If he knows what's good for him then he better stay away from you!"

"Did you mean what you said, am I your woman?" I smile up at him.

"Do you want to be my woman?" He wraps his arms around my waist.

"Can I think about it for a while?" I ask in the most serious way possible.

"On second thought, I think you and your ex is too much baggage for my liking." He jokes as he pulls away from me.

I slap him on the chest, "Hey!"

He laughs, "Of course, you are mine and I will let everyone know it." Leaning down, he kisses me for all to see.

TAVEN

With everything that I have on my plate, Liz's ex has to show up and start shit too! I want to go into a rage when I see him with his hands on my mate, but we are in public, and I don't want Liz seeing my vamp side of me yet. Not until I tell her anyway. I will find that motherfucker and take care of him, just you wait! If I hadn't been running behind, the asshole wouldn't have been able to get his hands on her, but Mika is on the move, and we have been tracking him.

Mika. That is another son of a bitch that has his day coming. It seems that he has started his senseless killing of vampires again, only he is using other vampires to do it! It makes no sense to me at all. The only thing that I can think of is that it isn't about vampires, but a vendetta. It all started when Jill was kidnapped by Jason and held prisoner for a few months. We eventually found her, and Duncan killed Jason, the man behind her kidnapping, and took Mika's arm as well. He has tried pointless times to get Jill again and Duncan has almost died twice during the process. Jill apparently shot his dick off the first time Duncan almost died, and that really pissed Mika off. Now he is making vamps and so again, I think it's more vendetta than anything.

He is trying to draw us out by killing innocent vampires. I have been on the phone all day, calling the surrounding Elite groups to come help. I've also called in a favor to one of my long-time vamp friends who works on the police force, Coco. She has informed me that her boss knows what she is and that he keeps her secret hidden well. She will discuss the situation with him and get back to me.

By the time I look at the clock, it's already after eleven. I feel bad that I haven't checked in with Liz tonight after the incident with her ex. I am beat, and I want to hold her in my arms. She seems to melt all the stress away when I am with her. I make my way to her room, making sure nobody sees me, and I sneak in. I can tell she is already fast asleep by her breathing, so I quietly kick my boots off and undress. Crawling in beside her, I slip my arms around her and pull her close.

"Long night?" she mumbles.

"Long day. Go back to sleep, love, I didn't mean to wake you."

"I am usually a light sleeper. Except for when you fuck me into a deep sleep." Her voice tells me that she is smiling.

"Mm, I like hearing that. Why don't you go back to sleep. It's late and you have work tomorrow."

"You are being a fun hater."

"Unless you want to quit your job and let me take care of you, you need to sleep." I chuckle.

"Fine, but I suggest you come to bed sooner tomorrow. If you want to be my man, you need to start pleasing me whenever I need it!" she jokes.

"I will definitely start calling it a day now that I know this!" I kiss the top of her head as she snuggles in closer.

Waking up to my cock throbbing because Liz's mouth is molesting it, I moan as she licks her way down my hardened shaft and then back up, swirling her tongue around the tip and then repeating it.

"Fuck, that feels good, don't stop." I move my hips up and down to her tempo. She uses her other hand to massage my balls. When she licks back up and swirls her tongue, she opens up and devours half of my eleven inches and uses her other hand at the base. She begins to move up and down, pumping my cock in her warm mouth, while working me at the base with her hand. I entangled my fingers in her hair and tighten my grip, putting pressure on her head as she goes down.

"Yes, take it. Just like that!" I close my eyes and bite my lower lip.

She picks up the tempo as she licks and sucks and then scrapes her teeth along the vein, causing an ache in my balls. I start pumping myself faster into her mouth and then I burst, holding her head so the tip of my dick is at the back of her throat.

"Swallow it, baby. Every... last... drop." I thrust with my last three words. She obeys and does just what I tell her to do. She then proceeds to clean the rest of my dick off with her tongue.

"Fuck, baby. What was that for?"

"That was just me starting your day off on a good note." She smiles, kissing me before getting out of bed.

"You going to let me return the favor?"

"Not right now. I have to get ready for work." She winks at me and disappears into the bathroom.

I hear the shower turn on and I smile. Getting out of bed, I head to the bathroom. I rip the shower curtain open, startling her, "That's too bad, because I'm going to do it anyway!"

I step in behind her and bend her over. I shove my finger into her pussy to make sure she is wet enough. Oh yeah, she is wet! I disengage my finger and shove my cock into her instead. She is holding on to the wall in front of her as I bang her from behind and pulling her hair, so her head is cocked back. Reaching around her, I help keep her steady and tease her clit at the same time. I can feel her pleasure building and using my thumb, I shove the tip of it into her ass, causing her to come instantly.

Once her orgasm is over, she tries standing up straighter, but I hold her down, "You're not going anywhere, sweets. I'm going to get off again, but this time it will be inside of you." I grab both sides of her hips and start fucking her harder and faster, using a little bit of my vamp speed. It sends me over the edge, and I take her with me once again.

After dropping Liz off at work, I head over to the police station to meet with Coco and the Chief. I had received a text from Coco when we were done with our shower, telling me that the Chief wants to meet with me. I fill Liz in on who Coco is and about the meeting. I think she might have been a little jealous, because she made this cute little face as if she didn't believe that I could be just friends with a female, "She sounds like a stripper," she says to me, and I can't help but kiss her for that one.

They are both in her boss's office waiting for me when I arrive.

"You must be Taven. Coco has told me a lot about you and your warriors. I am Chief Bently, it's a pleasure to finally meet you! Please, sit down." He offers me a chair. The Chief seems to be a pretty nice guy who looks to be in his early forties. He's got a head full of dark hair and friendly brown eyes. He could probably lay off some of the donuts, but he seems fit enough.

"So, Coco here, tells me that you two have been friends for quite some time and that you are like her?" He raises a brow.

"Yes, it's been what… a good hundred and ten years now?" I look at Coco.

"Sounds about right." She grins.

The Chief speaks up again as he looks at me, "So tell me. What exactly has been going on? Coco said something about vamps and people teaming up and killing more vamps? That hardly makes sense."

"I totally agree, it makes no sense, but then again, Mika isn't all that sane anyway." I go on to tell him the whole story. I also tell him that we have Jenny and Samantha holed up at the Compound. Not that Jenny is really a prisoner anymore. She is able to walk around freely, as long as it's within the Compound walls. She is actually a pretty nice woman who happened to get manipulated by Mika. Samantha on the other hand is still stubborn as ever.

In the end, the Chief agrees that Mika's group needs to be stopped and that he will put his "Special" crew on it. Meaning Coco and five other vamps within the police force. Once they are caught, they will be brought to the Elite Compound. The Chief is relieved to be working with us, but he still wants it all kept secret, so anything having to do with vampires, will be dealt with through us. I thank him for his time and promise that we will send over all the information that we have on the group of Hunters.

Coco offers to walk me out and I am glad for it, because I have one more favor to ask of her.

"Coco, are you familiar with a lot of the druggies that come through here?"

"Most of the regulars. Why do you ask?"

"Well, I have an issue with my mate's ex-boyfriend, and I need information on him. I only have a first name though. I don't really want Liz knowing that I am looking into this problem."

"Gotcha… so, what's his first name?"

"It's Dean. He used to be an accountant at one time, but I guess he got messed up into drugs and only who knows what. He was harassing Liz about giving him money just recently, even though it's been some time that she has even talked to him."

"If it's who I am thinking, I know him well and he is definitely trouble! I will look at his file and send you his mug shot, so you can let me know that we are talking about the same guy."

"That is great. I can't thank you enough Coco. You should swing by sometime and see the guys. I am sure they would be thrilled to see you!"

"Even Dane?"

"I am sure he will be happy as well. It's been what… twenty-five years now since you left?"

"Twenty-six, but who is counting?" She winks at me.

"I better get going, but I will watch for your message, thanks again!"

"No problem. And Taven, maybe I will stop over later this week, as long as it's okay with Dane."

"Sounds good! I will let you know."

On my way home, I think back on the conversation with Coco, and I smile at the memory. Coco used to be an Elite, the only female Elite and it was a sad day when we lost her. Her and Dane were hot and heavy for a few years until she got assigned a detail and found her mate. She was the only one to find their mate until Jax found Cassie. We all assumed that it was easier for the females to find their mates than it was for us males. Anyway, she broke things off with Dane and he was heartbroken over it, so she left. He has never spoken of her since. Man, I sure hope he will be fine with her stopping by. We could all use a little Coco in our lives right now. She always made things interesting. Cassie and Jill both are a lot like her, so they should get along great. The only obstacle in the way is Dane. This should be interesting!

FOUR

LIZ

I'm in the shower, shaving my legs and daydreaming of what kind of things Taven will be doing to me the next time we are alone, when I cut my leg with my razer, "Shit!" I get out of the shower and look for any kind of bandage, but no such luck. I throw my robe on and limp down to medical in search of bandages. As I look through cupboards, I see a fridge and of course, I open it up just to be nosey.

"What the fuck?" I wonder out loud. There in the fridge, are shelves full of blood bags. "Well, it is a medical ward, Liz." I say to myself, but as I go to shut the door, something catches my eye.

A blood bag with writing on it. More specifically, Jax's name on it. I pull it out to read it and see that it says Jax: For Cassie. That is really weird, so I look through a few more and I see Duncan and Jill's name on some, just like the first. Pulling a few more, I see a few other warrior names on them, including Taven's.

"Can I help you with something?" Raven's voice makes me jump.

"Sorry, yeah. I am looking for some bandages and I hold my leg up."

"You thought they would be in there?" He nods to the open fridge.

"Well, no, but I am nosy, which is a bad habit, I know." I giggle nervously.

Raven smiles and shakes his head as he bends down to examine my cut, "I hate to say this, but you should probably glue this shut. How did you cut yourself so deep?"

"Ugh, shaving and not paying attention."

He snickers and instructs me to sit down on the nearest bed. As he begins to clean the cut, I casually ask, "So what's with all the blood bags?"

"Oh those? That is just in case one of the guys get hurt in battle and need blood."

"What about the ones that say For Cassie and For Jill with their husband's name on them?"

"You are nosy, aren't you?"

"Yep... sure am!" I smile down at him.

"There you go, all done." He says, ignoring my last question.

"Thank you so much, Raven. I appreciate it."

"No problem at all. That's what I'm here for." He turns and starts walking to his office.

"Hey Raven." I call out.

He turns back and looks at me, "Yeah?"

"You never answered my last question about the blood bags."

I see him hesitate for a moment, "I think you need to talk to Taven. He can answer that for you, it's not my place. I will see you later." He turns, and hurries back to his office, closing the door.

I guess I will have to ask Taven then. I don't see what the problem is, but oh well. I look at the clock and swear. It's almost time to head for work. I practically run back to my room to get dressed.

Ten minutes later, Taven comes strolling into my room with a yogurt and a banana in his hand, "Good morning beautiful!" He leans over and gives me a kiss on the forehead.

"Morning hot stuff. How long have you been up?"

"Oh, a few hours now. Are you about ready?"

"Yep, I just need to grab my purse. Thank you for grabbing my breakfast. I knew I was keeping you around for something." I wink.

"Oh? You are only keeping me around for this?" He holds up the items in his hand, "I thought it was for my body and the things that I do to you." There is an evil glint in his eyes.

"I suppose that too!"

"You are lucky you are beautiful, minx! Let's go, before I call you in sick, so I can make love to you all day." He grabs my hand and pulls me out the door.

Once we are in the SUV, I decide to bring up the blood bags. "Hey, what's up with the blood bags down in medical? The ones with Cassie & Jill's names on them? Raven told me that I should ask you about it."

"Of course, he did." He mumbles.

"Why is it such a secret? Is it that big of a deal or what?"

"It's just a long story. Why don't I take you out to dinner tonight and we can talk about it?"

"SOOO… like a date?" I wiggle my brows at him, and he chuckles.

"Yes, a date! What, can't I take my girl out on a date?"

"Your girl, huh? I guess it's okay. I'll have to clear my schedule for the rest of the night though. I plan on utilizing the whole night for this date." I seductively run my hand up his thigh, stopping right before the bulge in his crotch, but not before grazing it with my pinky finger.

"You are asking for me to take you right here, aren't you" He growls.

"No, but I am letting you know how you can expect the date to end." I lean over and place a peck on his cheek, then hop out of the SUV with a big ass grin on my face.

Taven is waiting when I step out the door after work. He gets out and opens the passenger side door for me, grabbing my ass as I climb in. I give him a stern look, but I can't help but chuckle when I see the goofy grin on his face. Once he is back behind the wheel, I glance at my outfit and then look at what he is wearing to make sure I am dressed appropriately for dinner.

"So, where are you taking me?"

Showing me his most charming smile, "It's a surprise."

Fifteen minutes later, he is driving us down the private drive of the new Compound and pulling up to his house. I give him a confused look, but all he does is smile and wink. He gets out and walks around to help me out. I take hold of his hand and allow him to lead me around the side of the house. When we turn the corner at the back of the house, I stop and stare at the most perfect setting. He has a gazebo down by the lake with a table set up with candlelight and wine chilling... I look at him and see that he is watching me intently, I'm assuming for my reaction.

We make our way down a small slope and step up into the gazebo.

"It's perfect, Taven!"

He wraps his arm around my waist from behind, "Just like you." He nuzzles my neck as he says it. I lose his warmth as he moves away to pull out my chair for me, and I pout for a moment. I have never had anyone do anything like this for me before; I can feel tears well up in my eyes, but they never fall.

"So, what's on the menu?"

Taven leans over by his chair and pulls out two large pizzas, "Italiano!"

A laugh bursts from my lips, "Perfect!"

We make a little small talk during dinner and then make our way to a padded two-seater swing closer to the lake with our wine. Before I can even bring up the blood bags again, I hear Taven sigh and then he begins to speak.

"Have you ever turned away from something or someone, because it or they were different from regular people?"

"Not that I know of. At least not on purpose. Why?"

"Have you ever believed in something that you knew wasn't real?"

"I'm confused by the question. If I know it isn't real, then why would I believe in it? I mean, I guess I believe in soul mates even though I haven't found mine. Is that what you mean?"

He smiles, but it doesn't reach his eyes, "Yeah, kind of." He takes my hand and holds on to it tightly, "You know that the Elite warriors are good, respectable men, right?"

I am not understanding where this line of questioning is going, but I continue to answer. "They are the best men I know, including you. Taven, where is this going?"

"I'm getting there. What I have to tell you is very important, not just for me, but for all of the Elite."

"Okay…" I'm kind of getting worried now, because I can see how hard it is for him to get out what he is trying to tell me.

Taven brings my hand to his lips and kisses it tenderly, "Liz, I want to first tell you that I am totally head-over-heels- in love with you. I have been from the very first time I saw you. You are my heart. I love your boys as well and will do everything in my power to keep all three of you safe! I want you in my life always.

I know you see how Jax and Cassie are, as well as Duncan and Jill, that will be us. As long as you understand what I am about to tell you, and after everything you hear, you choose to stay with me. There is no one else for me, you are it."

A tear runs down my cheek and he wipes it away with the pad of his thumb, "Those words mean so much to me, Taven. What is it you are trying to tell me?"

"Liz, I, we, all of the Elite warriors, we are all vampires." He stares at me intensely.

I stare back for a moment, taking in every word he just said, and then burst into laughter. I'm laughing so hard, that tears are rolling down my face, "Oh… my… God! Now that is funny shit! You had me going for a moment!"

He sits there the whole time, not saying a word. I finally get over my laughing fit, wipe my eyes, and look straight at him. My smile fades as I see the hurt look upon his face.

"Taven, what is it? Tell me that you are joking."

I lose eye contact with him as he turns and looks the other way. Oh, my God, he isn't kidding. He really believes that he is a vampire.

Did I get myself involved with someone who should be locked in an insane asylum? I pull my hand from his grip and stand up, moving so I am standing in front of him.

"Is this a joke? Why are you saying these things?"

"It's no joke and I am telling you, because it's the truth. This was the other secret that I wanted to tell you. I honestly didn't know what your reaction would be, but it certainly wasn't you laughing about it." His voice sounding so saddened.

"Of course, I am going to laugh. What you are telling me sounds absurd! Vampires are fictional. They are not real."

"Do you need proof, Liz, because I can prove to you that what I say is true. I just don't want to scare you."

"If you can prove that you are a vampire, then yes, I will believe you."

"Well then, I prefer that you sit down. I don't want you passing out or fainting or anything. You will be safest sitting down."

I take my seat beside him again and stare at him, waiting.

"Just remember, there is nothing for you to be afraid of. I would never hurt you. You know that, right?"

"I do know that Taven. I trust you with my life."

As I gaze at him, he changes before my very eyes. His eyes are the first to change. Not to the swirling storm that I have seen, but to a bright blue that has a glowing effect. Next, I watch as his canines grow into fangs, and lastly, his nails turn into sharp claws. I don't know if I should be turning tail and running for my life or run my fingers over his pearly white fangs. A normal person would be running, but I have never been considered normal. Besides, I know that Taven would never hurt me. Well, at least when I thought he was human.

I can't help but to reach out and touch the point of his elongated canine. It's sharp and draws a dot of blood to form on the pad of my finger. I stare at the blood and then look at Taven. For some unknown reason, I lift my finger to his lips and allow him to suck the blood from it. I begin to feel a tingle down in the deepest region of my belly. Almost as if desire is building within my core, and a small moan slips past my lips. Taven releases my finger and the feeling goes away.

"Sorry, I haven't got to the part of explaining what all this could mean for us. I need to know where we stand, now that you know the truth."

"I honestly don't know. I mean, it's a lot to take in. What was that feeling I was getting when you sucked on my finger?"

He grins, "That is what happens to you if I were to drink from you. It's euphoric, especially during sex."

"Oh, I see."

"Liz, please talk to me. What are you thinking?"

How can I explain to him my feelings on this, when I don't even know. I don't want to hurt him, but this is a huge deal! It's not like it's a room full of toys that adults play with. How could I not have seen anything all these months while at the Compound? I tell him the only thing that I can tell him.

"Taven, thank you for dinner, but I need you to take me home now."

TAVEN

Well, that didn't go as planned, but it didn't go as bad as it could have either. I certainly didn't expect her to reach out and touch my fang or for her to offer me her finger. Her blood was divine. I have never tasted anything like it before. I hope that it won't be the last time. She is my mate; I need her in my life!

I keep glancing her way on the drive back. She has remained silent this whole time and refused my hand when I tried to help her into the SUV. I know it needed to come out at some point, but it was harder than I thought it would be. Why couldn't it be as easy as it was for Jax and Duncan?

We pull up to the Compound and before I can even turn the SUV off, Liz is out her door. I had to flash to her before she could open the front door, which in turn, startled her.

"What the…?"

"Sorry, just another perk to being a vamp. I wanted to say something before you went inside."

She won't look at me, so I gently grab her chin and tilt it up, "I know this is a lot to take in and I will understand if you do not want to continue on, but just know, I will always be looking out for you and the boys, no matter what. I love you, Liz." I see tears well up in her eyes and my heart aches. I know I am going into a danger zone with what I am about to do but fuck it. I dip my head and claim her lips. She responds at first, but then pulls away and walks inside.

I feel helpless and my emotions start to spin out of control at the thought of losing her. I punch the wall of the Compound, cracking the cement all the way to the ground. The door swings open a few seconds later and Jill stands there staring at me and then at the crack in the wall.

"You told her didn't you." I see the sympathy in her eyes, and it is too much for me to take. I push past her to go inside, but she stops me, "Just give her a little time, Taven. Cassie and I will talk to her. Liz is a good-hearted person who has had nothing, but shit dealt to her. Aside from her boys, you are the only good thing that has come into her life. She isn't stupid. She knows this, and she cares for you deeply. I don't think she can walk away from you, just like you can't walk away from her."

Without looking at her, I thank her and head to my office. There is a new bottle of Crown Royal with my name on it, sitting in the bottom drawer of my desk.

I throw myself into the moving of the Compound over the next few days, trying to keep my mind off Liz. I get glimpses of her here and there, while she is helping Cassie and Jill get stuff situated, but she never acknowledges me, not one time; it is as if I'm not even here. I know better than that, though, because my eyes are always on her, and I can see her tense up every time I am near.

Cassie and Jill both keep trying to talk to me about her, but I always claim to be too busy. I wish I could say 'fuck it' and move on, but it doesn't work that way when it's your mate. I really need to just have faith that it will all work out, I mean, why else would fate send me my mate, just to take her away from me?

All the guys pretty much stay clear of me, knowing what has happened and what frame of mind that I am in because of it. Most of them just give me sympathy looks, which is worse than anything else. It is Jax and Duncan who approach me first, telling me that I need to snap out of it and let things work themselves out. They are right, of course, I have important shit that needs to be done and as Head Elite, it is my job to do it.

As I am getting my new office straightened out, my phone buzzes with a text message. I look and see that it is Coco. She sends me a photo of the Dean that she knows from him being arrested all the time and sure as shit, it's that lousy bastard! I shoot her a text back thanking her and letting her know that it is the same guy, so she can send me a copy of his file. She then asks if it's okay if she stops over on Saturday. Shit! I completely forgot to talk to Dane about it. I go in search of Dane before I answer her.

I find Dane and Cooper unloading the trailer that has transported all the weight room equipment and wait until he puts one of the weight benches down.

"Hey Dane, can I talk to you for a moment?"

"Sure, what's up?"

"I have an old friend helping with one of our cases and they are hoping to come by on Saturday and see everyone, since they haven't seen you guys in years."

"That's awesome. Who is it"

"It's Coco, Dane. She really wants to see everyone, but not if it's going to make you feel uncomfortable."

"Why would I have an issue with it? It's been twenty-six years."

The fact that he knows the years right away without having to figure it in his head, and the tick he has going on in his jaw, tells me that he is not okay with it.

"Hey, I can tell her to come over the next time you are away on detail if you want. This is your home and you have a say in this."

"Honestly, I will be okay. If I am not, I am a big boy and can leave the room."

"Are you sure?"

"Yes! I am one hundred percent sure. You just threw me off at the mention of her name at first, but I am fine." He chuckles, and I believe him.

"Okay, great." I walk away as I reply to her text.

It takes us three whole days, with everyone helping, to move everything over to the new Compound. Liz's boys were in awe of the indoor swimming pool and playground. I have added a surprise for them and put in an indoor laser tag arena as well. Let's just say that they didn't get in any body's way for the whole three days we were moving. I love those boys like they are my own, and it saddens me that I may never get to be their stepfather.

Friday night, a few of the men and I are in the arena playing with the boys when Liz comes looking for them. Of course, it's dark in there and a person needs night goggles, but Liz isn't wearing any. I see her long before she knows I am there and I can't help but stand here and watch her feel along the walls as she makes her way towards me, calling out for the boys.

She walks right up to me and starts feeling my chest. She jumps back quick when she realizes that it isn't a wall that she is feeling. I lean down so I can whisper in her ear.

"It's just like being blindfolded, isn't it?" I hear her heartrate go up and I can smell the arousal that my words cause.

"I am looking for the boys. Are they in here?" So, she thinks she can change the subject, huh?

"They are somewhere in here, with the others, but it's just you and I here right now."

"I just wanted to make sure they were alright. I'll leave you alone." She turns to go back the other way, but I move quick, so I'm in front of her again.

"What? You don't want to play with the big boys?"

"Taven, please let me through."

I have it, so her back is against the wall, "If memory serves me, you like being touched when you can't see." I press my arousal against her, "I miss you, baby, so much. I miss your lips, I miss the feel of your touch, and the warmth of you in my arms. I need you to come back to me." I dip down and kiss her neck, "Please say you will come back to me. I need my mate by my side."

"Taven." She pants.

"Yes, love. I'm here."

"Why are you doing this to me? I need to think." Her mouth is saying one thing, but her body is telling me something all-together different.

"Tell me that you don't want me, and I will never bother you again." I nip at her earlobe before running my tongue down the column of her neck.

"Wanting you was never the issue." She is breathing heavily as her desire starts to build.

"Then come with me, otherwise I may take you right here." I slide my hand down to her crotch and can feel the heat permeating through her jeans. She moans, and I take her lips to muffle the sound. She returns my advances and wraps her arms around my neck. I lift her up and before she can change her mind, I flash us to my house and up to my bedroom.

I strip us both down as quick as possible and lay her down beneath me. I watch as emotions dance across her face, some of doubt and some of desire. I can't go on until I know for sure that she wants this as much as I do.

"Sweetheart, tell me, what do you want?"

She looks at me and I can see the passion in her eyes, "I don't know."

"I can stop if you want. Is that what you want?"

"Yes, no, maybe."

"Let me love you, Liz, the way you deserve to be loved."

"Okay." That was all it takes.

As much as I want to take her to my playroom, I want to make love to her more. Show her how loved she is. I will give this woman anything, because she is giving me everything I thought that I would never have.

FIVE

LIZ

I am more confused as ever! As much as I want to be with Taven, our future worries me. Cassie and Jill have talked to me extensively about their relationships with their mates and have explained to me how vampires exist. I get it now, and it isn't a question as to whether I am afraid of them, because I have seen first-hand what type of men they are. I understand that if I choose to go through the mating ceremony, I will live forever, as long as I drink from Taven. I guess what scares me the most is that I will outlive my boys and how do I explain all this to them?

I need some company. Sitting in my room is driving me crazy and I need to take my mind off the whole mating thing. My stomach rumbles, so I head to the kitchen to grab a snack and find Carrie and Paige sitting at the table enjoying their own snack.

"Mm, smells delicious! What are you ladies eating?"

"Oh, my God, Max has just made the most delicious brownies ever! They are still hot. Grab one and throw some ice cream on top. It's so gooey and delicious!" Paige says as she licks her spoon clean.

"I will have to take your word on that. I eat that, and it will all go to my ass." I profess. I open the fridge and pull out a yogurt before joining them at the table, "So, where is everyone anyway? It feels like a ghost town in here."

Carrie is the one to speak up, "Not quite sure, but a visitor came a short while ago and Taven took her into his office."

"A woman is here visiting Taven? What does she look like?"

"Yes... a very gorgeous woman!" Carrie smiles mischievously, "She has short dark hair, brown eyes, kind of a darker complexion. She has a warm smile and seems really happy to be here. Looks to me as if she and Taven knew each other." Carrie smirks at my reaction. Everybody knows that Taven and I have a "thing" for each other.

"Hmm... wonder who it is?" I shrug it off like it doesn't bother me and stand up to leave.

"I think they are still in his office." Paige informs me, "His door has been closed this whole time."

"It's most likely business then." I say as I walk out.

I am not usually the jealous type, and knowing how Taven feels about me, I try not to let it bother me, but my nosiness gets the best of me, and I find myself headed in the direction of his office. As I near, I hear a woman's laughter and then hear Taven tell her how much he has missed her.

Now the little jealousy bug has hit me, and I give a sharp knock before opening the door, not waiting for an invite. I walk in expecting to find an intimate scene, but instead, the woman is sitting in a chair in front of Taven's desk, while he is sitting behind his desk.

"Ah, here she is! Liz, come in. I want you to meet Coco." He motions for me to come stand by him, but first I shake Coco's hand.

"So nice to meet the woman that has captured my brother's heart! I have heard so much about you Liz." Coco smiles warmly at me.

"Brother?" I question.

Taven speaks up, "Coco used to be an Elite here, but she left us once she found her mate. It's been years since she has been back among us."

"Oh? Why didn't you stay here? If you don't mind me asking."

"That is a story for another time." She chuckles, "Maybe we can have a girl's night some time."

"Sure, sounds fun." I look up at Taven, "I will leave you to your visit. Oh, is there anyone that can run me and the boys to the mall quick? They both need new shoes, and I can't order them online, because they have outgrown them, and I need their feet measured."

"Oh, I can take you. I am sure Coco understands."

"Gosh no. You stay and visit, and I will go find someone."

"Are you sure? I really don't mind."

I reach up on tip toe and peck his lips, "Yes, totally sure." As I'm leaving the room, Taven calls out to me, and I spin around.

"Why don't you find Dane and see if he is up for the drive." I notice a look that he and Coco exchange, but I don't question it. I bet the whole reason for her leaving has to do with Dane.

"Okay, will do." I go in search of Dane, before trying to round up my rug rats.

Dane is more than willing to take us once I tell him that Coco is here at the Compound. It just confirms my suspicions. Another question to ask Taven when we are alone.

It takes us a full hour in the mall until the boys finally find the shoes that they want. Dane refuses to let me pay for them myself, informing me that Taven insisted on putting all purchases on his credit card. Not being able to argue with him in front of the salesman, I let him do it, but I am far from happy about it.

We stop for blizzards at DQ on the way home and joke about this and that. Even Dane joins in. We are just on the outskirts of town when Jack shrieks from the back seat. A second later, the SUV is tumbling over in the air from an impact that only Jake saw coming. It feels like we tumble forever until the vehicle slams into something and stops us.

I groan as pain streaks across my head, and I reach up to feel wetness, knowing that it is blood before I even look at my hand. My head is fuzzy for a moment, but as it starts to clear, I think of the boys and start yelling their names, but I get no response. I can't see them, because I am hanging upside down, being held up by my seatbelt. I see Dane start to move and then a curse rips from his mouth.

"Hold on Liz, I will have you and the boys out in no time!" I watch as Dane uses his claws to cut himself out of his seatbelt and then kicks out the smashed windshield, so he can get out.

He disappears for a moment before yanking my door open. "No, get my boys out first!" I yell.

"Their wounds are serious, Liz. I can't move them without a proper medical team. I don't know the extent of their injuries and I don't want to make them worse. I've called into 911 and sent a text to Taven."

My heart stops at Dane's words as he is telling me about my kids. I start bawling and lashing out, trying to get myself out, so I can go to my boys. Dane reaches in and carefully cuts me loose and helps me out. I drop down to my knees to get a better view of Jake and Nate and my stomach drops. They are both covered in blood, cuts everywhere. Jack looks the worst since it was his door that took the hit. I go to grab for him, but Dane holds me back as I struggle to break free.

Next thing I know, I am in Taven's arms screaming for them to save my boys. I don't when Taven got here, but he makes it before the rescue squad does.

"Why can't you save them?" I shriek as I look up at him with blurry vision.

"Baby, if they are too far gone and we give them blood, they will turn like us. I don't know how that works with children. I don't want them to be stuck this age for eternity. Do you want that?"

"There has got to be something that we can do!" I look to him and even he has tears streaming down his face. It calms me a little, to where I stop yelling at him. I know he loves my boys as his own and would do everything he could to help them. He feels helpless as well.

"All we can do is wait for the Rescue Squad to get here and get them to a hospital as fast as we can. Praying is all we can do at this point." He holds me tight while I cry like a baby in his arms, as he cries too.

At the hospital we are told that Nate has sustained a serious head injury that has left him with no brain activity and that Jack is bleeding internally and needs to have surgery. The doctors try to talk me into letting Nate go, but as his mother, I just cannot do it. Taven and I are sitting by Nate's side as we wait for news on Jack. Jax, Cassie, Duncan, and Jill are out in the waiting room waiting as well.

While we wait, Taven calls in Dr. Howard, a mate to a vampire who is also a great doctor, so she can look over the boy's charts and give us her input. Before she can get here, the surgeon comes in and informs us that they have done all that they could, but that his injuries are just too bad and that they can't get all the bleeding to stop. He suggests that we say our goodbyes, because it won't be too long before he passes. I fall to the floor, my wails bring the others from the waiting room, running into Nate's room. I don't hear anything, I don't see anything, all I feel are arms rocking me back and forth.

TAVEN

The ache in my chest that I feel, continues to grow. Losing a child is not something that any parent should go through. I feel so helpless. I promised Liz that I would never let anything happen to her or her boys, and I let her down. I am rocking her back and forth, while sitting on the floor, trying to sooth her the best that I can, when Dr. Howard rushes in. I motion for Cassie to take my spot, so I can talk to the doctor in private.

The moment we are alone, I turn to her, "Tell me what our options are?"

"I am not sure yet, Taven. I haven't had a chance to look at their charts."

I repeat to her what the doctors had told us, just so she would have some sense to what we are dealing with.

"If what you are saying is true, we should be able to give them vamp blood to heal both injuries."

"I sense a but coming on."

"The amount of blood that Nate would need to reverse the injury that he sustained, will turn him, Taven, and for Jack as well. Are you prepared for that?" She asks me worriedly.

"I need to know all the facts first. How does it work with kids who are changed? Do they stay that same age, like we adults do?"

"I only know of one case where a child was changed. It was a patient of mine. She continued to grow like any other child, except, she had all the magnified senses like a grown vamp. I can't say when she stopped aging, because the family moved away, and I haven't heard from them since."

"At least it's something, though. I can't let Liz lose her boys if there is a way to help them live." I am a ball of emotions right now.

"There is another concern, Taven. How are you going to do this without the doctors knowing? I mean, we can change Nate's care over to me and say that Liz wants him having home care, but Jack doesn't have much time. There is no way he can make a miraculous recovery in the time that he has."

"Shit! You are right. We need to come up with something." Then it hits me. "Wait right here." I instruct Dr. Howard. I go back to Nate's room and whisper for Jax to follow me.

When I return with Jax, I explain to him our options, "I know you hate doing it, but could you please make an exception and use mind control on the doctors and nurses who are taking care of Jack? It's our only option." I plead with him. Jax is the only vamp that I know who can use mind control and read minds, but he hates doing it. He is our only hope.

He hesitates, but then nods his head, "I'll do it if it means that we can save him."

"Thank you so much. I owe you big time for this!"

"No thanks necessary, and you don't owe me anything; I love the little guy."

Dr. Howard goes off to talk to Jack's doctors and nurses, taking Jax with her. The plan is to have them believe that Jack came out of the accident with a few minor scratches. While they are working on the staff, I go into Jack's room and feed him my blood. I give him more than I think is necessary, just to be sure. I can hear his heartbeat getting stronger by the minute and I sigh a breath of relief. I know he will be asleep for a few hours, so I head over to Nate's room, finding Liz still on the floor with Cassie, I shut the door and take over for Cassie.

"Hey, baby, can you hear me?" I give Liz a little squeeze to try and get her attention when she doesn't answer me. I figure I might as well just come right out and tell her.

Leaning in closer to her ear, hoping she hears me, "Jack is going to be okay, love. Do you hear me?"

She stops rocking and turns her head towards me, "Really? I thought the doctor said there was no hope?"

"Yes, he did, but I also promised you that I would always take care of them, and I'm not breaking that promise."

Looking confused, she asks me how, "By doing the only thing that I could do. I fed him my blood." Gasps were heard throughout the room, but my only concern is for the woman in my arms.

"W-What about N-Nate?" she stammers, but a little bit of her light is back in her eyes.

"I will do the same for him, but I can't do it here. You will need to sign over his care to Dr. Howard and we will tell them that he will have home care. Nate isn't in any immediate danger at the moment, but the sooner we can get him back to the Compound, the sooner we can take care of him too."

Liz throws her arms around my neck, thanking me. I hug her back before I pull away to look her in her eyes, "Sweetheart, do you understand what this means, me giving them my blood?"

"Yes, it means that I am not going to lose either one of my boys." She smiles.

"Yes, it does mean that, but it also means that they will be one of us."

"But they will be alive, right?"

"Yes, that they will."

"That is all that matters."

Once the initial shock of the accident wears off and we know the boys will be okay. I ask Dane about what happened, and he can't tell me, just that he never saw another vehicle coming. I find the whole thing suspicious, because the police labeled it a hit and run and that it is under investigation. Damn right it is! I have a feeling that our Hunter friends have decided to start another game of cat and mouse.

I assign each warrior a detail around town, and they are to report back to me each night. We are going to get this son of a bitch once and for all! I don't understand how one person like Mika can keep slipping through our fingers. He has hurt too many of our loved ones and we are going to enjoy his demise; there will be no easy death for that guy.

The days following the accident are tenuous, having to explain everything to the boys. From how vampires are real and that they are now both one, to what they can and cannot tell people about us. Jack is old enough to understand, but we worry about Nate. Liz decides that they need to be home schooled until they are both old enough to control themselves in public and trusted not to say anything. The boys themselves are stoked to find out that they are vampires now and can't wait until they were old enough to train for the Elite.

I run into Liz on my way out the door. My plan is to turn in early, until I see her, and my thoughts go to other places. Snatching her up against me, I claim her lips and grab onto her ass, hauling her up against my bulge.

I break the kiss only to nibble on her ear, "I need to be inside of you." I say in a hushed tone, "Will you come back to my place with me tonight?"

"What if the boys wake up and I am gone?" She asks between pants.

"After how hard they played and practiced learning how to use their vamp senses? They will be out cold all night, I promise."

"I don't know if I should."

"I am not beyond begging for your time and your body, Liz. I need you; it's been way too long." I continue to press myself into her and squeezing her ass.

"Will you take me to your playroom?"

That is the last thing I thought I would hear coming out of her mouth, but I smile, "Are you willing to submit to me if I do?"

"Yes, Sir."

Those two words do me in. I pick her up, cradling her in my arms, and flash to my house. Setting her down on her feet, I take the key out of my pocket and unlock the door.

"I want you to go in and undress. Pick which toys you want to try, and I will be back in five minutes."

"Yes, Sir." I lift her chin to have her look at me.

"I love you, Liz." I give her a tender kiss and then smack her ass as she walks into the room.

God, I'm one lucky son of a bitch!

I wait the allotted five minutes and go into the room. I gave her the time to pick her pleasures, so she won't be embarrassed by me watching. She is still learning, and I want her being as comfortable as possible in the beginning.

I stand before her and my eyes sweep over the front of her, then circle around to the back and do so again. I walk over to the bed and can't help but smile. She has a small flogger, a vibrator, a set of velvet-lined cuffs, and a blindfold. I can understand that she sees the innocence of these tools, but what she doesn't realize is that they are not as innocent as they look, and I plan on teaching her that lesson tonight.

I grab the blindfold and slip it over her eyes, then guide her over to stand below the eyehole in the ceiling. Choosing the rope that I want to use, I lace it through the hole and let it hang. I pick up the cuffs, restraining both of her wrists, and lift them up over her head. I attach the cuffs to the rope before tying the other end of the rope to the bed post. I stand in front of her and roll her nipples between my fingers and then twist and pull on them. She doesn't make a peep. I flick each nipple at the same time, and she gasps.

I drag my finger down her stomach until I reach her clit, rubbing it good while I nibble on first one nipple and then the other, before I continue down and reach the wetness between her legs.

"Fuck! You are so damn wet, Just the way I like it. I go to my knees and spread her legs farther apart, "Do not move your legs, no matter what."

"Yes, Sir."

Using both hands, I pull her lips apart and practically salivate at how delicious her pussy looks. I swipe my tongue quick, and she jerks. I do it again and her legs buckle. I reach a hand around and slap her ass.

"Don't move. You need to train yourself to be able to take what I give you. I will never give you more than I know you can handle, but in case you feel different, tell me a safe word that you will use when you need me to stop. It cannot be a word that could accidentally be called out during pleasure."

"Purple"

"Okay. Whenever you need me to stop, just say purple."

I continue the assault on her pussy using my tongue and fingers until she has her first orgasm, drenching her opening. Undressing quickly, I pick up the flogger and lightly run it over her ass before flicking my wrist and bringing it down on first one cheek and then the other. Her skin breaks out in goosebumps, and I do it again quickly, she moans. I bring it down on her right thigh, then her left, earning me grunts.

"You may scream if need be. In fact, it turns me on more when you do. This room is so soundproof, that even vampires can't hear the screams. I flick the flogger across her chest, stinging her nipples, causing her to cry out. I lick each one to deflect the sting, but then flick it across them again.

I bring it up and the tails of the flogger connect with her pussy. A few more flicks of my wrist and she is coming all over again. While her orgasm is at its height, I lift her up by her hips and bring her down over my cock, slamming her down on me over and over until she spirals up and over again. I keep thrusting into her, watching her tits bounce in front of my face, until I am filling her with my hot cum.

I reach up and untie the cuffs, allowing her hands to lower, but remained restrained. I take her over to the bed and lay her down, connecting the cuffs to the bed this time. I take the blindfold off and she blinks, trying to adjust her eyes.

"I want you to keep your eyes on me this time. I want you to watch me fuck you with this vibrator as I jack off."

"Yes, Sir" Her face has ecstasy written all over it as I spread her legs wide. I pick up the toy of her choosing and hold the tip of it against her clit. I turn it on. Her hips buck, so I hold her down as I continue to torture her sensitive nub. She is just about to come, when I pull it away.

Her face puckers in displeasure at me, but I let the transgression go for now. I slowly push the toy in and watch in fascination as it slides in and out with ease from both of our releases. I grab my cock with the other hand and start pumping myself, only taking my eyes off the toy fucking her pussy to make sure her eyes are trained on me pleasuring myself. When I look up, I see the desire in her eyes, as she bites her bottom lip and gyrates her hips to my tempo.

She is going to come, and I am almost there. I fuck the toy harder and faster into her and she explodes. Making sure the vibrator is in to the hilt, I leave it going while I move up by her head. I grab the hair on top of her head gently, "Open up for me, baby. I have a big load for you!"

She opens wide just as my dick erupts with sticky cum, shooting into her mouth. She swallows like a trooper until I am bone dry. I remove the cuffs from her wrists and then slide the cum-coated vibrator out of her. Holding it up to her mouth, she licks her own juices from the toy. I take her mouth with mine, tasting our mixed essence, which gets me hard all over again.

I flip her over, so her ass is in the air and her head is down, "This, my little vixen, is for the displeasure you showed me earlier."

I drive my cock into her over and over while I smack her ass continuously, she is screaming louder than I have heard her scream before, turning me the fuck on even more. I lean over her and speak while still slamming into her.

"Do you submit to me fully?"

"Yes, Sir!" She pants.

"Does that include letting me drink from you?"

She doesn't answer right away, but then I hear a "Yes, Sir", and I am sinking my fangs into her neck. She tastes better than I remember. I come so hard; I don't know if I will be able to come for days. She screams out my name as she lets go.

"Fuck me... TAVEN!"

SIX

LIZ

I'm laying here, wrapped in Taven's arms, still in his playroom. I am not sure what time it is, because there is no clock in here and I do not have permission to check my cell phone that is laying with my clothes on the other side of the room. I think back to a few hours ago, when I submitted and let Taven drink from me. I'm not going to lie; I was scared shitless. Fearing that his bite would hurt, but on the contrary, it was sheer bliss. Granted, there was a slight sting at first, but then it was forgotten when the desire started to build right after. I was a little upset that he would use my submission to be granted my blood, but when I think about it, would I have let him drink from me otherwise? I think it would have taken a lot longer to reach that part in our relationship if he hadn't, and I believe he knew this. Now that I have experienced his bite, and all that it awakens inside of me, I cannot wait until he drinks from me again. Even now I am craving it.

First and fore most though, I need to relieve myself in a bad way. I rub his arm that is lying around my waist, and hope that it is okay to do so while we are in this room. Then again, his punishments for me defying his rules are most pleasurable.

I feel him stir, so I use my voice, "Sir, may I use the restroom?"

He tightens his hold on me and I feel as if my bladder is going to explode from the pressure.

"Sir!" I say a little bit louder and he finally wakes up.

"What is it?" He asks and nuzzles my neck.

"I really need to use the restroom. May I be permitted to go?"

"Yes, but hurry back." He kisses my neck and releases me.

I shoot up from the bed and practically run to the bathroom. In record time, I empty my bladder and wash my hands. I glance in the mirror and see that I look like I have been thoroughly fucked, which I have, and I smile. Then I see the two little puncture holes in my neck and I run my fingers over them. The area is a little sore, but remembering the moment it happened, makes me want to go back out and beg for him to do it again. I won't of course. I run my fingers through my hair quickly, trying to comb through some of the tangles, but then I say, "fuck it" and I journey back to the bed.

Taven is getting up as I am crawling back into bed, and I watch as he bee lines for the bathroom himself. When he comes back, instead of getting back into bed, he comes over to my side and picks me up. Carrying me towards the door to his bedroom and I look at him confused.

"You have sated the demon inside. We do not need to remain in the playroom. Now, I want you to be yourself." He dips his head and gives me a quick kiss.

When I wake again, I am able to see the clock on the nightstand and it says that it's a few minutes before five in the morning. My head is resting on his massive chest, while my legs are entangled with his. I begin tracing his chest with my finger lightly until I hear him say "Mm" while his eyes are still closed. I know I have his attention.

"I need to head back over to the Compound, so I can shower and get ready for work."

"You can shower here, in fact, I will join you." He mumbles to me.

"I don't have any clean clothes here. I can't put my dirty clothes on after I have showered." I giggle.

"I have clothes in the closet for you." Still he keeps his eyes closed while he talks to me.

"You do?" I get up and walk to the closet to examine the items. I stare in disbelief at all the new clothes hanging up for me. Suddenly, he is behind me, sliding his arms around my waist. "Why would you have all this hanging in your closet?"

"Well, I was going to wait a few more days, but you are here now, so…"

"Wait a few days for what?" I ask him.

"I would love it if you and the boys would move in here with me. What do you think?"

I turn and stare up at him in disbelief, "You want us to move in with you? Are you sure about that? I mean, it's not just one person, but three!"

"Why do you think I had so many bedrooms built into the house?"

"I don't know, I never thought about that."

"I designed this house with you and the boys in mind, Liz."

"What? We weren't even a thing when you designed it."

"I knew you were my destined mate and that we would be together eventually, that's why." He gives me his devilish smile.

"Oh, did you now?" I cock an eyebrow at him.

Taven turns all serious on me, "I want us to be a family Liz. I want you to feel loved and cherished and I want your boys to have a father."

I gawk at his words, "Are you proposing to me?"

"Well, kind of, yes, but not officially until I find a perfect ring for you. I just want us to start our lives together. I do have a question for you though."

"And what is that?" My face is beaming with happiness.

"Once we are married, I would love it if you would allow me to adopt the boys." He quickly continues, "They can still keep their last name and carry on their father's legacy. I just want them to know that I think of them as my son's as well and that I love them as if they were my own."

My face is wet from the tears that are rolling down my face. He is waiting for my answer, but I cannot speak right now, so I nod my head up and down and throw my arms around him.

I am on cloud nine all day at work today, not even my asshole boss can put a damper on my mood. I'm finally able to catch up on all my work that I missed after the accident and work a head a little bit as well.

It's about ten minutes to five, and my supervisor pokes her head into my cubicle, "Hey, can you run the bag of shredded paper down to the recycling bin for me? I am already late for a meeting."

"Of course, no problem." I don't mind being asked to do these extra things when it's coming from her, because she would do the same for me.

I shut down my computer and get my things together, so when I get back from running the recycling out, I can grab my stuff and go.

I grab the big red bag that is sitting by the door that leads to the back stairwell, and head down. I open the outside door and shove the door stopper underneath it, so I don't lock myself out. Walking the ten feet to the bin, I swing the bag over the top, and toss it in. As I turn back towards the door, I am startled to see three men blocking my path. I recognize all three.

Dean is standing there looking all smug and his two cronies from that night, years ago, who wanted a piece of me, are standing on each side of him, smiles on both their faces. Alarm sets in. I look around, but there is nobody else around.

"What do you want Dean?"

"You know what I want, darling."

"I told you that I am not giving you any money! Besides, I don't have any extra money to be able to just hand you, even if I did want to help." I cross my arms at my chest and hope that I don't look as scared as I feel.

"Well, then, we have a problem."

"Why is that? Why are you even contacting me after all this time?"

"Because I have missed you, baby!"

"You sure didn't seem like it when we were still together, and you were fucking around on me."

"Is that why you left? Honey, none of those whores meant anything to me. You were the one that I wanted to spend my life with, I swear."

"Funny way of showing it. You wanted to share me with your two cronies there!" I nod to the two standing beside him.

"They are my best friends and we share everything, don't we boys?" Dean looks back at them.

"We sure do." They both say in unison.

"Well, that's too bad, because I am not a whore that will let myself be used by the likes of any of you! Now, let me through!" I try to walk around them, but they are quick and one of them grabs me by my hair, while the other one removes the door stopper and lets the door slam shut.

I go to scream, but a hand covers my mouth and muffles the sound. An arm comes around my waist, holding me in place as Dean walks over to us.

"I told you last time that I would bring my friends with me the next time. Doesn't look like your boyfriend is here to save you either."

Pain shoots through my stomach as Dean slams his fist into it. I can't even double over, because I'm being held too tight. The other one comes over and rips my shirt open, exposing my chest. Oh, my God, this can't be happening!

"We have been here every day waiting for a chance to get you alone. Your over bearing boyfriend is always in the way though, but not today. Today you are going to learn the hard way that you don't deny me anything!"

Next thing I know, I am being thrown to the ground and being held there. I watch as Dean swings his foot and it connects with my rib cage, agonizing pain follows. He kicks me two more times and then bends over and delivers a few blows to my face.

"Now lay still while we get to enjoy you!" Dean sneers as he undoes my slacks and pulls them down. My mind is fuzzy, and I can barely see through my already swelling eye.

Through my good eye, I see him stand straight up and undo his own pants. I hear rushed movement coming towards us and then an unfamiliar voice, "Dean, we have to go! Her boyfriend just showed up!"

"Are you a pussy? He doesn't even know that we are back here and besides, there is one of him to our four!"

"I don't know about this, Dean?" This coming from the one holding me down.

"Just shut the fuck up and hold her down! You," he points to the third guy, "cover her mouth so she can't scream. We will be through with her in no time."

The relief that I feel when I hear that Taven has pulled up, has now vanished. I start squirming and kicking out, regardless of the pain shooting through my body from his assault. I try screaming through the hand that is over my mouth, but barely any noise comes out.

Dean smirks down at me, "I like it when they are feisty. Makes my dick even harder!" He pulls his pants down and out pops his sorry excuse of a dick. I close my eyes and wait for this nightmare to end.

TAVEN

I pull up to Liz's work and find it strange that she doesn't come out right away. She is always waiting just inside the door, watching for me. My gut is telling me that something just isn't right. I turn off the SUV and go inside. I know she works on the second floor, so I take the stairs two at a time. I ask the first person I come to where I could find Liz's desk and they point me in the right direction. I look in Liz's cubicle and see that her things are still sitting on her desk. I turn and see another woman getting ready to leave for the day.

"Excuse me, do you know where Liz is?"

"Oh, you must be Taven! Lord, she said that you were hot, but that was an understatement!" She states as she fans herself.

I smile at her patiently, "Thank you. Have you seen Liz?" I ask again.

"I'm sorry, yes. She went down to take a bag to the recycling bin. Now that I think about it, she should have been back by now. That was ten minutes ago."

Fear rips through my mind, "Which way did she go?"

The woman points to a back door, "That door will take you down the back stairwell and the bin in just outside the door at the bottom of the stairs."

"Thank you." I walk quickly to the back door and then flash down the stairs. I hear voices on the other side and I burst through the door.

First thing I see is Liz's beaten body, her clothes half torn off. Her ex standing over her with what looks like his dick sticking out of his pants, but I can't be too sure, even with my magnified sight. I unleash the anger that boils over, but I keep the vamp at bay, for now. I grab Dean by his neck and throw him into the building with a roar. I then turn to the two that were holding Liz down but are now stumbling back on their asses trying to get away.

I advance on them. I bring out my claws and slash through one, killing him instantly. The other one tries to stand, but I grab him, showing him my fangs and enjoy seeing the horrific look on his face right before I snap his neck.

I spin around to go finish Dean off, but he is gone. Liz moans and I kneel beside her, while I take my shirt off and gently put it on her. I see the bruising on her ribs and flinch as I look upon her beautiful but beaten up face. Anger rises in me once more. Thankfully, I got here just in time. Her pants are down, but her underwear is still intact, so they hadn't gotten that far.

"Hang on, baby!" I kiss a spot on her face that is unmarked by bruises. Pulling my phone out, I speed dial Xavier.

"What's up boss?" He answers.

"I need a clean-up team behind Liz's work place. She was attacked, and I did what needed to be done. There are two bodies here."

"Shit! Okay, we are on our way." I end the call and lift Liz up into my arms. I place her so she is sitting up against the wall. While we wait for clean-up, I move the two dead bodies, so they are hidden between a dumpster and the recycling bin.

Liz calls out to me, and I am there in a flash, "I'm here, baby! Tell me where your pain is." It hurts seeing my mate broken like this. I am going to kill that motherfucker!

"It hurts everywhere. Thank you for coming for me."

"I will always come for you, know that."

I am guessing she is trying to keep her spirits up, because she looks at me and asks, "Would you still take me home, looking like this?" She tries to chuckle but groans in pain.

"Oh love, you could be covered in boils, and I would still take you home!"

"Please don't make me laugh, it hurts to damn much." A smile appears through her swollen lip.

"I'll have you back to yourself in no time, once we get you back to the Compound. I need Raven to check you out before I can give you my blood." I see the clean-up van make its way over to us. Xavier, Duncan, Ryder, and Cooper jump out and get to work. Within ten minutes, not a trace of a struggle could be seen. Duncan walks over to us and whistles when he sees the damage to Liz.

"Who the fuck did this?"

"Her ex druggie boyfriend, Dean." I sneer.

"Were one of those bodies his?"

"Unfortunately, not. He got away while I was busy killing these two fuckers. They were the ones holding her down. I have Dean's file at the Compound already, so we will be visiting him very soon!"

"Good! I want to be there when you end him." I nod.

"Can you go grab my SUV and bring it back here?" I ask, handing him my keys.

"Sure will."

I turn to the others, "Thank you for getting here fast and cleaning up my mess."

"It's what we do, boss. You would do it for us, too." They climb back into the van and leave us to wait for Duncan.

I am sitting beside the bed, holding Liz's hand while Raven finishes up examining her.

"Well," Raven informs us, "nothing is broken. She most likely has a few cracked ribs, but they should heal fine."

"So, I can give her my blood now and she can heal?" I ask hopeful.

"I don't see any reason why you can't. She will be as good as new in a few hours if she drinks now."

I look at Liz, "Do you want my blood, so you can heal faster?"

"I can try, I don't know if I will gag or not. The thought of drinking blood nauseates me, even if it is yours."

"Believe me when I tell you, drinking a mate's blood gives you nothing but pleasure."

"I will try it. Does it have to be from a bag, or can I drink it straight from you?"

"Which would you prefer?"

"I'd rather drink from you."

"You just want to give me a raging hard on, don't you?" I smile at her.

"Oh, I actually didn't think about that, but that is a very good incentive." I can see the smile within her good eye.

"Well, that is my cue to leave the two of you alone." Raven clears his throat, "Let me know if you need me for anything else."

"Thank you Raven, for taking care of me." Liz says to Raven.

"Hey, I never mind helping a damsel in distress. I just hope one of these days it's my own damsel." He chuckles, and we join in.

Once we are alone, I carefully move Liz over a little bit to make room for me to lay beside her. I want to make it as comfortable as possible for her. I climb up and lay on my side, supporting myself with my elbow, so I can lean over her.

Looking at her, "Are you ready?"

"As ready as I'll ever be!"

Releasing a claw on one finger, I slice myself at my jugular and lean into her mouth, "Drink, baby."

Seeing the hesitation on her face, I am about to urge her on, but then she opens her mouth and I move my neck to her lips. Her first pull causes my cock to twitch and then continues to grow with the more she sucks. She moans, and I know that she is loving the taste of me. I undo my pants and pull my dick out, so I can stroke it.

"Fuck, baby. This feels better than I ever thought possible! I pull her shirt up, that way when I come, I can squirt it on her flesh, and make it easier to clean up, "That's it, keep drinking. I'm going to fucking come all over your stomach." My balls are aching and then I am spilling my cum all over her creamy skin, "Ahh… that's it. Yes! Fuck me, baby. I can't stop coming. You are going to kill me here!"

She takes one last long pull and another load shoots out. "FUCK!" I roar. I continue to pump my cock to make sure everything comes out and then I tuck myself away. I look down at her stomach and see all the cum that I unloaded on her.

"I'll grab a rag." When I return, I see Liz run a finger though the mess and then lick it off her finger, "Now that is fucking hot! Do it again." I feel my demon trying to come out, but I know I need to keep him at bay. At least until Liz is back to feeling like herself.

"You taste so good, Taven. Your blood, your cum, it all tastes musky but sweet."

"Now you know how I feel when I drink from you and eat you out." I grin. I clean my mess off her tummy and pull her shirt back down before climbing back in beside her.

"Drinking from you has left me all horny. Will you take care of it?"

"As much as I would love too, you need to let your body rest and heal. I will gladly return the favor later tonight. I kiss her gently and then wrap her in my arms, so she can sleep.

I leave Liz sleeping in medical and go in search of Jack and Nate to make sure they are staying out of trouble and to reassure them that their mom is going to be fine. I find them where I always find them since moving here, in the laser tag arena. They are just getting ready to head back to the Compound to take their nightly showers.

"Hey boys, did you play hard?" I rub the top of Nate's head and mess up his hair.

Giving me a toothless smile, "We play hard every day. We need to practice our shooting, so when we are Elites, we won't miss hitting the bad guys!"

"Is that right? Well then, you better practice every day." I inform him.

"Oh, we will!"

"I have a question for you boys. How would you like to move into my house with your mom? You would have your own bedrooms and everything!"

"That would be cool." This coming from Jack, "Can I ask you a question?"

"Of course, shoot."

"Are you and our mom going to get married?"

"Would you like us to get married?"

"Well, you would make a pretty awesome dad and I know mom really likes you."

"Does she now? What about you Nate, what do you think?"

"I think what Jack thinks. You are awesome."

I can't help but grin at these boys and the space in my heart for them just grew bigger.

"Well, I'll tell you what. How about in a few days, the three of us go shopping and find the perfect engagement ring for your mom?"

"What's an engagement ring?" Nate asks.

"It's a ring that you give the person that you ask to marry."

"Yeah! Let's do it!" Nate begins to jump up and down.

"Now, how about we go and pack up all your stuff, so we can move it over to my house? We can get it all moved in while your mother is resting and then we can surprise her when she wakes up later."

"Okay." They say in unison and then they run off to go start packing. We haven't taught them how to flash just yet, because we still have the three women in the Compound who are still unaware of who we really are. I can only imagine Nate flashing from room to room. I smile to myself and shake my head. That boy is definitely going to be a handful, but I'm going to enjoy every minute of it!

SEVEN

LIZ

After the attack, I decide to take some time off from work. I am completely healed, but just the thought of going back to that place, unnerves me. Taven has been great, especially with the boys. He had moved us into his house the night of the attack, while I was healing, and the boys have been on cloud nine ever since. I was a little worried that they wouldn't adjust, but apparently, they think that Taven is the coolest person they have ever met and love the fact that they get to live with him.

I love that my boys have bonded so well with Taven, and that maybe one of these days we can be a real family. Some people may think that I am out of my mind for shacking up with a vampire, but in all honesty, I have met a lot of shady men that do not come close to the kind of man that Taven is.

"Hey gorgeous. Fancy seeing you here!" I feel strong, welcoming arms wrap around me from behind, and I smile.

"You may want to be careful. My boyfriend may see you and that won't be pretty." I tease.

"I think we may have time for a quickie before he catches us. What do you think?"

"Well, seeing as we are in the Compound, there is no place to have a quickie. Duncan and Jill ruined that for us." I giggle, "Although, I don't think my boyfriend will be home for quite some time, we can go back to his place and see what kind of trouble we can get into."

"Mm, I like the sound of that!" I feel a nibble on my earlobe before I am spun around and kissed fully on the mouth.

Taven pulls away from me and smiles, "As much as I would love to find a quiet spot, so I can screw your brains out, I am actually on my way to go meet with Coco. Can I get a reign check?"

"I don't know, my schedule is pretty full, but I can try and fit you in."

"Oh, I think we both know that you can fit me in!" He rakes my body salaciously, "God, have I told you how much I love you?"

"Every morning, every night, and many times in between. I am not bothered by hearing it more than that either." I slide my arms around his neck and meet his lips as they come down to mine. We stand there in the hallway, not caring who would see, but it ends way to soon, "I don't know if I have told you, but I love you, ugly mug and all." I give him a teasing grin.

"Actually, you have never said it before, but I was willing to wait until you were ready. No matter how long it took. Say it again."

"I love you Taven…", I stop and realize that after everything we have been through, I don't even know his last name! "Do you realize that I don't even know the last name to the man I love?"

"Really? Are you sure?" He asks quizzically.

"I am one hundred percent sure. I would never forget it."

"Well, Ms. Brady, my last name is Anderson. It's a pleasure to meet you." He lifts my hand and kisses it tenderly.

"How did you know mine? I know I never gave it to you."

"Come on now, Liz. I am head of the Elite. I know everybody that lives under my protection."

"Well, I guess you are right, but it doesn't make it less creepy or stalker-like." I chuckle.

"I will stalk you to the ends of the earth, until my last breath, babe. Look I really have to go. I will see you this evening." With a quick kiss, he is gone. I wonder what he and Coco are working on.

I let that thought go and turn my mind towards my boys again. I haven't seen them all morning and I am seriously hoping that they did not find trouble to get into.

I find Jack and Nate at the pool with Cassie, Jill and the babies, and decide to run back to the house and change into my swimsuit. It's been a while since I actually spent some quality time with my boys, and I am looking forward to it.

I walk into the pool area and whistles come my way from the girls. Rolling my eyes, I take a seat in one of the chairs next to them.

"Look at all this hotness, Jill! I think I had better cover myself up, so I don't look so hideous sitting by her!" She teases and winks at me.

"No kidding! Where have you been hiding that body for all these years?"

"I usually don't wear my swimsuit in public. As far as my body goes, I'm always self-conscience about it, so I don't wear too tight-fitting clothes." I say as I try to cover myself with my arms.

"First of all," Jill pipes in, "I wouldn't call that a swimsuit. It's more like two pieces of scrap material thrown together. Wow! Second of all, what is there to hide? You are like a perfect ten!"

"Shut the fuck up. I am not!"

"Pfft... whatever you say." Cassie and Jill both roll their eyes at me.

The boys call for me to get in the pool with them, so I stand up and walk to the edge. I'm about to jump in when the door opens, and I hear men's voices. I sit at the edge and slide into the water.

"Hey ladies, who is your friend? She is smoking hot from behind!" I hear Kai ask Cassie and Jill. I turn around to face him and his eyes are about ready to pop out of his head. Cassie, Jill and Duncan, who walked in with him, all burst into laughter as I turn a light shade of red from embarrassment.

"Open mouth and insert foot as always." Duncan shakes his head.

"I am so sorry Liz. I didn't realize you were so hot. I mean, not that you're not, but I didn't know your body looked like that!"

As the girls laugh even harder at Kai's sorry excuse of an apology, Duncan grabs him by the shoulder, "Quit while you are ahead, because you are making it worse."

"I am truly sorry, Liz."

"It's okay. I will forgive you this time." I smirk.

"You better hope that Taven never hears of this!" Cassie says with an evil smile.

"Taven will only hear about it if you say something about it!"

"Oh, I don't know. I have a feeling that you will be the one to say something. You can't seem to keep your mouth shut."

"Wanna bet?" He asks.

"Sure!" Both Cassie and Jill say in unison.

"You will definitely be losing this bet, because there is no way that I am going to tell Taven that I was checking out his mate's fine ass!"

"YOU WERE DOING WHAT?!" Taven's voice booms through the pool area. The girls are holding their stomachs and laughing.

Kai's eyes widen for a second time as he turns slowly, "It was a complete misunderstanding, boss! She had her back to me, and I didn't realize it was her!"

"Kai, why don't you go and suit up before I lose my shit!"

"Yes, boss!" He quickly heads for the door.

"Oh, and Kai? Jill and I will catch you later for our pay out!" Cassie calls after him.

He raises his hand and flips her off, "Bunch of fucking cheaters!" More laughter follows his response.

I look at Taven cautiously as he walks over to the side of the pool.

"I really can't blame the kid. You do look smoking hot in that bikini!" He wiggles his eyebrows at me, "I should ban you from wearing it again, but the men will have to learn to not look."

"What about you?" I ask as I hold on to the side of the pool and make it so my cleavage plumps up.

"Baby, if I didn't have to leave right now, I would go all cave man on you and drag you back to the house!"

I pout my lip up at him, "Where are you all going anyway?"

"Coco got a lead on where Dean has been staying and we are raiding the place. That mother fucker will pay for what he did to you."

"Oh, I see."

"You don't sound too happy about it? Why is that?"

"No, it's not that. I just thought back to that first year that we were together. He was such a good man. It is sad that he got messed up in the bad life. He deserves to pay for what he did."

"Well, I don't want you worrying too much about it. It will be taken care of today. I always protect what is mine, and you my dear, belong to me." He reaches down and takes my lips, "I love you, baby." He says as he pulls away.

"I love you too. Please be safe."

"I will. I have you and the boys to come home to now." He runs his thumb over my cheek and then stands up and turns to Duncan. "Are you ready to roll?"

"Sure am, let's get this fucker!" Duncan slips Jill a kiss and walks out with Taven.

TAVEN

Walking into the pool area and hearing Kai talk about Liz like that, really made me have to hold the vamp back. I wanted to tear his head off! I realize that he means no harm, but the vampire in me only wants to protect its mate. Kai needs to know when to keep his mouth shut if he wants to continue living. I shake my head at that kid. Always getting himself into trouble with his smartass comments. I think it's time to have a little talk to him about it. For now, I just want to concentrate on raiding Dean's place and bringing him in.

My meeting with Coco earlier has had me amped up and ready to go. I will not let him slip past us. Coco has informed me that one of her informants in the drug scene had told her that Dean has been a regular at a drug house on the east side of town. He should be there in the next few hours, so we will go and watch for him to show up and then bring him in. The rest, Coco and her crew will bring to the local police station.

Now that I have met the Police Chief and know that he is on our side and is willing to work with us, it takes a huge weight off my shoulders. Staying in hiding and trying to protect the innocent has been hell. We now have the extra help and resources to do our work more efficiently.

We have been sitting here for an hour, watching people go in to get their fix and then leave stumbling, but none are Dean. The tick in my jaw is getting worse with the longer I have to wait. My body is tense, and I am worried that I will not be able to hold my vamp in once I have him in my sight. I think about sending Duncan for him, but I want to be there the moment of his capture.

Finally, after an hour and a half, Dean is spotted walking down the road in our direction. We are parked two houses down from the location that he is going to, so we wait until he starts to pass us. He is looking down at his cell phone, so as he closes the distance, he isn't aware of the blacked-out van that is waiting for him. Just as he starts to pass, Duncan, Ryder and I jump out and circle him. Yeah, we could have just flashed and nabbed him at the same time, but what kind of fun is that? Mama always told me not to play with my food and I always listened to her, but mama isn't here anymore, and this vamp wants to play, just a little.

"Well, well, well, what do we have here? Where are your cronies, Dean? Oh, that's right... they are rotting six feet under!" I sneer.

"W-What d-do you w-want?" He stutters as he tries to find a way around us.

"We just want to talk. Why are you looking so scared?"

"W-what about?"

"Oh, you know damn well what about. How about you come take a ride with us?"

"I'm not g-going anywhere w-with you!"

I turn up the heat and let my eyes glow as I stare him down, "Now Dean, is that any way to talk to an old friend?"

"What the fuck are you?"

"I don't know what you mean, Dean?" I lengthen my fangs just a little.

"Y-your eyes! Your t-teeth!"

"I see you are hallucinating again, huh?" I hear Duncan and Ryder snicker.

"Don't come anywhere n-near me or I'll s-scream!" The fear on his face is priceless. I pretend to clean a fingernail as a claw replaces the nail and I smile down at him.

"Do you want to do this the easy way or the hard way? Easy, being that you come with us and hard, is dying a slow death right here on this sidewalk." I inform him.

"You are going to kill me anyway, so what does it matter?"

"Hm, Duncan, would you like to explain it to him?" Duncan flashes around Dean, scraping his claw down his mid-section as he does so. Dean howls in pain even though Duncan only scratches him.

"There is more of that," I speak up and nod over to Ryder, giving him the signal. Ryder flashes around him next and bites down, taking a chunk from Dean's arm, causing him to scream bloody murder, "and a little more of that if we stay here."

Holding his arm to staunch the blood flow, "People will see!" He shrieks, "They will call the police!"

"Look around you, Dean. You are in drug town, USA. Do you truly believe that someone will call the police to come? Besides, how do you think we got intel on you? The police know we are here."

"Lies! The cops would not allow you to torture and kill someone!"

"Are you sure about that? I guess if you want it the hard way…" I nod at Duncan, but Dean yells.

"Okay, okay! I will go with you."

"That's a good boy. Ryder, cuff this piece of shit!" I get back in the front passenger seat while the guys secure Dean in the back of the van.

Now that we have Dean nice and secure in one of the cell blocks, I go and search for Liz. I find her at our house preparing supper and enjoying a cocktail. Strawberry Strippers are her favorite, so I always keep the ingredients at her disposal.

She turns towards me when I enter and gives me her best smile before coming over and wrapping her arms around me.

"I see you are in one piece. How did it go?"

"It was a piece of cake. I just wanted to stop in and see if you had anything that you wanted to say to the asshole before I end him?"

I can see that she is struggling with the idea of if she wants to or not, but in the end, she nods yes. She chugs the rest of her drink down, I'm assuming for some liquid courage, and takes my hand as we head to the Compound.

The underground level is bright, and each cell block is made up of impenetrable glass. The first cell we walk by is Samantha's; she's had the most comfortable cell. She has been coming along nicely with her therapy and I believe that she will eventually be freed, but that decision is all on Xavier. He is her maker, and it is his decision.

A few cells down is Dean's. As we approach, he stands up and smiles when he sees Liz.

"I knew you wouldn't let them kill me! We meant too much to each other at one time and you have a soft heart, Liz. Thank you!"

Liz straightens her spine and lifts her head defiantly, "You are right about two things, Dean. We did mean something to each other at one time and I do have a soft heart, but you ruined it all. You couldn't just leave me alone, could you? Instead, you and your friends held me down, beat me, and would have raped me had Taven not shown up! You expect me to have them give you mercy after all that?" She sneers at him, and Dean realizes that he had it all wrong.

"This isn't you, Liz! These monsters have brain washed you!"

"The only monster I see here is you!"

"You don't know? He has eyes that glow, and fangs! Liz, he has fangs for shits sake! You are going to tell me that he isn't a monster?"

Liz looks up at me and smiles, then comes and stands in front of me, leaning against my chest.

"Taven is no monster, Dean. He is the love of my life and I, his. He will do anything to protect me and keep me safe."

I want to laugh at the horrified look on Dean's face as I extend my fangs and sink them into Liz's soft, creamy neck, looking at him the entire time. Liz moans and starts to rub her ass against my arousal. Of course, we won't do anything right in front of him, but he gets the gist of it. I retract my fangs and Liz turns in my arms as I slice my own neck open, for her to sample my blood.

"You are fucking insane! How can you succumb to these beasts, Liz? What about your boys?"

Liz spins on him, "You don't get to talk about my boys, Dean! You lost that privilege a long time ago! Now, I'm going to take my boyfriend here and go fuck him senseless. Maybe that way he will be lenient with you and your death will be quick. That is all I am willing to do for the likes of you."

Dean's jaw drops, and he stares as Liz grabs my hand and pulls me back towards the entrance. Although, I am so turned on right now that I can't wait until we get back to the house. I open the door to the guard room and see that Kaid and Phoenix are on duty at the moment.

"Go take a thirty-minute break." I demand.

Kaid looks back and forth between Liz and I and then breaks out into a smile, "Breaking your own rules, I see! Just don't forget to change the sheets on the cot before you leave." He and Phoenix walk out chuckling and shaking their heads.

I slam the door and lock it, before turning back to Liz.

"You were so fucking hot back there! Later on, I am going to take you to the playroom and reward you properly, but right now, I just want to fuck your brains out!"

I don't waste time. I pull her shirt off and then her bottoms, so she is just in her bra and panties, "Fuck, you are a sight to behold!" I slam my mouth against hers and demand that she open for me. She does, and our tongues begin dancing to their own tempo. I am so fucking hard; I can't take it any longer. I break free of the kiss and spin her around, bending her over the desk that sits in the middle of the room.

"Don't fucking move, sweets!" I kneel down behind her and spread her legs far apart. I can smell her arousal and know that she is already wet and wanting. I tear her panties off her and run my tongue through her gentle folds, lapping at the juice that is already flowing. I use my hands to spread her lips apart, before shoving my tongue into her pussy. God, her taste is to die for! I reach up with one hand and pinch her clit before I roll the nub between my fingers making her moan.

"I need more Taven." She pants, "I need to be fucked right now..."

I slap her ass hard, "I will fuck you when I am good and ready, but not before I have you coming on my face!" I continue the assault on her pussy, licking her folds and then thrusting my tongue in and out, all while rubbing, pinching, and rolling her sensitive nub within my fingers.

I remove my tongue and insert first, one finger, and then a second one into her wet entrance. I begin to finger bang her hard and fast and just as her breathing increases, I lick her puckered bud before taking it with my tongue. She explodes in a tidal wave of pleasure, and I pull my fingers out and shove my face back into the cradle of her thighs, allowing her sweet nectar to run down into my mouth.

I don't give her a chance to rest. I stand up and thrust my cock into her, penetrating her over and over, until she is about to come again, and I pull out. She groans.

"Please!" She begs, so I fuck her even harder than the last and pull out again, before she explodes.

"Tell me what you want me to do to you, baby. It needs to be dirty, not a simple "please" will do if you want me to let you come again."

She hesitates a moment, "I want you to let your vampire out. I want to watch as your vamp fucks me with the ferocity that only he can. Let him out Taven, and you can have free reign to my body."

Fuck! The second the words are out of her mouth, the vampire in me breaks free. I grab her up and spin her, so she can see all of me. Not only my eyes, fangs and claws, but even my cock grows in girth and length. Her eyes are glazed over with desire as she stares at the vampire in me.

"What are you waiting for? Fuck me now, show me no mercy."

That's exactly what I do. I pick her up and slam her against the wall as I enter her at the same time. I am fucking her so fast that to the human eye, you wouldn't be able to tell. I have her come three times within a minute at this speed, but then I slow down, continuing to drive into her hard as I sink my fangs into her. My balls ache for release, but I hold off until she comes one more time. I don't need to wait long, though. She screams my name as she claws my back like a wild cat, while her orgasm hits her hard. I let myself go, thrusting my cock all the way in as I erupt. I pull out a little and thrust back in to fill her up a little more. I do this three more times, until I am finally drained, and she is holding all of it inside.

I remain inside of her as I lay her down on the cot. I want to keep as much of my cum inside of her, in hopes it seeds itself. I know we haven't talked about it, and I know she is on birth control, but I am desperate to watch her belly grow with my child.

We only have about five minutes left before the guys come back, so regretfully, I pull out and walk over to the sink and wet a towel down, so I can clean us off.

"How are you feeling, baby? I didn't hurt you, did I?"

"You could never hurt me; you are wonderful." She says this as she begins to fall asleep from exhaustion. I can't help but smile, knowing that I do this to her every time. I finish cleaning her off and dress her quickly. Picking her up, I open the door and find both Kaid and Phoenix leaning against the wall, grinning from ear to ear.

"Wow, boss, total exhaustion? You are definitely doing it right!" Kaid chuckles as he slaps me on the back and walks back into the room, "Man, it stinks of raw, hot sex in here! Phoenix, grab the air freshener, will you?" I smile as I climb the stairs and carry Liz back to our house.

EIGHT

LIZ

I awake to the sound of the door clicking shut and to the delicious aroma of the lasagna that I made earlier. I sit up quickly at the thought of supper still in the oven and here I am, lazing around in bed, but Taven is here, carrying a tray.

"Hello sleepy head. I thought I would bring you some supper to get your strength back up." He places the tray over my lap and sits on the edge of the bed.

"You must be ravenous." He gives me his devilish smile.

"I am, and if you would stop putting me into a sex induced coma, I wouldn't feel like this!" I look at him sternly.

"I can stop doing that at any time, but that would mean not ever making love to you again. Do you really want that?"

"That is not fair. You know damn well that I am addicted to you and that I will take being comatose over never having you fuck me again."

"Ah, that's what I like to hear." He nibbles on my earlobe a moment and then pulls away. "Don't think I have forgotten about your little reward either. I'm having my urges again and need you in the playroom in a bad way."

"What will be my reward? I thought earlier was reward enough." I flush just a little. I love the playroom. I don't know what he has done to me, but I look forward to him trying new things on me. I have started to yearn for more, for him to show me just how much he can torture me. I've yet to say the safe word and I trust him enough that I know I will never have to use it. I will do anything to calm his demon. That room lets me be a completely different person, submitting to him and his needs is pure ecstasy.

"That my little sex kitten is for me to know. The only thing that I will tell you is that my demon is very pent up at the moment and I will warn you, he will do things that you can't even imagine yourself doing. You will not be Liz in that room tonight. Tonight, you will submit to whatever my demon deems necessary. Do you understand? Are you willing to go through with whatever is demanded of you?" I can't help the way his words turn me on or the tingles I have running through my body as he runs his fingers through my hair and whispers the words in my ear.

"Yes, I will submit to all of it. Only for you. Let your demon do what he wants, whatever it takes to calm him. Can we go now?" I am wet and panting for him, my supper forgotten.

Taven looks me in the eyes, and I see the storm brewing within his lids, "Not yet, love. What I have planned for you will take most of the night. That is why you need to eat up, and I promised the boys that we would go for ice cream as soon as you are done." He chuckles and then kisses me, taking my breath away in this one little kiss. He pulls away and stands up. "Eat up, I will be back in a few minutes."

Thirty minutes later, we are in the SUV and heading for Dairy Queen on Civic Center Dr. The boys are chatter boxes the whole way, and I can't help the overwhelming love that I am feeling right now, as I gaze upon my children and the man I love, talking and laughing together. Taven looks over at me and smiles as he takes my hand and squeezes it.

When we get there, the boys run ahead and grab one of the tables in the corner for us. Taven orders his and the boy's dessert and then looks at me for my order. I think it's weird that he already knows what Jack and Nate want since it was never discussed on the way over, but he orders exactly what they like, so I don't mention it.

Taven and I make our way to the table and sit down to wait for our ice cream to be delivered to the table. Nate starts telling us knock-knock jokes, but then turns them into "your mom" jokes and I can't help but laugh at some of the ones that they come up with.

Our order finally comes, and the boys attack their dessert as if it is going to disappear. "Slow down," I reprimand, "You are going to get brain freeze!"

Taven keeps looking over at me, his eyes smiling each time he does, "How is your sundae?"

"It's pretty good. What about yours?"

"The same."

I am about three quarters of the way done with mine, when I feel something hard in my next bite, "What the...?" I spit the mouthful out in a napkin and look down. "What is this?" I don't bother looking at anybody, I am too confused at what I am seeing. "Oh, my God, someone lost their ring while making my sundae!" I hold it up for the three of them to see it.

All three of them are wearing goofy grins on their faces, which confuses me more.

"Here, let me see that." Taven takes the ring from me and wipes it completely off. The next thing I know, he is getting down on one knee in front of me and holding the ring out to me. I realize what he is doing, and I feel my eyes start to fill up.

"Liz, you and the boys mean so much to me. You have been my salvation when my world turns to darkness, and I want to spend the rest of eternity with you and the boys by my side as a family. I want to be the husband and father that you all deserve. Will you do me the extreme honor in marrying me?"

Tears are now flooding my face and my hand is in front of my mouth. I have waited a lifetime for someone like Taven and now, here he is wanting not only me, but my children as well. I look over at the boys who are smiling and nodding their heads yes. Turning back to Taven, I remove my hand and hold it out to him.

"Yes, I will marry you!" He slides the ring on my finger and hauls me up to spin me around. The rest of the patrons and employees cheer and applaud at us. Taven smashes his lips to mine in a deep and passionate kiss and more cheers erupt.

He finally breaks away from me and gazes into my eyes, "Thank you, Liz. You have just made me the happiest man on the planet, I love you!"

"Thank you for loving me and my boys the way that you do!"

"Loving you three is the easiest thing to do, baby."

As the boys finish up with their desserts, I stare at the gorgeous ring on my finger. It must be almost two-karat, with clusters of little diamonds all around it, but what stands out to me the most are the four gems within the cluster of diamonds. Each gem is our birthstones, intermingled. I absolutely love it!

I look at Jack and Nate, "Did you boys know about this?"

"We sure did!" Jack says, "He asked for our approval first and we helped pick out the ring." His bright smile brings more tears to my eyes.

Nate goes on to add, "It was my idea to do it here and to put it in your favorite dessert!"

"It was?" I ask surprised. I love it when he gets so excited over things, and he is tickled pink about his part in this occasion.

I look back at Taven and grab his hand, "Thank you for including them. This is the best proposal ever!" He winks at me and gives me his most dashing smile.

The boys are already in bed, and I am just finishing cleaning up the kitchen when I hear a low baritone voice in my ear, "Go to the room, strip, and kneel on the floor as you wait for me." Arousal floods me instantly.

"Give me two minutes."

"No. I said to go now."

"Yes, Sir." I look at him as I turn to head upstairs and his eyes are the deep, dark blue storm clouds. Shit! It's the demon talking. I don't waste any time making my way upstairs. I see the playroom door is already open, so I quickly walk in and undress. I kneel in the middle of the floor, hands behind my back with palms facing up, and my head is bowed. Excitement coursing through me at what is about to take place.

I hear his footsteps coming towards me and then I see his bare feet as he stops in front of me.

"That was a naughty thing you did downstairs, disobeying me. For that you will be punished. You will be my little slut tonight, among other things. Look at me Slut!"

I look up at him and see that he is completely naked, his cock hard as a rock.

"Get up on your knees." I do as he commands never taking my eyes off his. He takes a step closer and rubs his cock all around my face, stopping at my lips. "You are going to blow me until I come in that slutty little mouth of yours. Do you understand?"

"Yes, Sir."

"Good, now open up for daddy." I open up and he pushes himself in. I reach up to stroke him with my hands, but he quickly pulls back out, bends down and squeezes both my nipples until I cry out. "I never said you could touch me with your hands. I am going to fuck your mouth, no touching with any other body part!"

"Yes, Sir... sorry, Sir."

I open up again and this time he grabs my hair and gently pumps himself back in. First, he starts slowly and then he picks up speed. All I can do is swirl my tongue and suck him off as he continues to push my head back and forth with my hair. My body is on fire, and I want to feel him in me, but I am sure that it will be a while before we get to that part.

He is thrusting faster now, and I can feel the pulse in his cock as he gets ready to come. Hot, thick liquid erupts in my mouth, and I begin to swallow.

"Give me your hand." He commands, and I do as he says. He pulls his cock out while he is still coming and wraps my hand around it, "Pump the rest out and cover your tits with my semen."

I start pumping fast, pointing his tip towards my chest as his cum squirts out all over me. When he is done, he tells me to lick him clean and I happily oblige. Holding his hand out for me to take, he helps to stand me up. I expect him to clean me off, but all he does is stare at the mess on my chest and smiles.

"Now you are my dirty slut." I am so turned on at this moment that I don't care what he calls me, as long as he releases this fire that is burning inside of me, "Come, I'm going to introduce you to something new and you are going to enjoy it."

He walks me over to what looks like a sawhorse, except it has padding on it and places for your arms and legs, each with cuffs attached.

"Climb up and straddle the horse here." He points to where he wants me to straddle. It feels weird on my crotch as I sit with the padding against my wet sex.

Taven then leans me forward until I am laying on my stomach, the padding resting between my breasts, and my head turned to the side on a head rest. He then moves both arms to the armrests, my elbows bent, and cuffs each wrist. Moving to my legs, he bends my knees as he lays them on more padding and then cuffs my ankles.

There are two more straps, one for my neck and one for my waist, which he wraps around me. I am truly strapped in and at his mercy. He bends down so he is at eye level with me.

"Now the fun can begin. Do you remember your safe word?" For a moment, I see the swirling storm in his eyes leave and it is just ocean blues, Taven, not the demon, asking me this.

"Yes, Sir."

The demon is back as soon as I say those simple, but very important two words.

TAVEN

She is per-fucking-fection, as I gaze upon her restrained form. Never have I seen anything more beautiful. The demon in me wants to punish her for disobeying, but all I want to do is give her sheer pleasure. Granted, the demon will not hurt her, but there will be slight pain before the pleasure.

I run my hands over her naked form, feeling the creaminess of her unblemished skin. Yes, we will mark her, but again, it's all out of pleasure. Tonight, I am taking it up a few notches, and that is why I wanted to make sure that she remembers her safe word.

I go to my chest of drawers and pull out different anal plugs. Yes, I will be working that hole tonight until it fits around my cock like a glove. Moving over to my floggers and crops, I choose one of each. Grabbing lube, I make my way back over to where my dirty little slut is waiting. I can smell her essence as it seeps out of her, and I can't help but to lean in and swipe my tongue deep through the lips.

"Mm..." I say as I see a shiver run through her, "Warm apples is my new favorite flavor." I run the crop lightly up her folds before giving it a quick little slap, making her body jerk. "You like that, slut?"

"Yes, Sir."

"Tell me you want me to do it again." I command her as I run it up and down her lips.

"Please, do it again, Sir!" She begs, and I bring it down harder, but quickly lick over it to reduce the sting.

Putting the crop down, I pick up the smallest plug and lube it up before carefully inserting it. She tightens her ass up and I slap her cheek, "Do not do that again. Relax and let me do what I will to this glorious piece of ass."

Once she relaxes, I push it the rest of the way in and smack her ass cheeks where it is inserted. Hearing a moan spill form her lips, I smack her again, "That's it, take it you little harlot. That's right, you are mine, to do with as I please. I will call you whatever pet name that is befitting at the moment."

I whack her again and then massage the area. I hear her whimpers and walk over to her, so she can see me, "Are you doing okay?"

"Yes, Sir. I want more. Please give me more..." I run the back of my hand down her cheek.

"You, my little slut, are everything that I need. I will have you begging for release in no time."

I go back and I change out the plugs, putting a bigger one in. Using the flogger, I slice it across her backside as I reach between her and the padding and play with her clit. I continue this until she is creaming herself.

After switching and putting the big plug in, I start to thrust it in and out of her bud while I fuck her with my fingers.

"Oh... Oh... don't stop, please... don't stop!" She screams as her orgasm bursts forth, claiming her body.

"I'm not done with you yet, you little trollop. You are going to feel my dick take possession of that tight little bud and then you will really be screaming."

I situate myself behind her and lube myself up. Slowly, inch by inch, I shove through the tight canal until I am as deep as I can go.

"How does that feel? Do you like being full of my dick?"

"Oh, my God, Yes, Sir." She's panting heavily, but her body is relaxed.

"Good. Now hold on, because I'm about to fill your ass up with my cum."

I begin thrusting into her, slapping her ass every so often. God, she is so tight, it almost hurts, but it's a good kind of hurt. I lean over and start playing with her nipples, squeezing and then rolling them between my fingers. My balls slap against her pussy and then they start to pull up and I know I don't have long.

My dirty little slut is screaming in pleasure and as I feel her start to tighten up, I let myself go, filling her ass up to the brim. As I pull out, I slap her ass again for good measure.

After I clean us both off, I release her from the restraints and carry her over to the bed, where I restrain her once more. It gets me so fucking hot seeing her there, open for me. I have her spread eagle, making the perfect picture.

I go to the drawer in the night stand and take out the round packet of pills that she insists on taking. Standing there with my hands behind my back, I urge her to look at me. I can still see the desire in her eyes as she looks upon me.

"Tonight, I will be making you my official mate. My demon needs to be one with you, as do I. By submitting to me fully, it is my choice, but this too can be stopped by saying your safe word." I wait a moment to see if she will say it, but she remains quiet, "So, since you are willing, there is one last thing, which is non-negotiable." I bring my hand up to show her the birth control pills, "There will be no more of these." I crush the whole packet in my hand, turning it to dust, "Do you understand me?"

"Yes, Sir." Her teeth dig into her lower lip.

"I am going to fill you up with my seed every day until you conceive. I have waited centuries for you and to start a family and I refuse to wait any longer now that I have you." I crawl over to her and line my tip up to her opening and thrust into her, "You are going to grow with my child many times and you are going to enjoy every minute of it, as will I. Say you are willingly to give me this."

"I've submitted to you, Sir, and I would love nothing more than to give you a child."

"Are you ready to become one with my demon?"

"Yes, Sir." She is panting and grunting the harder I fuck her, and I know she is almost there. I bring my vampire to the surface and slice my neck open for her.

"Drink, baby. Let me fill you with my seed and my blood." I lean down, and she latches on as I sink mine into her. It's like an electrical shock goes through me and it swirls within, my own body's desire building until I can't hold it in anymore and it all comes pouring out tenfold. I feel little sharp teeth break my skin and I know that we are now bonded for eternity. She pulls away from my neck and lets out an ear-piercing scream of pleasure that puts a very satisfied smile on my face.

I release her from her bonds as we come down from the best high ever, and I wrap her in my arms, kissing her forehead.

"This will be the only time we break role in this room. Please repeat after me, okay?"

"Okay."

"Liz Brady, I promise to love you, cherish you, and protect you forever."

"Taven Anderson, I promise to love you, cherish you, and protect you forever."

I claim her lips with mine and begin to make love to her, this time as my beautiful Liz, my mate.

It's the wee hours of the morning when I carry Liz to our bed. I start to climb in beside her when my cell begins to buzz. Looking at it, I see that it's a text from Kole saying that he has some urgent news and that I need to come to IT as soon as possible. I lean down and give Liz a kiss before getting dress and closing the door quietly behind me.

Kole is pounding away at his keyboard when I walk in, "This better be good! You pulled me away from my mate and we just made it official."

"I am so sorry Boss, and congratulations!"

"Yeah, thanks. Now, what is it that is so urgent?"

"Ten vampires have come up missing, not dead, just missing, and it has Mika's name all over it! I have some footage of one of the abductions. It is a female and it looks like they are using the tranquilizer darts that they had used on Duncan."

"That doesn't mean that it is Mika, though."

"The one who shot her with it is that Frankie guy from the club. The one that is now a vampire. Xavier already confirmed it."

"I don't get it. First, they are killing Vampires, then they are making them, and now they are kidnapping them? It doesn't make any sense."

"All ten vamps have been in a twenty-mile radius, but I have only found the one video footage so far."

"Has there been much activity at his house?"

"Nope, just the woman and the kid."

"As much as I hate to do it, it looks like we are going to have to do a little bit of kidnapping of our own! Get a cell ready and make it as comfortable as possible. Bring some toys in and whatever else will be needed and then send a team in to grab the woman and child. Do not hurt them! This is not who we are, but we need to do what we must to capture the mother fucker once and for all!"

"I'm on it, boss!"

"I'm going to go finish spending my mating night with Liz. You are in charge until I get back in a few hours."

"Copy that. Congratulations again, Taven. You definitely deserve it!"

"Thanks, Kole. We all deserve it!" I smile and then turn and head back to my bed that has my sleeping mate in it.

NINE

LIZ

I wake up to the loud sound of dishes being clanked together. I throw the pillow over my head, but it only muffles the sound a little bit, "What the fuck?" I say to myself. I throw the pillow aside and open my eyes. Bright light greets me, and I have to close my eyes again. "God dammit! What the fuck is wrong with me?"

Hearing a chuckle beside me, I turn and look up at Taven who is holding a tray of food for me, "You will get used to it. I will teach you how to tune out a lot of it."

"What are you talking about?" I can't think straight at the moment.

"Your heightened senses." He states with a smile, "When we became bonded mates, your senses became magnified. You also can extend fangs to drink from me, and you will live for eternity. I thought Cassie and Jill told you all of this?"

"Ugh, I think they left a few parts out."

"It will be okay. Your boys are adjusting to it just fine and their senses are magnified more than yours."

"Are you serious? My boys have to deal with this?"

"Baby, it's all part of who they are now. Just like it's part of who you are now. Everything will be fine, I promise." He sits on the bed and kisses me on the tip of my nose.

"Mm, is anything else magnified?" I ask as I rub the bulge in his pants.

"Is someone feeling a little frisky this morning?" He puts the tray down on the table and stretches out beside me.

"Maybe just a little. Do you have time?" I cock a brow at him. He flashes to the door, closing and locking it and next thing I know, the t-shirt that I was wearing is in shreds beside me and I have a bare ass naked Taven standing beside the bed.

"I can definitely make time." He picks me up and sits on the edge of the bed, so I am straddling him. He lays down on his back and smiles up at me, "I want you to ride me, so I can watch your girls bounce." His smile deepens.

Reaching between us, I pump his shaft a few times, but it is already hard and throbbing. I bring myself down on him and begin to move up and down. Taven grabs hold of my hips and meets me with his own thrusts as I throw my head back and groan at the searing heat that is building within me.

Taven sits up and continues his counterthrusts as he pulls a nipple between his teeth. One of his hands find my nub and the flames of my desire build even stronger. Just as I'm about to come, I bite down on his neck and feel his enter mine. We tumble over the edge together, me screaming his name and him grunting as he thrusts hard one last time before we both collapse. It doesn't matter if sex is an hour long or just a few minutes, like now, it's always amazing with this man.

"I think I will leave it for you to explain to the boys why you were screaming dad's name." He spins me around, so I am on my back, but never pulls out.

"The boys are still here?"

"They were finishing up their breakfast when I came up."

"Oh my God, why didn't you say something?"

"Babe, they are going to hear us eventually, so it doesn't really matter."

"Ugh, don't you have some where you need to be?"

"I am right where I need to be for a little bit longer."

"Oh, well I kind of have to pee."

"You are not moving from this spot either."

"What is up with you this morning?" I ask giggling.

"Nothing. I just meant what I said last night about seeing you grow with my child. I filled you up and now I'm holding it in for a few minutes to give it a chance to seed itself."

"You're serious!?"

"Of course, I'm serious! I want us to have a baby right away."

"I'm not talking about that part, babe. I'm talking about the part where you are not going to let me up to pee!"

"Fine! Just know that you owe me an extra helping of that delicious pussy, since you are wasting my seed now!" He rolls off me and then slaps my ass as I jump off the bed, making me squeal.

I eat my cold breakfast that Taven leaves me and then shower and get ready for the day. Taven has to get to the Compound and meet with the guys over the whole Mika issue, so I go in search of the girls to hang out for a little bit.

The Compound is a buzz with the new development with the Hunters. Even the women are talking about it in the rec room, which is where I find all five of them.

"I so hope that they get him this time! I would like to return home soon. Hell, it's been almost a year now, that we have lost, because of these whack jobs!" Carrie is complaining, and I can't really blame her. I would be in the same boat if it weren't for me and Taven finding each other.

"Yeah, my poor Pookie must be lost without me! Thank God my parents took him in!" Paige is pouting.

"Well, I'm not going to complain. My life has been so much better here, then it was before!" Ally pipes in.

"Why is that?" Jill asks her.

"For starters, I have no family. The only two people that I did consider family was my boyfriend and my best friend. That was before I caught them in bed together; the fucking skank."

"Wow, maybe your life is better her." Cassie states.

"Do you think they would let me stay once they catch the douchebags?" Ally asks hopeful.

"That, I do not know. You would have to take that up with Taven." Cassie responds.

"I can always ask him about it, and I can talk him into it if he says no." I give them my evil grin.

"You would, you hoe!" Cassie laughs.

"I am not a hoe if we are engaged, now, am I?" I hold out my hand and look up at the ceiling.

"No fucking way!" Jill jumps over the back of the couch to get to me first, "When did this happen?"

"Yesterday. He and the boys were in on it together; I said yes. I mean, I might as well since we are already living together." I chuckle.

"Oh wow, that ring is amazeballs!" Cassie gawks.

I went on to tell them how the proposal went and how he had asked the boys first. It was truly amazing, and I couldn't have asked for better.

"I want a warrior for myself!" Ally whines, "I've flirted with a few, but they don't seem to be interested."

"Don't take it personal. They are all waiting for the right one and it seems as though they all have a sense as to when they do meet her." Jill pats Ally's back trying to sooth her.

"What is everyone up to today?" I ask.

"Not much. Just being couch potatoes and baby feeders." Jill quips, "With the guys so busy, there isn't much else for us to do."

"I was going to start googling teachers who do home schooling. The boys need to get back to their studies."

"What are you doing that for? Why don't you do it yourself? Jill and I have been reading up on it, because that is what we plan on doing with our kids when they are old enough." Cassie informs me.

"Because some of us need to get back to a real-world job, that's why."

Cassie and Jill look at each other and then back to me, "You are marrying the head of the Elite warriors, Liz. Why on earth would you want to go back to working a full-time job?" Jill questions me.

"I don't want to be dependent on a man, that's why. What if it doesn't work out?"

"I think we are going to hit the pool." Carrie informs us as she points to Paige and Ally.

"Okay, see you ladies later." I reply. We watch them all walk out of the room and then Cassie starts in.

"Alright, now that we are alone, we need to have a serious talk!" Cassie holds her hand up when I open my mouth to say something "No! First of all, when you and Taven complete your bond, you...." I cut her off.

"We did that last night."

"What!? Why didn't you say anything?" Jill shrieks.

"Um... I don't know. Maybe because there were three people in here that don't know about the "situation", duh!"

"Okay, you are right." Cassie says, "So, now that you are bonded, there is no such thing as it "not working out". You will be together for eternity. Aside from that, Taven is loaded. He has more money than you could ever dream of. You don't have to work, and I will put twenty dollars down that he will bring it up to you now that you are bonded. These warriors don't want their women to work, they want to take care of them in every way."

"Well, maybe after we are married and only if he brings it up first, because there is no way I am just assuming that he will be okay with it."

"Fine, suit yourself, but I know I am right." Cassie smiles smugly.

"Anyway," Jill breaks in, "Cassie and I can home school your boys until you decide to quit your job. We need something to do, and we had planned on doing it any way."

"You two would do that for me?"

"Why not? You are one of our best friends and it's not like you can bring just any regular person in here, not with Nate." Cassie chuckles, "That one there is after my own heart."

"Wait a minute...I am not so sure that I want you two teaching my kids anything anyway!" I'm not even playing; I know how my friend's minds work and I don't want that rubbing off on my boys.

"Oh, come on. There is an actual curriculum that we have to follow, so it's not like we teach them about what we have up here." Cassie points to her head.

"I don't know. I will have to seriously think on it." I smirk.

Jill shoves me, "God, you are such a bitch!"

"Yeah, and that is the only reason why you two are friends with me!"

"Very true story!" Cassie winks at me, "So, anything else going on that you haven't told us about?"

"No, not really."

"What do you mean by that?" Cassie crosses her arms over her chest.

"Taven is trying to get me pregnant. He literally crushed my pills into dust and told me that I am forbidden to take them."

Jill's anger is very noticeable, "You mean to tell me that he is telling you what you can and can't do with your body?!"

"I don't know, I find it kind of hot. It turns me on when he tells me what to do." I smile.

"I would have never thought that him, of all people, would be so controlling!" Jill is fuming at this point.

"No, you have it all wrong. It's kind of a private thing that we have going on, but he is never like that outside of the bedroom."

I see Cassie's eyes light up, "You fucking slut! You are his submissive, aren't you?"

"SHH... don't talk so loudly!"

"She is a what? I'm confused." Jill really does looks lost.

"Come on, you know! A Little bit of BDSM?" Cassie says softly behind her hand.

"Oh, my God, get out of here!"

"What? There is nothing wrong with it." I say defensively.

"I'm not saying there is anything wrong with it. I think it's fucking hot! Although, I myself would rather be the Dom, not the sub, but to each there own!"

"Anyway! The whole pregnant topic is the only thing that he is firm on. To the point that we have to lay there for a little bit to make sure none of his seed gets wasted." I chuckle, "It's actually kind of cute."

"Sounds like you are on board with getting prego." Jill teases.

"Kind of, I guess. It would be nice to try for a girl and I do miss my boys at that young stage. Seeing you two with your kids, makes me miss it more. So, yeah, I guess I am okay with it."

Callum starts to fuss and before Jill can get to him, he wakes up the others and it's a chorus of wails. I go to Colin and pick him up, while Cassie picks up Jace. The three of us are standing there trying to rock them back to sleep when Jax and Taven poke their heads in.

"Which one is causing all the problems this time?" Jax asks as he walks over to Cassie and takes Jace from her arms.

"That would be Callum." Jill sighs, "Hey Liz, do you mind watching Colin for a few moments? I think this little guy is hungry."

"Sure, go ahead." I smile down at the little tike. I feel a hand on my lower back and turn to see Taven standing behind me.

He grins down at me, "I see you are a natural. I can't wait for you to hold and comfort ours." He presses his lips against my head.

"What? Are you expecting?" Jax looks at me.

"No, not yet anyway. He sure is trying though!" I wink up at him.

"That's my man!" Jax hi-fives Taven while Cassie and I shake our heads.

"We just wanted to stop by and let you ladies know that we are stepping out for a bit. Elite business." Taven squeezes one of my ass cheeks.

"Okay, please be careful. I love you." I raise my lips for him to kiss.

"I always am. Be back as soon as we can."

TAVEN

I decide to go with the men to retrieve Mika's woman and child. I don't want any mistakes made and even though my men are capable, I feel the need to see this through for myself. The ideal time would have been at night, but since we don't want to wait any longer, we will have to depend on our vamp speed to keep us unseen.

I hit the button on my earpiece, "Kole, do you have all possible cameras down in the vicinity?"

"Working on the last one now."

"And you know that she and the child are alone?"

"Those are the only two infrared bodies that I am picking up. You are clear to go in now."

"Thanks buddy."

I turn towards Xavier, Duncan, Jax, and Cooper, "You four are with me. We will flash in there, grab them and flash back. Do not hurt them. I don't like this anymore than you do, but desperate times call for desperate measures. The rest of you keep on the look-out. If you see anything or anyone, take care of it. On my go!"

I look at all of my men and couldn't be prouder. This isn't a dangerous mission, but the need for them to be here in case anything unexpected goes down, that is called brotherhood.

"Let's go!"

The five of us flash into the house. Duncan quickly holds a cloth with chloroform on it, up to the woman's nose and mouth, so she doesn't scream. Jax and I head for the kid's room and find her taking her afternoon nap, so Jax carefully picks her up and cradles her in his arms. Xavier and I are pretty much there as look-outs in case the guys missed something outside.

As we are about to flash back, I spot a red light up in the corner of the living room and realize that it's a camera. I smile at it.

"Let's be quick. There is a camera and I don't know if he can see us in real time." I lift my hand to my earpiece once more, "We are coming out with both packages, be on the look-out, he has us on camera."

We all flash back to the men and the waiting vehicles. Once both civilians are secure, we take off and head back to the Compound.

We bring the woman and child in through the back door, so none of our guests will see them, taking them straight to the large cell that we had set up for them downstairs. The woman should be coming to at any moment now and luckily, the child has stayed asleep the whole time. I feel like dog shit, doing this to the child, knowing that she will be totally confused upon waking and being in a strange place. I just keep telling myself that I had no other choice. It's bad enough that the child will be left without a father when this is all said and done, even if that father is a sick son of a bitch.

I sit outside of the glass cell until the woman stirs, rubbing her eyes as she sits up on the bed. I can see the confusion on her face as she looks at her surroundings. Her eyes finally land on me and widen in fright.

"Who are you and where am I?"

"More importantly, who are you?" I ask with a cocked brow.

"I'm Marie, but if you don't know who I am, then why am I here?"

"You are here, at the Elite Headquarters, because of Mika." I scoff.

"What? What did my husband do? He has been out of town on business for weeks!"

"Ah, so you are married to him, and the kid," I nod towards the sleeping child, "she is his as well?"

Just now noticing that her child is there with her, she shrieks and runs to her.

"Don't touch her!" I command of her, and she stops dead in her tracks, "There is no need to wake her up while you are in this state. She is going to be confused enough."

"What did Mika do that would cause you to kidnap us and what are you going to do to us?"

"You have nothing to fear from us, that I can promise you." She scoffs at my words and goes back to sitting on her bed, "I am hoping that you can give us some answers, but if you can't, then we will use you as leverage to bring your husband in." The woman seems to be completely unaware as to what I may be talking about. The fact that she didn't even flinch when I mentioned the Elite, tells me that she has never heard of us.

Raising her chin in defiance, "You can ask me all you want, but if it's something that may incriminate Mika in any way, I will not answer you."

I smile at her, "Marie, what exactly does your husband do for work?"

"He's an investor and is always traveling around."

"Are you aware on whether or not he belongs to any groups or clubs?"

"He does not have time for that, so no, I am not aware of any."

"Hm, I see." I stand up and begin to pace back and forth in front of the glass, "Have you heard him mention the name Hunters or anything close to that?"

She scrunches her nose up, "No, what is it?"

"Hunters is a group of people, like a club, who has decided to follow one man. It actually started with Jason. Do you know who he was?"

"Jason Murphy? Why yes. He and Mika were best friends since grade school, up until he died about a year ago."

"Yes, he did, which is when Mika decided to form the Hunters." I go on to explain about the kidnappings, killings, and everything else. I leave the part about vampires out, "So, you see, your husband is not the man that you think he is."

"You are wrong! That doesn't sound anything like my Mika! My husband is caring and sweet, he would never hurt another human being!"

"I can see that you want to believe the best about him and that you will be no use to us for information. I guess the only choice we have is to use you as bait. Oh, one more thing. Do you know a woman by the name of Jenny?"

"No one comes to mind. Who is she?"

"Apparently, she was the woman that he was fucking and making promises to, before we captured her after she tried helping to kidnap a fellow Elite's wife."

"That is a lie! Mika would never hurt me like that! He loves me."

"I am sure he does, in his own way." I smile at her and then turn to leave, but stop, "I will send some food down for you and your daughter. Please let me know if there is anything else we can do to make your stay with us more comfortable." With that, I turn and walk away.

TEN

LIZ

I'm curled up on the couch at home with my lap top googling information for home schooling when Taven comes in and plops down beside me.

"Rough day, babe?"

"You can kind of call it that I guess." A long sigh follows his response.

"Let me reheat some supper for you and you can tell me all about, if you want to." I get busy making his plate and stick it in the microwave to warm up. Grabbing a beer on my way by, I head back over to him. I see he is busy scrolling through the information that I've been reading through until he came in.

"Freshening yourself up on schooling your kids I see." He smiles at me and thanks me as I set his plate down.

"Oh no, I don't have time to do it. I need to get back to work soon. Jill and Cassie offered to do it for me since they will be tutoring their kids." No sooner do I sit down; Taven moves my laptop and pulls me into his arms.

"You know, you don't ever have to go back to work. Let me take care of you now. You have worked hard enough and now it's my turn to take care of you and the boys." He nuzzles my neck, sending shivers up my spine.

"I really hate it when Cassie is right." I mumble, enjoying the feel of his lips against my neck.

"Mm, why is that?" His words are muffled against my skin.

"We were just having this conversation earlier today. She said that you would tell me that I didn't need to work. I just don't feel right not pulling my own weight. I have held a full-time job my whole life. I don't know what I would do with myself if I didn't have one."

"I have a few ideas. Like being my sex slave for life and carrying my children." He chuckles, and I have to give it to him, they both sound wonderful.

"I can still do those things and carry a full-time job."

"Not if I keep you chained in my playroom all day long!" His hands are now fondling my breasts and I can feel myself getting worked up, "Besides, think of the boys. They need schooling and you, being their mother, should be the one to do it, because you know them best. Your day will be filled with teaching them. Except during your break times when I come to ravish you"

"That does sound perfect, not going to lie." He now has a hand at my crotch, rubbing my sex up and down. My hips begin to move against his hand.

"I need you, baby. Feel how hard I am for you." Taven grabs my hand and moves it to his crotch so I can feel how his cock is straining to be released, "Where are the boys now?"

I am trying to form a comprehensive thought, but it doesn't seem to be working, "In bed, I think. Yes, they are in bed."

Taven growls and rips my shirt over my head. I have a better idea and I slide down to the floor and kneel in front of him. I hastily work the opening to his jeans and free him, so he stands tall and proud. I take my hand and start to work his cock up and down, licking the pre-cum off the tip and then swirling my tongue around.

"Fuck, this is just what I needed to end my day! Take it all in, baby." He lays his hand on my head while I wrap my lips around his cock and slide my mouth down as far as I can take him. I set my tempo as I start sucking harder, my hand still pumping the girth of his base. Bringing my other hand into play, I roll his balls around, massaging them. His head his thrown back and he starts moving his hips faster. I can feel his balls tighten and I ready myself for a mouthful of thick goodness; he doesn't disappoint. Shoving my head down and holding it there, he shoots his cum into the back of my throat. Releasing his grip on my head to pump one or two times, he then holds it again as another shot bursts out, "FUCK!"

I clean him off with my tongue and smile up at him, "All better?"

He looks at me incredulously, "Are you fucking kidding me? You are the best! Now I'm hungry, so get that pussy over here!"

I squeal and take off at a run towards the kitchen, but of course he catches me. He spins me around, pinning my chest down to the kitchen counter. Nipping my earlobe first, I feel his breath on my ear, "Don't move from this spot!"

Air hits my ass as he pulls my pants and underwear down, taking them off completely. There is a sting to my right cheek when he slaps it, but then massages the pain away. He gives the left one the same attention, causing heat to erupt at my very core. Not wasting any time, his face is all up in my pussy licking and thrusting his tongue inside.

I begin to moan and squirm as he attacks my clit, rubbing and squeezing the bundle of sensitive nerves. Waves of pleasure rip though me as he continues his assault. Lapping each drop until there is nothing left, he stands up and without warning, thrusts into me. His girth stretching me until he can go no further. Pulling out slowly to the tip, he slams back into me and doesn't let up. He covers my mouth with his hand as I begin to scream when another wave hits me, this time harder and longer. Still, he doesn't let up. Once my next orgasm hits, he lets his own release go, grunting and bruising my hip within his grip.

He falls on top of me panting while he rubs the hip that he held on to, "Damn baby!"

We both lay here for good five minutes before he starts to stir. He picks me up and carries me over to the couch, covering my nakedness with a throw blanket, "Lay still and let my men do their job." He smiles slyly, making me laugh at his ridiculous behavior.

All of a sudden, we hear a noise upstairs and Nate's voice calling out for me. Taven shoves me back down when I go to get up, "Don't make me tie your ass down! I said stay put. I will go see what he needs." Kissing me on the forehead, he buttons his jeans up and jogs upstairs.

Taven and I are lying in bed when he explains to me the mission they went on today. He told me how they took Mika's wife and child captive to use against him. I gasp, "How could you do that to a woman and child?" I sit up and look down at him. I would never have believed that he was capable of such a thing.

"I know, sweetheart! It's been tearing me up inside, but we have come to a standstill and now they are kidnapping vampires for only God knows what! What else could we do?"

"I understand your predicament and I know why you did it, but it is wrong to keep them in a cell down there! You need to let them up in the Compound. Especially the child! Put a tracker on them or whatever you have Samantha wear when she roams freely, but you will not keep them in a cell!" My voice is raised at this point, and I don't care.

"Are you trying to tell me how to run my Headquarters?"

"No, I am not, but this is inhumane! Even Samantha roams free and she isn't innocent! This mother and child are!"

"Okay, okay. I didn't like the idea of them being down there anyway, so I will let them up in the morning."

"Promise?"

"Yes, I promise. You can even come with me and help her get settled in, how is that?"

"Thank you. I knew you were a better man than that."

"You are lucky I love you and you are spoiled rotten!" He kisses my cheek.

"And you are lucky that you are fixing that asshat move you made, or else you wouldn't be getting any for a long time."

"Ouch! The boys definitely wouldn't like that."

I lay awake a long time after Taven falls asleep. I can't believe that he would do such a thing, that poor woman and child. Granted, they are Mika's family, but from what Taven has told me, she knows nothing about his secret life... or so she says.

My thoughts move back to earlier when Taven brought up exactly what Cassie said he would. Could I really quit working and just be a full-time wife and mother? I don't know how to live that kind of lifestyle, but I guess if it means my boys getting a good education and having lots of sex, I could probably handle it. I giggle loudly, slamming a hand over my mouth, so I wouldn't wake Taven. How does that saying go? Keeping me barefoot and pregnant? I may like that...

TAVEN

Bright and early, as promised, Liz and I make our way down to the cell blocks. I have Kole meeting us down here with two trackers. I don't think the child really needs one, but I don't want to take any chances.

We have to walk by Dean's cell to get to Marie's and he starts calling out to Liz, begging her to help him. Fuck! I need to figure out how and when to take care of him. I didn't think about him when I told Liz she could come down here. I place my hand at the small of her back and hurry her along.

"Sorry sweetheart, I didn't think."

"It's okay. I'm just surprised that he is still here."

"With everything going on, I haven't had time to deal with him."

She stops and looks up at me, "Is it necessary to kill him now?"

"What are you saying? You don't want him to pay for what he did to you?"

"It's not that." She looks back towards Dean's cell and then back at me again, "It's one thing to kill him in the heat of the moment or even right after you brought him back here, but he has been sitting in that cell for days now. How are you planning on doing it?"

I blow out a breath, "I honestly don't know. I thought about a quick breaking of his neck or maybe a duel, but we all know that it wouldn't be a fair fight. So, what are you suggesting?"

"I honestly don't know. I don't want to see him back on the street again, using and hurting people, or even coming back after me at some point. God, I never would have thought I would be standing here trying to figure out a way to kill my ex!"

"You don't have to. This is my responsibility, love. You just forget all about him and he will be taken care of." Grabbing her shoulders, I pull her to me and brush my lips across her forehead. She nods, and we continue down to Marie's cell.

"What do you mean you are letting us out? We are free to leave?" Marie looks at us with excitement.

"No, not quite. You will still need to stay within the Compound." I inform her and her smile falters.

Liz quickly speaks up, "We will keep you safe and no harm will come to you. You are not here because you did anything wrong, so I feel that you shouldn't be treated like a criminal. You and your daughter can walk around freely, but will wear a tracker on your ankle, so you don't step over the boundaries. I know it still seems as if you are held prisoner, but you need to understand, your husband hurt people. I, myself was shot, because of your husband. He needs to be stopped."

"Honestly Marie, we have known about you and your child for quite some time, but never once thought about touching you; this is our last resort. I have to give Mika one thing, he is smart. He has slipped through our hands every time."

"I still don't believe that he has done and continues to do what you are saying." The woman states but not with the conviction that she did in the beginning.

"I know you don't and it's understandable. Everybody wants to believe the best of their spouse, but we do have video and witnesses that will prove to you, what he has done." Liz tries to soothe her, but I don't think it's working.

"So, Emily and I can move around freely as if we are just visitors, until this is all handled?"

"Yes, as long as you both wear the trackers. You will not be able to get them off and if you do try, it will set off an alarm and we will have no choice, but to bring you back down here."

Kole comes walking up just as I finish answering Marie, "Ah, here is Kole now with the trackers." I take them from Kole and hold them up, so Marie can see, "They are not balky or ugly. They look like ankle bracelets almost, and they flex with your movements, so they are comfortable."

"Okay, I will do it your way for now, but I want to see this proof that you have against Mika."

"Done. Just let me know when you are ready, and I will take you to Koles office, where it's all kept."

"I would like to get Emily fed first if that is okay. Then maybe after breakfast you can take me?"

"That is perfect. Liz, will you show Marie and Emily where the kitchen is and have Max fix them up something?"

"Oh, definitely!" She smiles at Marie, "Follow me. Later, I will give you a tour of the grounds as well."

I listen to Liz's chatter as she walks away, smiling and shaking my head, "Let me guess, this was Liz's idea, wasn't it?" Kole chuckles.

"What makes you think that?"

"Your mate has a heart of gold, and I can't see her standing by while two innocents are held down in a cell. Especially when one is a child."

"You are so right, Kole. I won the lottery when fate gave me her." I smile, but then hear Dean calling for Liz again, "Shit! I need to do something with him!"

"What's your plan?" Kole asks.

"Him getting himself killed trying to escape." I stomp over to his cell and open his door.

"What do you want? I was calling for Liz, not you!" He spats. He is definitely coming down from all the drugs that he has been without and is at that hateful stage. This shouldn't be too hard.

"You will never speak to Liz again! Do you hear me?"

"Fuck you! I will talk to her any time I want. After all, it was my dick that was in her before yours!" He knows that he has angered me, but continues to run his mouth, "I don't know what she sees in you… you're a monster! You're not even human! I never expected she would open her legs and whore around with the likes of you!" He tries spitting in my face, and I am done. I upper cut him right in the nose and send him flying across the cell, the sound of bones breaking as he hits the wall.

Kole walks over and checks out Dean's lifeless form, "Well, that's done and over with. I'll send a couple of the newbies to come and take care of him." I nod and walk away.

I am escorting Marie to IT, where Kole has everything set up for her. Samantha has already been brought in and Jenny is supposed to be on her way. Jenny, now there is someone that has changed tremendously. I am pretty sure it is all thanks to Ryder. They have been thick as thieves ever since Jenny tried starving herself to death. I haven't quite figured out whether or not they are destined mates or if they are just enjoying each other's company, but I am happy that she is turning her life around.

I pull up a chair in front of the monitors for Marie and have her sit. She looks at her surroundings nervously and I notice that her hands shake, just a little bit. The most damning video footage is the one of Duncan's capture, so that is the one that we bring up.

"Marie," I get her attention, "If at any time you feel like you can't watch anymore, let us know. We are not here to torture you by making you watch this, but you wanted proof and what you are about to see, is all the proof you should need." She nods her head as she looks at me warily. I nod at Kole to proceed.

The video plays and I watch the different emotions as they dance across her face. I glance at the screen and there is Mika's face, clear as day, as he beats Duncan, screams in the background from Samantha during her fake rape scene, but Marie doesn't need to know that. You can see the cages in the background with the women who were kidnapped.

"Turn it off!" Marie yells, "I can't watch anymore!" Tears flowing down her face.

"I am sorry that you had to watch that, but you needed to see the type of man that you married."

Jenny and her shadow, Ryder, walk in, "Ah, Jenny, just the girl we were waiting for." I smile warmly at her.

"Sorry, I was running a little late." She looks over at Ryder and blushes. Interesting.

"It's all good. Marie just finished watching some of the video." I can tell that Jenny is nervous, who wouldn't be when being face to face with the wife of a man you were sleeping with, "Jenny, will you properly introduce yourself to Marie please?"

Jenny smiles sadly at me and takes the seat beside Marie, "Hi Marie, I'm Jenny. I'm...", she looks up to me and then to Ryder, who encourages her to go on with a nod, "Mika was my boyfriend... well, at least I thought he was. I never knew he had a family, and I am so very sorry! I would have never been with him if I knew about you and your daughter. He used me to try and get to Jill, so he could have her kidnapped. He had planned on torturing her and having her raped before killing her. He was going to video tape it and send it to Duncan."

Throwing her hands up to her ears, Marie starts screaming for Jenny to stop, "I can't hear any more of this... please stop!" Loud sobs burst out and her body shakes. I put my hands on her shoulders and Jenny begins to rub her back.

"I am sorry that you have to find out this way, Marie, but you needed to know why your husband has to be stopped."

"Don't call him that! Anyone that could do these horrible things is no husband of mine! Do what you have to do to take him down, but don't ever let him come near me or Emily again!"

"You are under our protection, Marie, he will not get to you, I promise." I say soothingly.

Samantha, who has been sitting in the corner this whole time, finally speaks up, "So, you don't need me after all?"

"No, I think she has heard enough. You can roam around freely today, within the boundaries, of course."

"Thank you, you are too kind." Samantha's sarcasm is heard by all.

"Watch it Samantha, or I will send you back to your cell!" She scurries away quickly before I make good on my threat.

"She is a prisoner here?" Marie asks.

"Yes, she was working for Mika and tricked us by acting as a victim, so she could get into the Compound. We are trying to rehabilitate her, but it's slow going at the moment." I hold my hand out to her, "Come on, I will take you to your daughter."

Marie and I find Emily playing with Jillian at the playground, while Cassie and Liz watch them.

"Hey, Marie. Looks like Emily found a new friend!" Liz smiles at her.

"I see that. It's good for her. Maybe this whole ordeal won't be as bad for her if she is occupied." Marie smiles sadly.

Liz stands up and pulls Marie in for a hug, telling her that everything is going to turn out just fine and that we are all here for her.

Marie pulls away and turns back in my direction, "Thank you for bringing us here and showing me everything. I would have never known what kind of monster he was if you hadn't."

"Again, Marie, I am sorry for all of this. I do not like being the one who disrupts your life, but we couldn't go on letting the vileness continue." I look at Liz, "Babe, will you come with me for a bit?"

"Sure, I will see you later Marie. Bye Bitch." Liz waves at Cassie, who in turn flips her off. Good Lord, our women are so classy sometimes, I chuckle to myself.

I lead Liz into one of the restrooms by the playground and lock the door. I urgently claim her lips with mine as I pick her up and sit her on the counter by the sink.

She tries breaking free, but I don't let her, I need her too much. I stick my fingers into the waistband of her yoga pants and panties, yanking them down and off, without breaking the kiss. She tries mumbling through our lips, so I slap the top of her ass cheek, "I need you, so I am going to fuck that pretty little pussy of yours until I fill that need. You will not say a word except to scream my name while you are coming on my cock. Do you understand?"

"Yes, Sir."

Those two little words undo me, and I rip open my own jeans, and feeling her pussy already wet and radiating heat, I plunge into it, making Liz gasp as I plant myself all the way in. I stop and take a deep breath, loving the feel of her walls clamping around me in a tight vice-like grip. I slowly pull out and then slam back into her. Reaching between us, I play with the bundle of nerves that brings her great pleasure. I push her back, so she is leaning back on her elbows, while I lift her shirt. Pulling her bra down, her tits hang out and I latch on, sucking and pulling on her nipples as she moans with desire.

I only wanted a quickie when I brought her in here, but fucking Liz is the greatest pleasure ever, and I find myself not getting enough of her. I continue to make her orgasm over and over again, until finally, I have to release myself, so I bring her back to a sitting position.

"Bite me while I come inside of you. I have a huge load here for you and your pussy is going to take all of it." I feel her sink her fangs into my jugular and I follow suit. Her blood takes my breath away every time; I can never drink enough of it. My balls ache for release and as I thrust into her harder, she screams my name and creams all over my cock. I let my own load shoot deep inside of her, and boy, is it a load!

As our routine lately, I stay completely and deeply seeded in her womb, hoping against hope that my guys take this time. I don't understand the urgency for which I have in impregnating my mate, but it's there. My demon needs it, I need it, and so it will be done.

I wait until I feel it's been long enough, and then I pull out. I scoot her back and lift he legs, planting her feet on the counter, so she is spread open for me. Just looking at her glistening pussy, makes me want her all over again, but I know we have to wait. Turning the water on and wetting some paper towels, I begin to wash her off, but I do it in slow massaging strokes, making sure I rub her sensitive nub just right. She is whimpering with desire, and I want to make her come again, but the demon in me smiles and makes her wait.

"Please, Taven! Fuck me, eat me, I don't care, just let me come!"

"Sorry, baby, but you will have to wait until tonight. I am going to torture you all day long and you will not, I repeat, will not pleasure yourself. You will wait for me to do it. Do I make myself clear?"

"Yes, Sir," She lets out a moan as she answers.

"That's a good girl. I will make it worth your while in the playroom tonight." I whisper to her before I take her lips again. Still playing with her pussy. The scent of her arousal burns through my nostrils, and I know I need to get out of here. With one final kiss and an "I love you", I flash out of the bathroom and down to my office, locking myself in.

ELEVEN

LIZ

Damn Taven and his sexiness! Turning me on and then leaving me high and dry and not letting me deal with it. I've had to change my panties twice since our little quickie in the bathroom this morning. Each time he has found me, he pulls me in somewhere and molests me, but never finishes the deed! He is up to something, and I don't know whether to be scared or excited. I know one thing; my plan right now is to stay hidden from him the rest of the day. I can't deal with him fondling me until right before I come and then stopping. At least not when I have so long to wait!

I knock on Cassie's door, hoping that she is home, so I can hide out. Relief floods through me when she answers the door and I shove my way past her and close the door.

"Please say that you have no plans for leaving your house." I peek out the window to see if anyone could have seen me come in.

"No, not really. What's going on?" She looks at me strangely as if I have grown two heads.

"Oh my God! I don't know what the fuck got into Taven today, but he has been on a mission since we left you guys at the playground." I go on and tell her about the bathroom scene and then about the other two times, "It's like he is trying to make me so hot that I go wild on him later or something, I don't know. It's crazy!"

Cassie is laughing her ass off at me, "Why don't you just take care of yourself. He doesn't have to know."

"Hell no! I am not taking any chances in him finding out, because I don't know what he will give me as punishment while in the playroom if I do. Granted, it's always pleasurable, but I don't need him making it worse while in there and not letting me finish!"

"Man, I need to have Jax build us one of those rooms! The things I would do to him in there! Fuck! Now you're getting me turned on, bitch!"

"Everyone should have one of those rooms, but you can't let Taven know that you know about his. I don't think he wants anyone to know."

"It's not like I'm going to ask him to use it! You don't need to tell me not to say anything."

"Thank you. So, I can just hang here for a little while?"

"Of course. I'm about to watch a movie while the kids are down for their nap." Cassie's phone buzzes with a text and she looks at it, "That's weird, it's Taven. He never texts me."

"What does he want?"

She chuckles, "Um… he wants to know if I have seen you. He's been looking for you."

"Just tell him you haven't seen me since this morning."

"Don't worry girl, I've got your back!" She smiles at me, and I plop myself down on the couch, "I'm going to pop us some popcorn."

I am looking through the movie choices that she has sitting on the table when there is a knock on the door. Cassie jogs over to the door and I hear her say hi to whoever is there and tells them to come in. I look up and there is Taven with a shit eating grin on his face.

"Well, hello gorgeous. I've been looking for you!"

I turn to Cassie who is leaning against the door jam, "How could you?! You said that you had my back!"

"Uh, yeah. Meaning girl, I'm going to help you better your sex life!"

Taven literally throws me over his shoulder and calls out his thanks to Cassie.

"Paybacks are a bitch Cassie, remember that!" I holler, hoping I wake the kids and ruin her quiet time.

"So, you thought you could hide from me, sweets? That wasn't very nice. Do you not like me touching you?"

"I love when you touch me, just not when you don't finish the deed! I'm tired of changing my panties!"

"Oh love, just think of how good it will feel later!"

We don't get too far from Cassie's place before Taven's phone starts buzzing. He answers it and after taking a few more steps, he halts and slides me down, planting me on my feet.

"Okay, I'll be there in a minute." He hangs up the phone and turns to me, "Looks like you get a pass this time, babe. I've got to go. Kole has a lead on Mika, and we need to move in." He grabs my face and kisses me, "I love you, baby." And then he is gone.

As much as I am a little relieved, I have this niggling feeling that something isn't right. Taven has told me how I can open up my mind and talk to him whenever I want to, but I haven't really been practicing, so I don't know if it will work, but I try anyway.

'Hey babe, are you there?' I wait and get nothing, so I try again and again. Finally, on the fifth try, I get through.

'Hey baby, I'm a little busy. What's up?'

'I just want to tell you to be safe. I have this feeling and I don't like it.'

'It will be fine. Everybody but Max, Kole, and Raven are going with us.'

'Okay. Just come back safely, please!'

'You know I will. Love you, baby, I gotta go.'

'Love you too.' That is the end of the conversation, but it doesn't calm my nerves any. I make my way to the Compound to talk to Kole and see what's going on.

Jill must have had the same idea as I did, because she is already with Kole in IT. They both look at me when I enter and pull up a chair by them at the monitors.

"I'm not getting a good feeling about this mission. What's going on? Taven didn't have time to tell me about it before they left."

"We got a tip on where they are hiding out now, but we know it is probably a trap." Kole looks at me and I see that there is a little concern in his eyes as well, "They are doing a little recon first and then coming back here to strategize an attack plan."

"Do recons ever go bad?" I am biting my nails as I ask.

"Not really. The only one that I know of that got bad was when Duncan's stupid ass thought he would go by himself!" Kole rolls his eyes at Jill when she slaps his arm, "Hey, you know as well as I do that it was a stupid move on his part."

"I know, but he was a man in love and heartbroken, so he wasn't in his right frame of mind!" Jill defends.

"Maybe if you weren't so uptight about getting taped having sex then he wouldn't have been heartbroken." Kole fires back.

"Stop being a creeper and putting up cameras all over the place and I wouldn't be uptight about it."

"I have an idea, why don't you keep the sex for your own bedroom!"

Jill is about to fire back, but I cut her off, "Both of you enough! Let's concentrate on what our men are doing now and not what happened in the past!"

They both looked at me, surprised that I am yelling at the two of them, "I am sorry, but I am nervous as hell right now and you two aren't helping."

They both say sorry and turn back to the monitors. Cassie comes walking in carrying Jace, "Hey, I guess you two had the same idea, huh?" She looks to me and Jill.

"I don't know, but my gut is telling me that something is going to happen." I look at her and she nods her head.

"Me too." She agrees.

"Me three." Jill pipes in.

"It's got to be a mate thing, because I don't feel that way at all." Kole chimes in.

We hear Taven come over the radio that they are there at the location, but it seems to be vacant, "A few of us are going to get a closer look and the rest will stay back."

"Roger that! Hey, I have three beautiful women here with me, so if I don't answer, I may be busy." He teases and winks at us. All at the same time, Taven, Jax, and Duncan throw expletives at Kole, and he sits there laughing. I hit him in the arm.

"Don't worry, babe. He isn't man enough to handle me, I'm all yours!" I reaffirm.

"That's my girl!" He calls out and then there is laughter. Kole is giving me the evil eye and I grin at him.

"You cannot be saying stuff like that when they are in the field, Kole! It's a good way to get them killed or hurt!"

"Ah, they know I am only fucking with them."

"You are not mated, Kole. You don't realize how the vampire reacts when something is said about their mate." Cassie states, "Even if the man knows better, the vamp doesn't."

"Guess I never looked at it that way."

We all grow silent and wait, watching the monitors. I watch on the infrared monitor, as three bodies move ahead from the others, and I know one of them is Taven. They are probably about a quarter mile ahead of the rest of the men when I see something in my peripheral view and look in that direction.

"Um, I think they have company," and point to the screen.

Just as Kole is about to push the intercom button to warn them, swarms of red bodies start to flood the area around the three figures.

"RETREAT, RETREAT!" Kole yells at them, "There is at least a hundred of them starting to surround you three!" It is too late, though. There are too many of them closing in on our three men, for them to escape.

The others start running towards the mass, but it's too late. The Hunters are already there and have the three men. Kole commands the rest of our men to fall back. "The rest of you need to get back here A.S.A.P.! We now need to plan a rescue mission. There are too many for you to take on."

"Copy that." Duncan's voice comes over the radio and I see Jill sigh in relief, "Just so you know, Taven, Jax, and Kai are in the group ahead of us." His voice raw with emotion.

"NO!!!" Cassie cries out. I know Taven would have been one of them, so it doesn't really come as a surprise to hear his name. Am I terrified, beyond belief, but I know it won't do any good. Jill and I both run to Cassie. I grab Jace out of her arms and Jill catches her as her knees buckle out from under her.

Kole's eyes meet mine and within them, I can see that this is not a good situation. All I can do is believe that we will get them back home safely… and soon!

TAVEN

Shit! How did we get ourselves into this mess? Better yet, how are we going to get out of it? Thank God, Kole pulled the others back, otherwise it wouldn't have been pretty. There had to have been at least a hundred of them and the majority are vamps. Although, they aren't very smart. If they were, they would have knocked us out for the ride back to their hideout and not just put a hood over our heads when we said that we surrendered. Unfortunately, they put each of us in a different vehicle, so we wouldn't try anything.

I wait until we are unloaded and brought into our separate cells before I try contacting Liz. It's a good thing that two out of three of us are mated and we can get our coordinates back to Headquarters. Now that all is quiet, I reach out to Liz.

'Hey baby, are you there?'

'Oh my God, Taven! Are you okay? Did they hurt you? Where are you?'

'Calm down sweetheart. We are all okay for now and no, they haven't hurt us yet. I need you to get a pen and paper and write something down. Can you do that for me?'

'Yes, I'm sorry. I've just been trying not to freak out, because Cassie is freaking out, and then I hear your voice....'

'Okay, baby, but I need you to pay close attention. I don't know what the plan is for us yet and I don't know how much time we have, so I need you to copy down these directions that I'm going to give you so Kole can get the coordinates and come get us."

'Sorry, yes, I'm ready.'

I have her write down all the steps I took from the time of our capture to where we got into the vehicles. Next are the turns we took and how far we drove and ended with the steps from the vehicle to where they placed me. I also informed her of any sounds that I heard nearby and any smells that I sensed.

'Did you get all that?'

'Yes. Want me to repeat it?'

'That's okay, I trust you. Hey, I'm going to be okay, and I will come back to you. I promise!' I can hear her tears even in her thoughts, 'I love you, Liz.'

'I love you too, with everything I've got! I can't lose you, so I'm holding you to your promise.'

'I'm here. I'm always with you, remember that! Now go get that information to Kole and make sure he calls in all other Elite and have him bring in Coco and her crew.'

I say my goodbye and concentrate on my surroundings to try and figure out what their plans are. I can see an open area with wooden crates and a few guards, but nothing that will help. I close my eyes and listen. There is a lot of chatter coming from different areas of this place, so I have to pick through the ones that may be important and ones that are not.

There are chains clinking together, which tells me that there are quite a few prisoners here. Probably the other twenty that were taken. The first thing they did was put me in chained cuffs, ones that I cannot break through.

I hear bits of conversation about blood and healing, but it's hard to make out, because there is a woman screaming for someone to get away from her. I move on from that area and hear another conversation, one where I know the voice. Mika. I strain to hear as much as possible.

"I don't fucking care what you thought! You should have used the tranquilizers on those three! I don't trust them." Mika was yelling at one of his goons. Yeah, they fucked up big time on that one. I grin.

"Sorry Boss, it won't happen again!"

"See that it does not! Which ones did you capture? Please say you got that Duncan bastard! I am still pissed that he got away. Him and his bitch need to pay for what they did to me!"

"I do not know the other two, but I did recognize the one from the face on the video when Marie and Emily were taken."

"Ah, so, we have the Head of the Elite, Taven! That is the only good news that I've heard tonight! Bring him to the room… and keep him chained up with four vamp guards."

"Yes, Sir!"

So, I'm going to have the pleasure of finally meeting the motherfucker! I contact Liz quick to let her know that they are taking me to Mika. Of course, she doesn't take that too well, but she is strong and will get through this. At least, as long as I survive it.

I am brought to a private room with no windows and only a chair in the middle of the room. These new fledglings think they are badass, acting like I should be scared of them. I let my own vampire out, flash my fangs and hiss at them and they all jump back. I throw my head back and laugh. Apparently, they didn't like that too well. One hauls off and sucker punches me in the gut and then in the jaw. He is a big guy. Too bad he is on the wrong team or else I'd recruit him for the Elite.

I'm left to sit here for about a half hour and then Mika comes strolling through the door with a smug look on his face, "Ah, Taven. I am so glad you could stop by. I see my men have been very hospitable towards you. I hope you find your accommodations comfortable."

"Well, it isn't the Ritz, but I'll manage."

He stands there for a moment, his hands behind his back and his legs shoulder width apart. "Tell me Taven, how did you know about my family?"

I shrug my shoulders, "A little birdie told me."

"Quit the shit! I made sure that nobody would ever find out about them, so I am going to ask you one more time. How did you learn of my family?"

I lean forward and motion for him to come closer. He leans in, "Go fuck yourself!"

Stepping back, he nods at one of his men and I feel the sting of a whip across my chest. Shit! The same kind that they tortured Duncan with. That wasn't pretty and I'm sure this won't be either. I smile up at Mika.

"Marie is a very kind woman, and your daughter, she's a peach. What do you think your wife would do if she were to find out about your little club that you have going on here?"

"She would never believe you. You had better not have hurt either one of them!"

"Hm, if you say so. Unlike you, we don't torture people, especially women and children! They are safe, for now. Tell me, how would your wife feel if she should run into Jenny? You know, your little girlfriend, that we had also captured?"

I saw the slight flicker of fear in his eyes before he got control of his emotions again. "Marie knows nothing of what I do, so there is no point in keeping her prisoner. Emily is too young to know anything."

"You do realize that they are where they are at because of what you are doing. Besides, they are not our prisoner. They are under our protection. It seems as though Marie doesn't take kindly to the kind of work that you do and, she doesn't like to share."

"What are you mumbling on about?"

Grinning, I shrug my shoulders, "I'm not quite sure. Let me think on it, my memory isn't the same as it was over two centuries ago." Another lash and then another slice through my chest. It takes me a moment or two to get my bearings back, "Tell me Mika, why are you now kidnapping vampires, better yet, why are you making new ones, if you despise us so much?"

"That's easy enough, I need an army to defeat you and the rest of your Elite Warriors." He thinks he is sly and gives me a satisfied smile.

"How do you expect a bunch of fledglings to win a battle against many Warriors?"

"Have you not seen my numbers? They exceed yours, by what, triple?"

Interesting. He doesn't know that there is more than one Elite team. Well, I am not going to be the one to tell him otherwise.

"What about the kidnapped vamps?"

"Ah yes! Now that, that is my favorite part. I have learned that your blood heals. Do you know that by harvesting vampire blood and auctioning it off to the highest bidders, that it will produce billions of dollars? Yes. I am selling their blood. You and your two buddies will be added to the collection as well."

I have no words as to how to respond. He is selling vamp blood? That is too fucking dangerous! I am glad that he is a talker, because I use the time to contact Liz again with what I just learned. She tries talking to me, but I cut our contact to listen in to what Mika is going on about.

"In fact, that smart mouth Warrior of yours is being harvested right as we speak." God no!

"What do you mean harvested? Do you drain all their blood? You will die for this Mika!" I go crazy, trying to break my chains, but I can feel the weakness from losing the blood from the lashes.

"Oh gosh no. We only take a pint at a time. You know keep them alive, so we can continue using them." Hearing this, calms me, but just knowing that they are taking my men's blood leaves me seething. Which one I wonder? Both Jax and Kai fits that description. At least they will not die, and I thank God for that.

Mika has his men beat me continuously, before taking me back. I am too weak to even contact Liz. My men will come, they always come. I just need to play it cool and keep what strength I do have and hope that they find us soon.

TWELVE

LIZ

No matter how hard I try, I can't get through to Taven since he last cut me off. Kole and the rest of the men are meeting now as they wait for more reinforcements. There are four other Elite teams joining our men, and Coco's crew as well. Jax has given Cassie the same directions as Taven gave me and Kole was able to pinpoint their location. Now, we wait. It's all we can do until the others join us. Jill is in helping Kole with all the monitoring, because Duncan won't allow her to fight with so many vamps, but she is doing a good job at keeping Cassie and I updated on the progress.

As the other Elite teams start to trickle in, I can't help but gape at the men. All of them big with muscle upon muscle, all flawless on the outside. Each one that I come into contact with, smile at me and wink. Maybe I should get in control of myself and stop drooling. I'm sure I make an amusing picture to them. "Think about Taven, Liz!" I yell at myself and come out of my trance. My nerves are shot worrying about the guys, and on top of it all, Jack and Nate keep asking me when Taven is coming home, that they miss him. I can't tell them what is going on, they are too young to have to deal with this kind of thing.

I've decided to just try and keep myself busy by cleaning up around the Compound. I even kick Max out of his own kitchen.

"You are a Warrior first and foremost, Max." I tell him, "You are needed in the rescue mission more than you are in the kitchen. I am here and will take care of the meals until this is over. I may not be you, but I do know how to cook, now go!" I am trying to shoo him out, but he isn't budging.

"I am the Compound chef, and this is my kitchen. I can do both jobs with my hands tied behind my back!" He fires back at me, which only aggravates me more.

I throw my hands on my hips and glare up at him, "I understand that you can do both, but right now, your brothers are more important than making sure the others are getting good cooking! My man is out there, and I will not let any of you be too rundown, because you are taking on too much! You all need to have a clear head and be at your best!" I step up to him and begin poking him hard in the chest, "You are banned from this kitchen until all three men are back home, do you understand me?" I'm glaring at him at this point.

"Fine! I will go, but only because you are Taven's mate, and he will kick my ass if I stand here and argue with you." He smirks down at my finger still poked into his chest, "As much as I don't mind the touch of a female, I must insist that you remove your finger from my chest." I quickly do so, as I continue to glare at him, "Have you ever fed an army of seventy-five plus warriors before?"

"No, and that is why you need to leave now, so I can get started! The other teams are starting to arrive, and you are needed there, so goodbye Max. I will let you know if I need anything, okay?" That seems to help him move his feet.

"Okay, I'll go, but you better call me if you become overwhelmed."

"Okay, okay! Get your ass out of here!" I blow a strand of hair out of my face as he turns and takes his leave, "Sheesh... that was harder than I thought!" I mumble to myself.

I have been up for twenty-four hours, and I'm exhausted as hell, but I get to work, pulling items from the cupboards and fridge to get started on breakfast. I decide on biscuits and gravy, since it's the easiest to make at this point, and I get started. Ten minutes into it, Ally walks in and offers to help me. Paige and Carrie show up around an hour later and I send them to go set up tables and chairs in the Gym, so the men could sit and eat. Within two hours, breakfast is ready, and the warriors gradually begin to trickle in.

The women's reactions to the new warriors mirror my own from earlier. Feeling amused, knowing that I'm not the only one with bad manners when it comes to eye candy, I elbow Carrie, who is standing closest to me.

"You should really wipe the drool that is running down your chin." I joke. She quickly brings her hand up to her mouth to actually check for drool and all I can do is shake my head.

"That wasn't very nice, Liz." Carrie scowls at me.

"I was doing you a favor, because it was very unattractive, the way you were eating them up with your eyes and your mouth hanging open." I laugh. The other two close their mouth at once.

"Holy shit, they are hot!" Ally loudly whispers, and a few men turn her way and smile, "Oh my God, they couldn't possibly have heard me!"

Oh, but they can, I say to myself amusingly.

The girls and I have just finished cleaning up after breakfast and are about to start preparing lunch when Jill finds me and informs me that the last group of Elites should be here my mid-afternoon.

"Kole is planning on briefing them while they eat and then they are heading out, so you may want to make it a big meal. We don't know how long they will be gone."

"Okay, thanks for the update. How is Cassie holding up?"

"Not too good." She whispers, "She is now freaking out, because there are only six of Jax's blood bags left for Jace, and she is worried they will run out."

"Do you think the guys will be back before that happens?" I am so worried. I still haven't been able to contact Taven.

Jill hugs me, "You know our guys won't give up until they are all back home. Have faith, Liz." I try to smile and shake my head. "Do you gals have this covered or do you need any help?"

"We have it covered, thanks. Why don't you go and stay with Cassie for a while. Keep her as calm as you can."

"Okay, that sounds like a good idea. Holler if you need anything."

"Will do."

I return to where the other women are, "Okay ladies, we have a feast to prepare for these men and not a whole lot of time to do it! Let's get to work."

Just as Jill said, the guys start to file in about one thirty and they definitely bring their appetites. Our team are the last to go through the line and each one praises and thanks us, causing Carrie, Ally, and Paige to blush.

Max pulls me to the side, "You have done a pretty good job, Liz, thank you! I may just start splitting the cooking duties with you, so I can have more time for details and missions." He winks at me.

"I will be happy to help out at any time. I think I have decided not to return back to work, and I will need more to occupy my time, aside from tutoring the boys."

"Taven will really be happy to hear that, you have made a good decision. We like to be able to take care of mates, not that I have one... yet, but it's what we do."

"You will find yours, Max, and she will be a very lucky woman." I actually make him blush before he turns and gets back in line for his food.

Once everybody is seated, Kole and Duncan stand at the front of the gym and signal for everyone to quiet down and listen. I stand off to the side and keep my eyes glued on the two of them.

Kole begins, "Our three men have been captive for almost twenty-four hours now. The last update was last night, which was reported that Mika is not planning on killing them but using them to harvest their blood and sell it to the highest bidder." There are gasps throughout the room and the warriors start whispering to each other, "Please," Kole calls out, "let me finish. I know this is upsetting to all of us, but we need to keep our heads clear and on the mission. Aside from our three, there are at least twenty other vampire's that were kidnapped and being used for the same reason. Their numbers are a little bigger than ours, but we have the experience and I believe that we will win this thing."

As Kole ends his part, Duncan picks up where Kole leaves off, "They are not expecting all of us and so they are cocky. This will give us an advantage. There is to be no prisoners taken. Everyone, and I mean everyone, are to be taken out. If you have to chase them down, you do just that. The only ones leaving will be us and the men and women that we rescue."

"What if they surrender?" Someone calls out.

"It makes no difference. They chose to betray their own kind for Mika, and they will die for it. This ends tonight! Everyone has a picture of Mika. He is the prime target. If you see him, you go after him and worry about the others after he is dead. We want that motherfucker's head."

I can't help to feel a little sick from Duncan's words, but I know what Mika is capable of and there can be no mistakes in killing him. I am just glad that I will not be there to see the gruesome site.

Everyone begins to file out of the gym to go suit up when the girls walk in, "What did we miss?" Ally asks.

"Oh nothing, just Kole and Duncan informing the warriors of the mission ahead." I said, relieved that they didn't hear any of it, because then I would be here all day trying to explain things, "Let's start cleaning up. Maybe hit the pool with a few margaritas when we are done."

"Sounds like a plan!" Paige responds.

I slip out for a moment and find a secluded spot. I reach out to Taven, hoping that he at least hears me, even if he can't reply.

'Hey babe, the Elite are on their way. Please hold on just a little bit longer! I love you, Taven, be strong.' Of course, I don't get a response back, so I go back and help the girls finish cleaning up.

TAVEN

They have taken too much blood from Jax and I over the last twenty-four hours and without the right nourishment, we are too weak. Kai on the other hand is doing okay. They send a female in to nourish Kai after each pint that they take, but seeing as how Jax and I are mated, we refuse to drink from anyone else. Mika refuses to care and continues to take before our strength is back up. On top of that, we are beat and whipped for refusing the nourishment, which makes us loose even more. We are slowly dying.

After taking another pint and throwing me back into my cage, I hear Liz's voice. I've heard her every time she has tried to contact me, but I haven't had the strength to answer back. Liz and the boys are the ones that are helping me to keep fighting. After living in the dark for centuries, I can finally see the light again. Liz has broken through and even though I can still feel the demon in me, it is easier to keep him at bay. As long as I let him out to play with our mate every once in a while, he is content. My Liz is my lifeline, my salvation from the darkness and I will fight with everything I have to get back to her and our boys.

I can hear her tell me that help is on the way and that I need to keep fighting. Relief washes over me. Soon, this will be over, and I will have my mate in my arms again. I close my eyes, remembering those last four words that she spoke… I love you Taven, and then everything goes black.

I wake up feeling lightheaded. There is a lot of shouting going on, along with glass breaking and splintering of wood. I try to adjust my eyes, but everything is so blurry. I start to hear screams coming from men and the sound of swords and knives clashing together. It seems to go on forever before I hear my name called and running footsteps coming my way.

"Taven, talk to me!" It's Duncan who is calling out to me. I try to look at him, but I have no strength. I feel something up against my lips before I even smell the scent of my own blood. Something wet is running down my throat and it is hard to swallow, but I slowly get some down. Little by little I finish off the blood and I can already feel my energy start to come back as my body begins to heal itself.

My sight begins to clear, and I can see my friend and brother in front of me, his face etched with worry. I smile up at him, "So, you finally decided to come for us. Took you long enough." I joke.

"You know me, always busy. Figured, I would get to you at some point." He kids back.

"I didn't interrupt you and Jill in another hall closet, did I?"

"Nope, we were using your bed this time. Figured you weren't home to use it." He laughs, which causes me to chuckle and then wince with the soreness that stretches throughout my body, "Here, I have two more bags of your blood. Drink them down.

Jayde comes running over, "Hey Duncan, Kole has Mika, but hasn't killed him yet. He thought that maybe you would like the honor of doing it."

"Have Kole bring him over here."

"Will do." Jayde rushes off again.

Xavier is helping Jax move towards us and of course Kai is walking on his own, rubbing at his wrists where the cuffs were. Looks as if I got the worse of the beatings out of all of us.

"Wow, don't you look pretty!" Jax teases me.

"I'm still the better looking one."

"Uh oh, I think he might have lost a little too much blood! He is talking out of his ass again." Jax looks at me and winks.

Kole clears his throat behind everyone, "Sorry to break up the reunion, but I have brought the entertainment for you."

We all turn towards him, and there is Mika, handcuffed and held tightly within Kole's grip, "Would you like to do the honors?" He looks to Duncan.

"Oh, I think Taven, Jax and Kai deserve to have a little fun as well." Duncan responds.

We all look at Mika and he has pure hatred in his eyes when he looks at us. I finally have enough strength to climb to my feet, "You are a disgrace to all mankind, and I hope you burn in hell!" I spit in his face, "Oh, and don't worry about your wife and child. They will be well taken care of." I smile evilly at him to make him think that my words have a totally different meaning.

Jax, Kai and I are handed two swords and a machete, while Duncan draws his own sword, "Do you have any last words asshole?" Duncan asks Mika with a sneer.

"Fuck you all! You may kill me, but there will always be a survivor that will take over!"

"Sorry to break it to you, but we have won. Every man of yours is dead; you are the last." Kole informs him and Mika's eyes pop out for a split second.

"You will never hurt another person or vampire again! This is the end of the road for you so-called Hunters." I look him dead in the eye as I slowly slide the sword through his gut. He doesn't scream, but a gurgling sound finds its way out. Jax follows suit with his sword on Mika's side and Kai uses the machete on his other side. Blood trickles from Mika's mouth as he blinks continuously at us. Duncan moves to stand in front of him, "And this you, ugly motherfucker, is for me and Jill... burn in hell!" He brings his sword up, Mika following with his eyes, and swiftly brings it down, slicing through Mika's neck with precision, and taking it clean off.

There is a sigh of relief that spreads throughout our little circle and I drop to one knee, not quite having my full strength back yet.

"Take me home, I need my mate." I say to no one in particular. I feel the strong arms of one of my brothers help me up and walk me out. I look up once we get out to the van and see that it is Jayde who is helping me, "Thank you." It's all the strength I have left. Axel, one of our newer recruits is at the wheel.

"It's good to have you back, boss. The same goes for you two." He nods at Jax and Kai.

"It's good to be going home. Now step on it." I command, and our heads whip back as he does what he is told.

We are just coming to a stop at the Compound when my door is ripped open. There stands my beautiful mate, her face soaked with tears. I slowly climb down off my seat, and she is in my arms, kissing me as if her life depends on it. Not caring if others are watching, she grabs hold of my hair tightly and pushes her body against me. The sounds of whistles, hoots and laughter drift over to us and she finally pulls away, but not completely.

"I think they want you to continue. I know I want you to." I smile seductively at her.

"I don't care what they want. I only care what I want, and right now, I want you all to myself." Her lips are swollen from our kiss, and I can see the desire building in her eyes, "But first, you need to go get checked out by Raven. Then I will take you home."

"Mm, I love the sound of that."

Next thing I know, I am being mauled over, not by Liz, but by Jack and Nate, "You're back, you're back!" They say in unison, while jumping up and down with their arms around me.

I chuckle, "You boys didn't miss me any, did you?"

"Yes! Where have you been?" Jack asks as he hugs my side. I look at Liz and she shakes her head, conveying that she didn't tell them what had happened.

"Sorry boys, I got stuck out on detail and didn't mean to be away for so long." I hug them both at the same time, "I won't let it happen again, I promise." I look back to Liz as I say the last part and I can see tears glistening in her eyes.

Letting go of the boys, they look up at me, "Hey, I kind of hurt myself, so I need to go have Raven check me out. Why don't you boys go back to the house, and I will be there shortly, okay?" They agree and hurry away in the direction of the house. Liz wraps her arms around my waist and helps me into the Compound and to the medical ward.

"Ah, I see the troublemakers are back!" Raven teases as he comes over and brings me in for a man hug, "You sure know how to make a good example, boss!"

"Yeah well, I definitely didn't see that coming. Lesson learned for sure!"

Raven checks all my vitals and looks over the wounds that are now almost healed, "I suggest you get bed rest for the rest of the day, maybe get some nourishment from your mate and you should be good as new by tomorrow. Nothing too strenuous, though!" He points to both Liz and I and we know exactly what he means. I roll my eyes at him, "I mean it boss!"

"Yeah, yeah, yeah."

Leaning back in my chair at the dinner table, my stomach full of the delicious food that Liz and the boys made, I gaze at my family. Yes, my family. I want to make it official as soon as possible. I wonder if Liz wants a big wedding. I mean, I know she had one with her first husband, but is she going to want one with me as well? I will give her anything she wants, but I will be happy with just having Cassie marry us and be done with it. I know, not very romantic, but I am just too impatient to wait much longer. I want to make her mine in every possible way, and I want to make her boys mine officially, just as much. These boys mean everything to me, and I want to show them the love that I never had growing up. I don't want them becoming like me, with a demon hidden beyond the surface, fighting to get out constantly. Liz has tamed that demon immensely, but in doing so, has made him fall in love with her as well and instead of completely disappearing, he waits patiently below the surface until it's his turn. He wants his turn now. I feel him stirring, and I don't know how long I will be able to hold him back.

"Hey boys. Have you had the chance to hang out with the other warriors?"

"No." Jack speaks up, "They have been super busy." The disappointment clear on his face.

"Well, they are not leaving until tomorrow and you boys have about three hours before you need to get ready for bed. Why don't you go hang out with them and see if you can learn any new cool stuff from them."

"Can we really?" Nate's excitement makes me smile.

"Yes, but you need to listen to them, do you understand?" I try to sound stern, but I know I'm far from it.

They both jump up and run out the door.

"What was that all about?" Liz cocks a brow at me, "You're not trying to get me alone, are you?"

"What if I am?"

"You heard Raven, nothing strenuous."

"Oh, I don't plan on disobeying him. Actually, I think I'm going to head upstairs and try to rest."

"Now that sounds like a good plan. I am going to clean up down here quick and I will come check on you in a little bit." She smiles at me, and my dick hardens.

I stand up and plant a kiss on the top of her head, "I love you, baby."

"I love you too. Now, go lay down and I will be up after a bit." It turns me on when she tries commanding me to do something. I turn and slowly make my way up the stairs. I am actually feeling pretty good, but I like how she takes care of me, so I'm going to milk it as long as I can.

Instead of laying down in our bed, I pull the key out of my pocket and unlock the door to the playroom. I know for a fact that she will follow Raven's orders outside of this room, so I am going to play the trump card. Within this room, she has to submit to me, and unless she doesn't set foot in here, I will bend her to my demon's will. I undress myself and lay down on the bed and wait for her to come check on me.

Ten minutes later I hear soft footsteps coming up the stairs and towards our room. They stop for a moment, but then I hear them again as they make their way over to the playroom.

"Taven? Why are you laying in here?" Liz pushes the door open and steps in. That's my girl!

"Shut the door, Liz."

"Babe, we can't. You know this."

"What did you just call me?" I ask her in a low baritone voice. She recognizes the demon in me just by my words.

"I'm sorry, Sir."

"That's better. Since you stepped into this room, the only orders that you will be following are mine. Remember your place here. In here, you are my dirty little slut, and you will show me how dirty you are when I demand it, and I am demanding it now. Now shut the door, lock it, and get that slutty ass of yours over here and strip!"

"Yes, Sir." She quickly walks over and undresses for me, dropping her clothes on the floor at her feet.

"Turn around, spread your legs, and bend over. I want you to spread your ass cheeks open, so I can see that pussy and tight asshole." I see a quiver run through her body as she obeys my command. I wrap my hand around my cock and start rubbing up and down slowly. "That's a good girl. I want to taste that pussy of yours as you come all over my face, but first, get your slutty ass over here and suck my cock."

She straightens up and crawls over to me seductively. I can smell her sweet nectar dripping from her pussy just from my demands. She loves it when I talk to her like this and that is why I continue to do so.

I spread my legs, so she can kneel between them. She watches intensely as I slide my own hand up and down, "Do you like watching me jerk myself off?"

"Yes, Sir." She licks her lips.

"What are you waiting for? Wrap that fucking mouth around my cock and get to work." I watch as she replaces my own hands with hers, and then dips down licking the precum at my tip. She wraps her lips around the head and gives it a suck before sliding all the way down. Lubricating my cock with her tongue swirling around, she comes back up, before taking me in again, "Fuck, I love possessing this hole and every other hole you have, which is what I will be doing tonight."

She continues to possess my cock, working me beautifully until my balls boil. Taking her hair, I start pumping into her sweet mouth fast and hard, hitting the back of her throat as I do so. Hot fire shoots down her throat with my release, and she begins swallowing as much as she can. I continue to fuck her mouth until I am done and as always, she licks me clean.

She looks at me, her eyes asking what her next command is. I know she is desperate to come herself, "I can smell your pussy. Bring it over here, so I can dirty it up. I want you sitting on my face while you come." She crawls up and straddles my head but doesn't sit all the way down. My tongue snakes out and swipes at her lips; she tastes so fucking good! Grabbing her hips in a bruising grip, I bring her down against my face, and take from her what I can. She is panting and moaning, as the pressure builds inside her. Tilting her hips forward, I reach and lick her tight bud, lubing it before inserting my thumb.

"Oh, my God! I'm going to come, Sir!" I continue to fuck her pussy with my tongue as my thumb fucks her ass. She rewards me with her release as it drips down onto my face and tongue. Licking and lapping it all up until I feel her body collapse once she is done. Moving her pussy from my face, she moves down and sits on my chest, still trying to catch her breath.

"I want you to go into the drawer and get the big anal plug." Her eyes widen at my command, and I bring my hand down on her ass when she doesn't move, "I gave you an order, now go do it!"

"Y-Yes, Sir." She jumps up and fetches the plug.

THE VAMPIRE'S SALVATION

"Now get on your knees while straddling my chest. I want your ass facing me." She is a good girl and follows my order. I bring her ass down to my mouth and begin to lick around her bud, occasionally licking further down to her wet lips. Using some of her juices, I slip a digit into her tight hole, and then another, "I want you to stick that plug in your dirty little mouth and get it all nice and wet for me." She works the plug with her mouth like she does my cock and then hands it to me; I lube it a little more with my own saliva. Removing my fingers, I slowly push the plug in while I reach around and rub her bundle of nerves. The plug slides in all the way, and she groans.

"That's my dirty slut; taking it all in like that. You like that don't you?"

"Yes!" She groans.

My hand comes down on first one cheek, and then the other "Yes, what?"

She cries out at the sting that my hand causes, "Yes, Sir!"

"You want more, don't you, you fucking slut! You want to be filled and stretched. You are going to turn around and slide that tight pussy over my cock and ride me like a bull. You will not stop until I tell you to. You will not come, until I tell you to. Do you understand?" I pinch her clit and slap her ass at the same time.

"ARGH... YES, SIR!" She turns around and grips my cock with her hand, guiding it to her waiting hole. As she slides down, I bite my bottom lip and grunt at the tightness that surrounds my dick, because of the plug in her ass. I can hear her whimpering as she takes me in.

"Fuck me! I am being squeezed; it feels so good!" I watch her as she finally takes me all in. Her head falls forward before she whips it back and groans with pleasure, "You like feeling full, don't you? I knew my dirty slut would love the fullness. You would like to be taken in both holes with two cocks, huh? Guess what? That will never happen, because I will never share you... ever! Now ride me."

She starts off slow but increases her speed as I begin to thrust into her hard. She is screaming my name as she bounces up and down on my cock. I squeeze and pull at her nipples, "That's right, ride it hard!" A few more pumps and I know she is about to come, so I stop and pull out.

"Please Sir, I want to come on your cock!"

"You are here to please me right now, and you don't get to come until I sink my fangs into that delectable neck of yours." I flick her sensitive nub with my finger to tease her. I sit up and make her lay across my lap, face down, "This is for speaking out of turn." I slap her right cheek hard, and then the left. I do it four more times, each one a little harder, until her ass is bright red, and she is panting with need. I massage her ass to help with the sting, but looking at her red ass, only makes me harder.

I flip her around and look down at the feast that lays across my legs. I slide two fingers into her pussy and rub her nub with my thumb as I pinch and twirl her nipples in my fingers.

"You are so fucking unbelievably beautiful, Liz." She looks up at me under hooded lids and bites her bottom lip, "Your vampire needs to take you now. I can't hold him back any longer."

"Yes, Sir. I am his for the taking." She says as she begins to play with her other nipple. I feel my fangs extend and the claws on the fingers that are not inside of her come out. I can see the glow of my eyes within hers and I remove my other hand from her pussy. Picking her up, I remove her from my lap and place her on her knees, shoving her head down to the bed.

"Is my dirty little whore ready to be fucked good and hard?" I whisper into her ear.

"Yes, Sir... please!" She pleads, and it's all I need to completely let go and let my demon out to play. I take her hard and fast; harder than I've taken her before. My cock has swollen up more since letting the vamp out and it's almost excruciating with the plug in her ass, but I will not remove it. I love watching my cock fuck her pussy, while her ass is being filled. I feel the familiar aching in my balls and know my release is coming.

"I am going to fill that pussy of yours up with my seed now, but I don't want you coming yet. Hold it in. If I have to stop, because you can't hold it off. The consequences will not be pretty!"

On the last word, my cock explodes. I grip her tight at one hip, while I slap her ass with the other, making her grab at the sheets while she moans, "Feel this cock fucking you hard. There will never be another one. You are mine forever, to do with as I please! I am going to fuck you every day until you grow with my child, and then I am going to do it again, over and over. You will always be carrying a child of mine. We will have a big family. You are my salvation woman, and this is how I will be thanking you for eternity…ARGH! FUCK ME…TAKE IT ALL!" I scream as the best orgasm ever takes over my whole body. I know I told her not to come, but I can't help my craving to taste her. Knowing that she won't be able to hold off, I lean over and sink my fangs into her neck, taking her with me into the tidal wave of desire. It feels as if we are soaring over the world, it takes us to a place of sheer ecstasy. I feel her cum all over my cock as I thrust harder, holding my wrist down to her mouth. Her screams become silent as she bites into my vein and has me coming all over again.

Finally, once we are both done with the tremors wracking our bodies, I pull out the plug and climb up behind her, bringing her up against my chest and holding her.

"I love you so much, Liz. I thank God for bringing you to me every day!" I kiss her temple. "I will not punish you for coming when I told you not too, because it is my fault. I couldn't resist, but know, that we will start working on that as well. You learning to hold back even when I'm sunk into that pretty little neck of yours."

"I love you as well, Sir. I also love Taven with all of my heart. Is it possible for me to hold off while you are drinking from me?"

"I am not sure, but I will have fun trying." My demon settles down contently, knowing that he is loved by this gorgeous woman and knowing that he doesn't deserve her love.

I am feeling stronger now that I have drank from my mate and I pick Liz up and carry her out of the playroom. She is sound asleep as I lay her in bed. I shower quickly and dress, leaving her for just a little bit, so I can go and thank everyone for their help. I stop at the door and look back at the woman lying in our bed. A smile plays at my lips for a moment before I shut the door, leaving her to her slumber.

THIRTEEN

LIZ

I am dreaming of Taven, touching me, kissing me, building the fires within me with his hands and lips, "I can never get enough of your sweetness, baby," he whispers right before I feel my legs spread and I feel his hot breath upon my lips below. I hear his grunts after each lick he takes "Mm, your blood and your pussy are all the nutrition I need."

I feel his tongue push through my entrance and realize that it isn't a dream. He is here, making love to me with his mouth. I let out a moan and grab hold of his hair; his five o'clock shadow rubs against my lips, causing a wonderful friction that sends electrical shock waves through my whole body. He rubs at my sensitive bundle of nervous while thrusting his tongue in and out of me.

"Don't stop, I'm going to… OH!" I ride the waves of pleasure as he continues to eat me, only faster now, while my hands hold him against the cradle of my thighs and I grind into his face.

As I begin to come down, his hand continues to assault my clit, but he moves his mouth over to my inner thigh. I feel a slight pinch and then I am there again, riding that wave as he drinks my blood. With each pull, I soar higher until I can't take the pleasure any longer, "Stop! I can't take it anymore, it's too much…AGH!"

He retracts his fangs with a chuckle, but doesn't lick the holes closed. He never licks them closed when he drinks from the areas hidden by clothes. He says he likes seeing them and knowing that it is his mark. Vampires are so possessive.

"Mm, you can wake me up like that every time..." I stretch out my limbs as I smile.

"I may just take you up on that, Gorgeous." He takes possession of my mouth and I taste myself on him.

"What time is it?" I ask as he pulls away.

"A little after eleven pm."

"Oh my God!" I jump up, "I need to get the kids to bed!"

Taven grabs me by the shoulders, "Calm down, love. They are already sound asleep. I helped them to bed a few hours ago."

I cup his cheek and smile, "How did I get so lucky? Who would have thought that I would find the love of my life with a vampire that has a heart of gold!?"

"I'm the lucky one, love." He kisses the tip of my nose, "And if you tell anyone that I am not the badass that I pretend to be, I will redden that perfect ass of yours!"

"Oh, do you promise?"

"Better yet, I will torture you with my hands, tongue, and cock and not let you come... ever!"

"Now that right there is a punishment!" I giggle.

"Come, let's go take a shower and get you all cleaned up."

Taven turns the shower on and adjusts the temperature while I grab a couple of towels. He leaves the bathroom as I am climbing in, but is back within seconds, rubbing his hard cock as he steps in. He has something in his other hand, but I don't get to see it, because he spins me around, so my back is too him.

"Lean over and put your hands on the wall." He commands.

"What are you up to, warrior?" I ask, smiling at him over my shoulder.

He leans in next to my ear, "I told you earlier that I was going to fill every hole. I plan on filling the last one now."

"But I thought that was your demon talking?"

"Oh, baby, the demon and I are one in the same. I'm like Dr. Jekyl and Mr. Hyde, remember? Two personalities, one just stays hidden away until it's time to play."

I swallow hard as my breathing quickens and my body becomes excited.

"Now spread your legs and relax for me. I have been waiting to fuck this tight little ass for hours." I feel something cold run down the crack of my ass and then Taven's finger rubs it around my bud before he slips it in. Pumping the digit in and out, I feel more of the cold gel and then another finger.

"Oh God, Taven… please!" I'm panting but whether it's with need, I can't be sure.

"Please what, baby?"

"Please... fuck my ass, but be gentle."

"It will be my fucking pleasure. I will not hurt you; I promise you that."

I feel the tip of him enter me and then the pressure when he pushes through a little more. He reaches around to play with my clit and there it is, the desire he brings to me every time, beginning to build. He slides out to the tip and then pushes back in more and more until he can't push any further. There's a bit of discomfort, but no pain.

"God, your ass is so tight! How does it feel to have my big cock in that little tight hole of yours?"

"I am so full right now. It feels as though you are hitting every nerve, sending tingles all through my body. I love the way you feel inside of me." I begin to move my hips but he stops me.

"No, let me. I am about to come, because you are so tight. I have to give myself a moment."

I give him what he wants. I don't have to wait long before he is moving in and out of me, picking up the tempo. He inserts his two fingers into my pussy, so I am getting fucked in both holes. God, who would have thought that getting fucked in the ass would feel so good!

"Come for me, baby! Come all over my hand and I will fill your ass with my seed." His voice is hoarse and sounds so sexy. The husky dominant sound of his words take me over and I release myself screaming his name, "Fuck, baby, here I go, get ready!"

I feel his pulsing cock in my ass as he gives me his load, slamming into me with each squirt of his seed. I straighten myself and twist my neck, so he can claim my lips. He grunts and groans into my mouth as the last of his cum enters me and his body relaxes. He pulls out of me slowly and turns me to face him, just to take my mouth again, this time in a slow passionate kiss.

We wash one another, soaping each other everywhere. There is no hurry, we just take our time. It feels so sensual, bringing our bodies to the state of arousal once more. Taven rinses us both off and then carries me to the bed, where he loves on me for another hour or so and then we fall asleep holding each other.

There is a huge difference in the air the next morning as we are saying goodbye to the other Elites. Laughter fills the Compound all morning long. Knowing that life is finally back to normal; no looking over our shoulders for danger anymore. We are even saying our goodbyes to Carrie, Paige, and Ally. There are tears among the women and promises to keep in touch.

As Carrie and Paige leave together, Ally stays behind. I'm a little curious as to what her plans are now that she as free to leave. I know she has no one waiting for her and she had thought about staying on with us, but she hasn't mentioned it since the first time.

"Hey lady, what are your plans? Do you still need me to talk to Taven about letting you stay?"

"No, that's okay. Actually, I kind of met someone and we really hit it off."

"What do you mean? Who did you hit it off with?" Ally points to one of the Warriors that came up from York County. He is a tall one, that one; with strawberry-blonde hair and hazel eyes. His V-neck t-shirt fits snug across his muscular chest, which tapers down to his waist. "Wow! He is definitely a looker! How did you meet him?"

"I met him down by the pool yesterday after they all came back, and we hit it off. We stayed up most of the night talking and then did a little kissing. I am hung up on his scent, I can't breathe enough of it in! I literally can feel sparks whenever he touches me!"

I chuckle to myself, knowing full well that another mated pair just found each other. "That's how I feel with Taven. You know it's the real deal when there are real sparks." I wiggle my brows at her.

The Elite walks over to us smiling at Ally before he looks at me, "Hi, I'm Breck.", he says and holds his hand out to me. I shake it.

"Hello, I'm Liz. I'm Taven's fiancé." I smile up at him and wink.

He turns back to Ally, "Are you ready to head out? We have a little bit of a drive and we are needed back in Sanford by lunch time."

"Oh yes! I'm all packed and ready to go. Are you sure it's okay? I don't want to inconvenience anyone." She frowns up at him as he wraps his arms around her.

"It's all good, I promise!" He dips his head and kisses her lightly.

Ally turns back to me and throws herself into my arms. We hug for a moment until she pulls back, "I am sure we will see each other at some point and I will call you. Apparently, there are no other females at their Compound, so I may be a bit lonely."

"Of course, I will come visit you soon and you can show me around. I haven't ventured that way before, so it would be nice to see another part of Maine. You better get going and not keep your man waiting!" I giggle as I nod towards Breck.

I watch as they leave hand in hand and I can't help but be extremely happy for them. I know he will treat her well. I feel arms snake around my waist and I lean back into strong arms.

"You aren't playing match maker like Jill does, were you?" Taven asks as he nuzzles my neck.

"Um no! Actually, they found each other themselves. I don't need to play match maker when fate is involved."

"You are right about that."

"Do you think we can go down and visit some time? She is the only female at the Sanford Compound and I am sure she would like the company every so often."

"I am sure that will be fine. Honestly, with the Hunters taken care of, I don't see why you women wouldn't be able to make a day of it and go down together."

"Really? You would let us do that?"

"Babe, you are not prisoners here. We just had to keep you here because of the Hunters. You ladies can come and go as you please. Just make sure you always come back." He says the last with a wicked smile.

"I will always come back for you; there is nobody else for me." I turn around and wrap my arms around his waist.

"That is what I like to hear." He kisses me and then pulls back, "I came over here to let you know that I will be in my office most of the afternoon working on paperwork. Feel free to interrupt at any time and I can take a quick break." He has the most handsome devilish smile that I have ever seen.

"Well then, I may just have to take you up on that. I mean, I wouldn't want you to overwork yourself, now would I?"

"No, you wouldn't." Kissing me quickly again, Taven heads towards his office and I remain standing here, watching that tight, muscular ass of his, as he walks away.

TAVEN

It is nice to get back into the old routine, where all we have to do is do detail on the streets of Augusta. The police chief does call us a few times to help with certain crimes, but we don't mind. It is still better than having the stress of always watching our backs and keeping our mates and the children safe.

It has been six weeks since we took the Hunters out once and for all and all has been quiet. Liz, Cassie, and Jill have taken off for the day to go visit Ally in Sanford, leaving the kids in the hands of the men. Not sure if that is such a good idea on Cassie and Jill's part, though. It's funny watching Jax and Duncan try and take care of crying babies, not knowing if they are wet or need a diaper change. Thank God Jack and Nate are older, so I just need to make sure they stay out of trouble.

I keep hoping that Liz gets knocked up, but we haven't had any luck yet. Not for lack of trying or anything. That's the thing, I come in her at least twice a day and nothing. I guess it's true what they say, the harder you try, the longer it takes. Maybe I should just stop trying so hard.

These are the thoughts going through my head as I'm walking over to the Laser Tag arena to check on the boys and my phone starts buzzing. I pull it out of my pocket and see that it's Kole, "Yeah, what's up?" I answer.

"There is a visitor at the front gate asking for you. He says his name is Miguel, but refuses to show his face to the camera, so I can ID him."

"Yep, that sounds like him. Let him in but keep an eye on him as he drives up. I'm checking on the boys and then I will head back."

"Ten-four big guy."

I hang up and flash to the arena. The boys are in the middle of a war with Kai, Phoenix, and Stone, so I just tell them to check in with me when they are done. I give Liz a lot of credit. She raised her boys well, being a single parent. They are good kids, just getting into trouble every so often, but what boy doesn't?

I flash back to the Compound just in time to see a Lexus pull up to the front. My old mentor steps out of the car and smiles broadly at me, "Ah, Taven! My favorite student! Come and greet your old teacher." Miguel says this and yeah, he is a few centuries older than me, but he still looks to be in his late thirties. He is of Mexican decent, and the women go crazy over him. At six feet nine inches, built like an ox and is easy on the eyes, he knows how to talk to women. Hell, he can make them cream their pants by just talking to them! I used to idolize him and envy him, but I outgrew that about a century ago when I witnessed how he actually treats women once he has them; it's not pretty.

"Miguel! So nice to see you! Why didn't you tell me you were going to be in my neck of the woods?"

"It was a last-minute decision and I had other business close by, but I wasn't sure how long that would keep me. I was over in Somerset County, and they informed me of the issues you were having for a while and that they had sent warriors to help you out. That was quite a story they told me. I wish I could have been here to help. Anyway, they gave me the directions to your location."

"Well, it doesn't matter what brought you here. I'm glad it you are here, I've missed you, old friend! Let's go to my office and chat and then I will give you a tour."

"I hear you are mated now. I couldn't believe it when I heard that! I am happy for you! Do you have any children yet?" Miguel slaps me on my shoulder, and I laugh.

"I have two stepsons. Liz and I are trying but haven't been lucky enough yet. That reminds me, do you have any idea on what age a child who is turned into a vampire, stops aging?"

I see him think about my question before answering, "I've met a couple of adult vamps who were turned during their childhood, they each stopped aging at different times, but always in the mid to late twenties. Why are you asking?"

I explain the situation with the accident and how we did what we had to do to save them, but we just don't know when they would stop the aging part. I am happy to hear that it will be quite some time yet before it happens.

"Wow, you find a mate and all this shit starts to happen. Makes me grateful that I haven't found mine yet." He chuckles, but I see the sadness in his eyes.

"Actually, Jax and Duncan also found their mates, and each have two kids."

"You have got to be kidding me! Jax, the workaholic, found his mate?"

"Yep. He was the first to find his. There is never a dull moment at the Compound with our three women around, I will tell you that much." I slap his shoulder this time, "Let's go find a drink, shall we?"

By the time Liz and the women get back, Miguel and I are so far into the liquor, that I am slurring my words. Liz knocks and walks into my office smiling.

"Are you throwing a party without me?" She pretends to pout.

"Baby! Come over here, I've missed you!" Liz walks over to me, eyeing me warily.

"Are you drunk?" She chuckles and then looks over at Miguel. I pull her down on my lap and squeeze her around the waist.

"I may be a little intoxicated, but it will wear off. I want you to meet a very good friend of mine and my mentor, Miguel." I slurred a little at the end.

"It is so nice to finally meet you, Miguel. Taven has talked about you... and I promise, it was all good." She smiles at my friend.

"It is a great pleasure to meet you as well! I have heard quite a bit about you today... sadly, it wasn't all good."

I feel a slight sting as Liz slaps my chest, "What have you been telling Miguel about me?"

"Thanks Miguel!" I look back to Liz, "I swear I haven't said anything bad about you! Miguel has a tendency to cause trouble." I rub my chest as if she actually hurt me and Miguel laughs.

"No, he is right. I have only heard good, but I like watching him get slapped by a female. He did not, however, mention how exquisite you are! You are a true beauty; I am very jealous." I watch as he winks at Liz, and she blushes. I don't like how he is looking at my mate, but I keep it to myself. I will have to watch him carefully while he is here.

"Will you be staying for a while, Miguel?" Liz asks. I can tell she is feeling a little uncomfortable under Miguel's scrutiny and she holds on to me just a little tighter.

"I am not sure. I was hoping to stay at least a day or so, if that is okay with Taven."

"Of course, you are welcome to stay however long you need or want to." I say but hope that he keeps to his own time limit.

Liz looks at me, "Should I make up a room for him here at the Compound or up at the house with us?"

"Miguel, which would you prefer?"

"I can stay at the Compound. It will give me time to catch up with Raven and a few others, along with meeting any new Elite's that you may have. I always love seeing what my teachings have done for others."

"Great," Liz pipes in, "I will ready the room next to Dane's room then. I will leave you two, so you can continue your little party, and I will go find my hoodlums." She gives me a quick kiss and goes to get up, but I hold her in my lap and take her lips again. This time for a more passionate kiss. Just making it clear that she is mine, I know how Miguel thinks. I also know how competitive he is, regardless of whether Liz is my mate.

I reluctantly pull away and Liz is blushing, "You have company. I'm sure Miguel doesn't want to watch you make out with me!" She scolds me and gets up.

"Oh, I don't mind. It's not like I haven't watched him before." I glare at him for saying such a thing.

"I see. Well, I'm not one to put on a show for anyone. If you will excuse me…" She glares at me and turns and walks out the door.

"Why must you feel the need to start trouble?" I scowl at Miguel.

"What? I was only stating a fact. It's not my fault you never told her about your past." He smiles.

"She does know about my past. The stuff that was necessary to tell her. She doesn't need to know about other women. I swear Miguel, your manners haven't changed one bit." I shake my head, "Thanks to you, now, I won't be getting any tonight!"

"Sounds like you could use a break anyway. Too much sex is turning you into a sap."

"No Miguel, it's called being mated. You couldn't possibly understand what it feels like to have a mate. I will love to witness the day that you find yours!" I laugh, because the day that a woman brings Miguel to his knees, will be a day that will definitely go down in history in my book! I kind of feel sorry for the woman; there is no telling what kind of mate Miguel will be.

I show Miguel to his room and then head on up to the house. There is a lamp on in the living room and Liz is snuggled on the couch reading a book. I plop down beside her and rub her thigh. I sobered up soon after Liz left, Miguel being my buzz kill. I glance over at Liz, who hasn't said one word to me yet.

"What's wrong, baby?" I ask.

She cocks her brow at me, "Do you really need to ask me that?"

I blow the air out of my mouth, "Miguel doesn't think sometimes before he talks. He is like Kai, just says whatever is on his mind. He also knows nothing about mates. He didn't realize that his comment would upset you so much."

"So, tell me, Mr. Casanova, how many women did Miguel watch you kiss?"

"Come on babe, you don't want to hear any of this."

"Oh, yes, I do!"

"Have you never been out with friends and made out with someone in front of them? That's all it was."

"As a matter of fact, I have never been big on PDA... at least not until meeting you. Miguel seemed to insinuate something else. Have you shared a woman with him before?"

Ugh, how do I answer this? Fuck it, might as well be honest, "As a matter of fact, yes, I have. You know how my past was, how bad I was with my demon. Sharing with him was sometimes part of it."

Liz literally turns a tint of green and my first thought is that she is going to spew all over me, "Is it really that bad? People share all the time. And before you ask, NO, I will never share you! I have already told you this."

"I know it happens all the time, but it doesn't sit well with me hearing how my mate use to do it! You would feel the same way if the tables were turned, would you not?"

Sighing, because I know she is right, "Yeah, you're right, I would be pissed. I'm sorry, it was long ago, can we just forget about it? I had, until he brought it up."

"I guess. He kind of made me feel uncomfortable, the way he stared at me and the compliments he gave me."

"I could tell. Just stay far away from him while he is here, because he is a big flirt and is very competitive when it comes to females. Like I said, he isn't mated, so he doesn't understand the ramifications of flirting with a mated woman."

"Awe, are you getting jealous?"

"Maybe just a little, but I know you are mine." I reach up and push back a strand of hair that has slipped out of her messy bun, "You are beautiful, Liz, and I need to get used to people complimenting you like that. I need to try and not want to rip out their throats."

She giggles, "Really? You would rip someone's throat out for me? How romantic!"

"Don't you know I would do anything for you?" I can't help the emotion in my voice, causing the smile to slip from her face.

"I know you would. That is why I love you so much." I cup her cheek and rub my thumb over the softness of her skin, "Taven."

"Hmm?" I glance into her eyes and wait to hear what she is about to say. I love the sound of her voice, but I absolutely love the sound of it when it's laced with need.

"Will you take me to bed? I need to feel you inside of me."

"Never feel like you need to ask me, love. I will gladly take you wherever you want to be taken." I smile lovingly at her.

"I want our bed, not the playroom. I only want Taven tonight."

"Then you will have me and me alone, baby." I pick her up and carry her up to our bedroom. The love we make is sensational, and in the end, I fall asleep with my mate embraced in my arms and my cock still buried inside of her.

FOURTEEN

LIZ

I wake up to find Taven's side of the bed empty and cold. Last night was perfect and I was hoping he would wake me up and do it all over again, but I see that is not the case. I grab my phone and open up the camera. Taking a selfie of me pouting and his side of the bed, cold and empty; I send it to him in a picture message. I get a text back right away from him, apologizing that he had to head to the Compound early to take care of a few things and he didn't want to wake me up that early.

I am extremely horny this morning and I am feeling kind of evil, so I take another selfie of me still naked and playing with my clit, telling him that I will just have to take care of myself. I see that he's opened my message, but never replies. I shrug my shoulders and close my eyes, preparing to get myself off. I insert a finger into my pussy and begin imagining that it's Taven's finger as I bite my lip and moan. A few seconds later, I start playing with a nipple and open my eyes. Taven is standing there, watching me with his dick out, running his hand up and down his length.

"You are so fucking beautiful right now!" Taven's voice is husky, "Don't you dare stop playing with yourself."

I watch as he strips his shirt off and then his jeans and climbs onto the bed, "Oh, now you want to play? I think I can take care of myself, thank you very much."

"I insist that you continue playing with yourself, but I am also going to insist that you suck my cock, while you play with that gorgeous pussy of yours."

"Really? Hm, I don't know if I am really in the mood to please you this morning." I am trying really hard to keep a straight face.

"Well then, maybe I should carry you into the playroom and then you will have no choice." He raises his brows at me.

Rolling my eyes, "Fine! I suppose I can take care of you as well. Get that big ass cock over here."

He smiles smugly, "I knew you would see it my way!"

Before I can retaliate with a comeback, his cock is in my mouth and thrusting in and out. I concentrate on pleasuring myself while licking and sucking the huge girth that is continuously hitting the back of my throat. The more he thrusts, the more I thrust my own fingers into my pussy, moaning. Taven feels the vibrations of those moans against his cock, causing his own groans until he starts to pulse in my mouth, "Oh Fuck, baby!" He gives one hard thrust and hits the back of my throat one last time just as the first stream of cum comes shooting out. He starts to squeeze and pinch my nipple and it sends my own desire up and over.

As I lick his cock clean, he lifts my fingers to his mouth and licks my own juices from them, groaning, "Your nectar is like warm apple pie, the sweetest taste that I have ever tasted."

I look up into his eyes and see the storm swirling within their depths. He grabs me and places me on my knees, my chest flush against the headboard. Holding my hands in his behind my back, he enters me from behind, taking my breath away in the process.

"I can't help myself around you, baby; you drive me crazy, especially when you suck my cock the way you do." Taven speaks these words low in my ear as he slams his cock into me over and over.

"Oh, my God, Taven, don't stop! Keep fucking me just like this... Oh... Oh!"

"You like that, don't you? Your pussy can't get enough of my cock. Don't worry, you are mine and I will fuck you whenever and wherever I want... and you will enjoy that too!"

"YES! I love it! I am always yours for the taking!" I feel his teeth sink into my neck and my orgasm hits me hard. I'm blown away by the desire each pull causes and I come over and over.

He licks the holes closed and starts pounding away harder and harder, until finally, he is filling me up to the brim with his seed, grunting as he pushes out every last bit.

"Shit, sweetheart. The things you do to me!" He nuzzles his nose into my hair and takes a deep breath, "I love you with all my heart, Liz. I can't even remember my life before you came into it, and I can't imagine a life without you in it, marry me!"

"I already said yes."

"No, I mean, marry me today. I don't want to wait any longer. I need to possess you in every way possible!"

"Today? You want to get married today? That's impossible!"

"It is possible if we have Cassie marry us, unless you want to have a big affair. I would rather not, but I will give you whatever you want, sweetness."

I think about it for a moment. I am not really wanting a big wedding anyway and I want nothing more than to be Mrs. Taven Anderson. I bring my lips to his for the briefest moment before pulling away.

"I would love nothing more than to become your wife today, warrior." I smile at the relief that floods his face. He laughs and squeezes me so tight that I could barely breathe, "Babe! I can't breathe..."

"Shit, sorry love. You just made me the happiest man alive!"

Staring at the man in front of me, with nothing but the love he has for me in his eyes, I know I am making the right decision. I have always dreamed of having the kind of love that we have. I just didn't realize that I would find it with a vampire. It's not just the love he has for me, but also the love he has for my boys. He already considers them his own and that means more to me than anything.

"You have no idea how happy you make me, Taven. No matter what your life was before me, none of that matters. The only thing that matters is now and the future we will have together as a family."

He slams his mouth against mine, blowing me away with how much passion is behind the kiss. Never before have I ever been kissed like this, making me lose all train of thought. He makes me forget all the bad that ever happened in my life, hell, I can barely remember my name at this point.

He slowly pulls away and smiles at me deviously, "I can smell your arousal, love, and as much as I would love to spend the day in bed with you, I need to go find Cassie. Once we say our I do's, I am all yours!" He flashes his sparkling white teeth at me.

"Go then. I will shower and see what the kiddos are up to." I watch as he walks out, his steps a little lighter than usual.

Taven is over at Cassie and Jax's place planning a quick ceremony for this evening, so I decide I will go talk to Max about preparing a nice dinner for everyone. As I come around the front of the Compound, I see Miguel greeting a beautiful woman, who is getting out of a taxi. The woman steps forward and embraces Miguel who then kisses the woman… and it wasn't a chaste kiss either. I slap my hand over my mouth, so my chuckle won't be heard.

I find Max in the kitchen as always. He is pulling out a batch of chocolate fudge cookies from the oven, "I see my boys talked you into making their favorite cookies." I snicker at him.

He smirks, "Are you kidding me? They give me a reason to make these bad boys! They are my favorite too, but I hardly ever make them for just myself. Gotta watch my girlie figure, you know."

"Oh, sure, now you can blame my boys when you start packing on the pounds!"

"Someone will need to take the fall." He winks.

"I'll just pretend we didn't have this conversation." I laugh, "Anyway, I was wondering if you would be okay with making a nice feast for tonight's supper? You know, something fit for a wedding?"

He looks at me quizzically for a moment before his eyes widen, and a smile spreads across his face, "The boss man is finally getting hitched tonight?"

I bob my head up and down, beaming. Max rushes over to me and lifts me up, spinning me around, "Congratulations, darling!"

I slap at him as my stomach gets super queasy, "Oh my God, I'm going to puke if you don't stop!"

He sets me down right away, "I am so sorry! I didn't realize that you didn't like spinning."

"I usually don't mind it." I feel the bile start to rise and I run over to the wastebasket just in time to empty the contents of my stomach. Max hands me a wet rag and I wipe my mouth. When I look up at him to thank him, I find him smirking down at me, "What? Why are you looking at me like that?"

"Is there something that the two of you are not telling the rest of us? Why are you really getting married tonight?"

I look at him confused, "Because we don't want to wait and neither one of us want a big wedding. As for the first question... I haven't the slightest clue as to what you are talking about."

"Hm, you're serious. Well, Ms. Brady, if I were to guess, I would say that the boss man will be a daddy in the next five months."

I look at him as if he's grown a second head. There is no way, my period isn't due for another week.

"I think you are getting a little head of yourself here, Max. I think I would know if I was throwing up because I was prego. It's nothing, my stomach feels fine now."

"Whatever you say, darling." He smiles at me, "So, what did you have in mind for supper?"

"Whatever you think will suit the occasion, surprise us. Thank you so much for doing this on short notice. I can help a little bit too, if you need me to."

"Are you kidding me? This is my gift to you guys, now take a cookie and get the hell out of my kitchen! You are not allowed in here the rest of the day." He snickers as he shoos me out the door. I scarf the delicious cookie and head out to Cassie and Jax's house.

Taven is still there talking to Cassie when I get there. Cassie squeals and comes running over to me, throwing her arms around me and squeezing, "I can't believe you are finally getting married! I am honored to be ordaining it for the two of you!"

"I'm not going to be able to get married if all my bones are crushed!" I laugh as Cassie jumps back.

"I am so sorry. I'm just super excited for the both of you! Oh, and Jill was here earlier, but had to get back to the twins, but she said yes to be your Matron of Honor."

"Oh, God, I hadn't even thought about that."

"No worries, I took care of it for you." Taven says as his arms come around me.

"Of course, you would." I smile, "You take care of everything. Although, I did talk to Max about cooking a wedding feast for tonight. He is all excited for us. He shoved a cookie into my mouth and booted my ass out of the kitchen!"

"Want me to rip his head off?" Taven teases.

"No," I giggle, "I love Max, I am just not liking him at the moment! Oh, by the way, did you know Miguel is having a friend join him?"

"Yeah, he mentioned it this morning. He said that it was someone that was helping him with a job. Why, is he here?"

"Well, yes, but it's she, not he, and I am pretty sure that she is more than just a friend."

"Why do you say that?"

"Do you go around embracing all your female friends and shove your tongue down their throats? If so, then Coco and I will be going rounds!" I laugh.

"Uh, no. I do not, and neither does Miguel. I wonder why he didn't say that it was more than just a friend. I suppose we should go up and welcome her."

"Why do I need to go?"

"Because love, as of tonight, you are going to be Mrs. Boss Lady and you might as well start acting the part." He snickers and then kisses my forehead.

"Ugh, not even married and you are already bossing me around!" I wink and then say my goodbye to Cassie, but she is busy writing out notes for the ceremony already. So, I grab Taven's hand and let him drag me to the Compound.

TAVEN

I find it odd that Miguel didn't tell me that he had invited a lady friend to the Compound. I am sure Liz knows what she saw. It's strange, though, that he would even have a lady friend as Liz described, seeing as he has never had female companionship in the past, unless he is screwing her brains out. He always kicks them out the door afterwards and never sees the same woman twice.

When Liz and I get to the Compound, there is no one around, so we go to my office. Liz sprawls out on the couch and grabs a magazine to read, while I go to my desk to go through some reports that I still need to sign off on. After five minutes of sitting here and the continued glances towards Liz, I give up trying to concentrate. She looks too tempting the way she is laying down. With one knee bent up and the other down, her other foot on the floor, she is spread open, and I can't resist the essence that oozes from her pussy.

I flash over, and I am on her in a heartbeat. She squeals in delight as I cover her body with mine, massaging her sex with my bulge, "Why do you tempt me the way you do?" I kiss my way up her neck and nibble on her ear.

Laughing, she wraps her arms around my back, "I wasn't doing anything! Just laying here, reading a magazine."

"With your legs spread wide open, offering yourself to me. How am I supposed to get any work done with a temptress like you around, huh?"

"I am sorry, I can go somewhere else."

"Not a chance! I have you now and we have yet to break in my office." I pull her shirt up and over her head and my mouth finds her nipple through the lacy bra, my hand rubbing over her heated core.

I have her panting in no time and just as I begin to unbutton her jeans, a familiar voice peals with laughter. It's a voice from a past that has been long forgotten since meeting Liz. I tense up and listen some more, maybe I was mistaken. Nope, there it is again. I jump up and grab Liz's shirt, handing it to her as she looks at me confused.

"I am sorry, love. We are about to have company and don't want anybody seeing you undressed, least of all Miguel." I kiss the top of her head and walk over to the door just as Miguel knocks. I take a very deep breath and blow it out, praying that I am completely wrong about who is on the other side of the door.

I swing the door open and see Miguel standing there, "Ah, Taven, I am so glad I caught you! I wanted you to meet my colleague." He moves to the side and there she is. She hasn't changed one bit since the last time I saw her, "Taven, meet Beth. Beth, this is Taven, an old student of mine and one of my dearest friends."

I just stand here, staring at her. I don't know what to say. My first instinct is to put a stake through her heart for what she did to me, but seeing her stand here, with an innocent look on her face, has me deciding otherwise. She speaks first.

"Hello Taven, it's been a long time. How nice to see you again." She gives me the smile that used to melt my heart, but no more.

"Mary-Beth. Wish I could say the same to you. You have guts coming here."

"Wait a minute, you two know each other?" Miguel asks.

"I'm not surprised that she didn't tell you. She tends to keep secrets really well. Miguel, meet Mary-Beth, my maker." I hear a gasp come from behind me and I turn to see Liz frozen in place. She knows my feelings about my maker, so she is aware that I am two seconds away from snapping. She regains her composure, puts a smile on her face and comes over to me, taking my hand in hers. Just her touch calms me tremendously.

"Miguel! So nice of you to stop by." She doesn't even acknowledge Beth and I smile on the inside.

"Always nice to see you, Liz. Could you ladies excuse us? I would like a moment alone with Taven." Liz tries to let go of my hand, but I hold it firm in mine.

"Miguel, whatever you need to speak to me about, Liz can hear too. My "mate" knows everything, and I don't keep anything from her." I emphasize the word mate to make it clear to Beth that I am off limits to her. Yeah, I saw the hunger in her eyes when she spoke to me. That ship sailed a long fucking time ago.

"Of course," Miguel says, "Beth, please give us a moment."

She stomps her foot like a little kid, "If she can stay then I can stay!"

I turn to her, "Liz is my mate and my soon-to-be-wife, you are not. You can make yourself comfortable down the hall in the rec room on the right." Miguel steps into the room and I close the door in her face. I wait until I hear her footsteps disappear down the hall before I turn and glare at my mentor.

"I swear to God, Taven, I didn't know she was who turned you! She has never said anything, even the few times that I mentioned you in her presence."

"What is she doing here?" I sneer.

"She has been helping me collect information on a case and asked if she could join me here."

"You can stay as long as you want, Miguel, she on the other hand, cannot!"

"I completely understand. Do you mind if she leaves in the morning?"

"Liz and I are getting married this evening and I don't want her here for that!" I am beyond pissed at this situation. I feel a hand on my arm and look down at Liz.

"Babe, it's okay if she stays until morning. She just needs to not join us for supper and the ceremony. She can eat in her room."

"I don't want her here. I am doing everything I can to keep from staking her!"

"I get it, and if you really need her to go, then we will make her go. I just figured that she has been traveling and maybe needed the rest before leaving again."

"I couldn't care less how she is feeling. She didn't give a damn when she took my life from me!" I must have said something that upset Liz, because her stature changes, and she is glaring at me now.

"I understand that you are pissed that she changed you, but the way I see it is, she gave me the love of my life and I can't help but to be grateful to her for it!" Without another word, Liz stomps out of the room and slams the door.

"Fuck!" I pick up a lamp and throw it across the room. She is right of course. I would never have Liz and the boys if it weren't for Beth, but I can't let go the centuries of hate that I have felt towards her.

"You are definitely going to have your hands full with that one!" Miguel chuckles. "Congratulations, by the way. I didn't know you were getting hitched today."

"We just decided to do it this morning, instead of waiting." I inform him. "Jesus Christ, Miguel, what the fuck do I do?"

"That is for you to decide. I can keep her busy, so she stays away from you if you decide to let her stay. Otherwise, I will let her take my car and have her stay at a hotel."

"What is it that you are working on anyway?"

"Honestly, it's a weird case and you probably won't believe it. I didn't at first until I started looking into it. I have been getting calls from other Elite groups about strange things happening. They called me to see if I had any answers. At first, I knew nothing, but the more I started digging and investigating, I learned something new."

"What is it that you learned?" I ask.

"That we are not the only ones that have different DNA."

"What is that supposed to mean?"

"There are humans out there that can change… or shift is what I like to call it."

"Shift? Like their bodies change or what?"

"That is exactly what they do. They shift into wolves."

I am blown away from what I am hearing. How can this be possible? The human body changing form, and into a canine no less! That has got to be excruciating, one would think.

"So, there is a such thing as werewolves?" I confirm.

"No, not exactly. They don't change into huge beasts, granted some are pretty damn big, but mainly just oversized canines."

"How is this possible?" I still can't wrap my head around it.

"How are vampires possible, Taven? The research I've done so far, leads me to believe that they were created the same way that we vamps were."

"And how is that exactly. The last time I asked you how the vampire race came about, you had no clue."

"Yes, I know. Our conversation that day led me into my research. What I found is still a little confusing and still has a few areas that are unanswered, but the gist of it is, about a little before my time, some kind of sickness took hold and spread like wildfire. They did what's called bloodletting, draining of the blood, but then they transferred new blood into the body, but not until the body was mostly drained of the tainted blood. From what I understand, the little bit of tinted blood that remained in the body is what changed the DNA and when the person came around, they were vampires. Now I am not sure how it caused us to grow our fangs, claws, our eyes to glowing, and senses, but they did. As for the shifters, the story that I am hearing is the same as ours, except when their DNA was changed, it was either under a Full Moon or a New Moon."

I am sure I look ridiculous with my mouth hanging open in utter shock, but who wouldn't when hearing everything Miguel is explaining!

"So, they are exactly like us except that our bodies don't change?"

"Exactly, and I am assuming that our bodies don't change, because it wasn't done under a Full Moon or New Moon, but everything else is the same. Just like finding their own mates. They have to have Type O blood, and each have a destined mate."

"Wow! So, why have we not heard of these shifters before now? I mean, do they know about us?"

"They have known about vampires for a few centuries, but they have been told that we are sworn enemies, so they have stayed hidden. I ran into a pack a few years ago and almost got myself killed! They held me prisoner for a while until their Alpha and I had a nice long chat. Since then, we have become friends and allies, but he and his pack are still wary of most of our kind. They are just like us, Taven, some good and some bad."

"Do you have locations to any packs, aside from the one you know of?"

"Not the exact locations, but there are at least fifteen packs between Massachusetts and Maine alone. They make their own little communities either right in the towns, or on the outskirts of town. Almost like what you have started here. No one is the wiser."

"So, how do we locate these packs? I'm sure there has got to be some way to find them."

"You do what I do, you search them out, but it is very time consuming. I haven't found any as of yet in this county, but I am sure there is one. My findings have found that there is at least one pack to each county."

"Why are you searching them out anyway, Miguel?"

He smiles at me, "Because Taven, even though they are a vicious lot and very cautious about vampires, if you can befriend a pack, they make awesome allies. They could have helped with your Hunter problem."

"That would have been nice. Well," I rub my hands together, "I had better get my ass in gear and get ready for this evening. If you ever need any help with searching, please let me know."

"I will for sure." He smiles at me.

"Oh, and Miguel. I better see your ugly mug at the ceremony! Beth can stay for as long as you NEED her to, but make it clear to her that she needs to stay far away from me."

"I wouldn't miss your wedding for anything, Taven. As for Beth, I could use her for a day or so, but I will warn her to keep away from you. I am truly sorry for bringing her here. I honestly did not know that she was your maker. If you need me to, once I am finished with her, I can end her. I have no qualms about doing it."

I can't help but be amused by his offer, "No need to do that. It seems as if she has nobody, aside from you, so leaving her to be alone will suffice. As long as she isn't going around changing people."

"Honestly, the way she has talked, she hates what she is, and I don't think she would do that to another. Well, aside from you that is."

I give a long sigh, "I think it was an accident with me, and she got scared and ran. I truly believed that she loved me, but that still doesn't excuse the fact that she left me to deal with being a fledgling by myself. Liz is right, if it weren't for Beth turning me, I would never have Liz and her boys in my life, so I can't be mad at her for that any longer, but Beth leaving me to fend for myself, not knowing what I was, I can never forgive that."

"You have changed, Taven. Your mate, she has changed you." Miguel mocks me, "Do you still have the cravings?"

"She has changed me, but that's what a mate will do, and you will see it once you find yours." The horrified look on Miguel's face is priceless, "As for the cravings, I do still get them, but not as bad. It seems as though my demon has fallen in love with our mate as well and Liz loves my demon as much as she loves me."

"Oh really? Your mate sounds like a very good time! Are you sure you don't want to share?" The devilish smile he gives me pisses me off as much as his words do.

"I will forgive you this one time for asking that, Miguel, but don't ever say anything like that about my mate again. She is completely off limits; my sharing days are over."

"Hey, didn't hurt to ask." He chuckles, holding up his hands in defense.

I walk out without saying another word and go in search of Liz to try and smooth things over with her on the whole Beth issue. Man, it's not even lunch time and my mind is swimming with everything that has happened already. Between seeing Mary-Beth again and then finally learning how vampires came about, and that there are shifters among us, I seriously need a little down time. My need to find Liz grows as I think about her laying naked below me as I sink my cock and fangs into her delectable body. Now that I am rock hard, I am desperate to find the one person that can ease the ache… my mate.

FIFTEEN

LIZ

I am hiding myself in our room, crying my eyes out, and I don't know why. I mean, Taven being pissed that Beth turned him is understandable, and I know he wouldn't change anything now, since the boys and I came along, but it still hurts seeing the anger he still carries. Just not enough for me to be acting the way that I am. I am feeling exhausted, all of a sudden, so I lay down for a little bit, but I must have really been tired, because soon I am fast asleep.

Strong arms wrapping around me wakes me from my nap. His musky scent drifts through my nose and I smile as I snuggle in deeper. A hand sneaks up under my shirt and fingers find my sensitive nipples through my bra. Soft lips sprinkle feather light kisses on my neck. Every touch is loving and soft, except for the arousal that is nuzzled against my back side.

I can never stay mad at this man. He knows what makes me weak, what makes me submit to his every demand. I should hate him for it, but to be honest, I know that he submits to me just as much.

"I need you, Taven." I barely whisper the words, but he hears them clear as day. I had taken off my jeans before I laid down, so he easily makes his way down into my panties, finding me soaked with my own arousal. I hear his growl to my response from his touch as he sinks in fingers into my wet opening. His thumb rubs at my clit and I arch into his now rock-hard cock. I reach back with my hand to find that he is totally naked, I grab hold of his cock, and begin to jerk him off.

"Is that what you want? Tell me… what do you want me to do with this big boy?" He nibbles on my earlobe.

"You know exactly what I want, warrior. I want to feel this bad boy deep within my pussy, fucking me until I cream all over it and milk every last bit of your cum until you are bone dry."

He tears my panties right off me and flips me onto my back, "I will give you everything you want, but first I need to have you coming so hard, so I can have my lunch. I'm starving for your nectar." He nips each of my nipples and then continues to nibble down over my stomach. He swirls his tongue over my sensitive nub and gives it a good suck before continuing down.

Spreading my legs wider, he takes a moment to stare hungrily at my glistening entrance. His eyes meet mine and he smiles as he descends towards what he wants most. He starts from the bottom and slowly runs his tongue through my gentle folds until he reaches my clit. I moan as I watch him take what I am offering. He pushes his tongue into my opening, but then he stops. Lifting his head, he looks at me a bit confused. He then pushes his face into my pussy and takes in a deep breath. He looks back at me and I see the storm clouds in his eyes. He moves up and lays his head on my stomach for a moment. Slowly turning his head to look up at me, I see a smile appear and watch as it spreads widely across his face.

"What are you doing? Don't stop, I need you right now!" I show him how annoyed I am at this point, but all he does is crawl up my body and braces himself on one elbow as he lifts one of my legs with his other hand, opening me up further for him. In one slow thrust, he is planted all the way in.

He is loving me slowly with his thrusts, smiling down at me as he does so, "Do you know how much happier you just made me?"

I am very confused at the moment, but whatever he is doing with his hips is causing me to forget the nonsense that he is spewing.

"Do you hear me, love?"

"Yes, now just fuck me." My head is thrown back and I can feel the fire building within.

"I am going to make love to my soon-to-be-wife... and the mother of my child." He says softly. It takes me a moment, but then I look at him and try to piece together the words he just said.

"What did you just say?"

He takes my lips for a quick, but passion-filled kiss, "You have my child growing in your womb, sweetheart."

"What? What do you mean? Why would you say that?"

"I can smell it in your essence, and I can hear its heartbeat when I place my head on your stomach. We are having a baby, Liz!"

Tears prick my eyes once I finally realize what he is saying. Taven brushes away the single drop that trickles down my cheek, "We are having a baby, are you sure?"

"Yes, baby. We have a bun in the oven." He leans down and kisses my lips again, "Man just thinking about you growing big with my child makes me even harder!" His picks up his tempo and soon he is no longer making love to me slowly but is driving his dick so far into me that he is touching places that have never been touched. Hitting nerves that send electrical shock waves through my body. I claw at his back trying to hold on and thrust my hips to his rhythm, urging him on.

"I'm going to make you come so hard, you won't be able to see straight." He tells me and I see his fangs grow just before they sink into me and takes me to new heights as he pulls deep.

I am screaming his name and thrusting my hips harder as orgasm after orgasm bursts through my body like fireworks on the Fourth of July. Once he releases my neck, I bite into his and send him soaring, giving me load after load of his own cum. I can feel it spilling out of me, as it runs out and down the crack of my ass, but I still continue, feeling ravenous as ever. He roars, and it feels like the whole house shakes.

He drops down beside me, taking me with him, but never pulling out of me. We lay here panting, trying to catch our breath, but it doesn't seem as though there is enough air, "Fuck me, warrior!" I say between gulps of air.

"I believe I just fucked you really good, my greedy little sex kitten." He chuckles and takes a gulp of air. He kisses my forehead and we just lay here; no more words are spoken until we can breathe easy again.

Just out of the blue I blurt out, "I got sick and threw up this morning."

"What? When?" Taven pushes his head back to look at me.

"When I was in the kitchen, talking to Max. He had picked me up and spun me around when I told him we were getting married today. Normally, spinning doesn't get me sick, but I thought that's what did it. My period isn't due for another week, so I can't be more than a few days along. Max guessed that I was pregnant, but I laughed it off. It definitely explains my mood swings today."

"It doesn't matter how far along you are. All that matters, is that we finally have a little one growing in there." He places his hand on my stomach and I place mine over his, "Thank you, Liz. I thought I was the luckiest man before, but now you have given me what I have only dreamed of. A family. Not only with you and our boys, but also a child from my own flesh."

He has me in tears at this point.

"Hey, Baby, please don't cry." He kisses my tears away.

"Well, then don't say such kind words to me." I smile up at him.

"Get used to it, because it's all I have for you."

For the next hour, we lay here in each other's arms as he relays to me everything he learned from Miguel. Shocked isn't even the word I would describe as to how I feel when he tells me all of it. To think, people can change their bodies into a dog… a big dog! That's another thing that is only seen in movies or read in books. I am now a believer in the impossible.

We walk down to the Compound's dining room as a family after we tell the boys that they are going to have another brother or sister. They are so excited and can't wait, of course. Jack would like to have a sister, but Nate wants a baby brother. He says girls have cooties and he doesn't want cooties. We laugh and Taven tells him that I'm a girl and I don't have cooties, but Nate says that it doesn't count, because I am a mom and moms don't carry cooties. That really had us laughing all together.

Everyone is already in the dining room, waiting on us to arrive. The room is full of excitement as we walk in and they all hoot and holler at us, causing me to blush.

"Okay, that is enough. Save it for when I finally kiss my bride later." Taven tells them.

Jill and Duncan bring us each over a drink. Taven takes his, but I decline the one that Jill is trying to hand me, "Just take it… it's your wedding day for Pete's sake!" Jill is trying to shove it into my hand.

Max walks up, "Don't feel like drinking on your wedding day? Are you feeling okay?" He smirks at me and then at Taven, who has been all smiles since we found out that we are expecting.

"You are a shithead, Max! Do you know that?" I scold him.

"Ah, but a shithead that is usually always right!" He winks at me.

"Am I missing something?" Jill looks between me and Max, completely baffled.

At that moment Taven asks for everyone's attention and the room quiets down. He looks at me and I nod for him to go on. I know it's supposed to be bad luck telling people before a certain time, but we figure that it's going to get out anyway and we prefer to be the ones to announce it.

Taven begins by clearing his throat, "Now I know all of you are wondering why Liz and I decided to get married this evening and I know some of you automatically assumed that my lovely bride-to-be is knocked up," he smiles at me, and I roll my eyes, "but that isn't the case. We had just both decided that neither one of us wanted a big wedding and so why wait?" He goes on, "A little over two hours ago, we did realize that we actually are going to be having a baby, so it's actually perfect timing!"

The room explodes in cheers and congratulations. I am getting passed around by all the warriors hugging me and kissing my cheek. By the fifth person, I have been spun in every direction and I am now facing the door as Dane brings me in for a hug. There is Beth watching us with what appears to be a murderous look on her face. It sends chills through my body and all I want is to get back to Taven.

I am relieved once all the hugging is done, and we sit down to eat. I lean towards Taven and tell him that I saw Beth watching and that she seemed really pissed. He kisses my hand and tells me not to worry about it, that he will take care of it. I know he will, but I am wondering now if it was a good idea to let her stay. It's obvious that she still has a thing for Taven.

TAVEN

Max had out done himself with the wedding meal, but if you ask me, I'd say he had a little outside help. He couldn't possibly have made everything that was out on the buffet table, but I will let him take credit for it all. The last time that I saw my men really enjoy themselves was at Duncan and Jill's wedding and of course, Jax and Cassie's wedding before that. It seems as though finding mates is good for everyone involved. We have led tough lives up until now, and even though we will continue to do so, having a mate by your side makes it so much easier.

Once supper is over, Liz and Jill leave to go get ready for the ceremony and the rest of us all head over to my house where the wedding will take place in the gazebo by the lake. The men must have been really busy today, because there are chairs set up and twinkle lights strung all around the gazebo and lining the aisle that Liz will be walking down. There is a stereo system set up which Kai is now standing behind and Cassie takes her place in the gazebo.

We don't have to wait too long, before Kai receives a text and then begins playing a soft wedding march. I take my place and both Jax and Duncan stand next to me as my Best Men and Jack stands as a

Groomsman. They are both my best friends and since we are not being traditional, I don't care what anybody says.

I watch as first Jillian and Nate come down the aisle as Flower Girl and Ring Bearer, then Jill walks down and takes her spot. All eyes turn to Liz as she makes her way down to the front. I can't take my eyes off her, not because of the white satin slip of a dress that she is wearing, but because she seriously looks like an angel floating towards me. I don't know if it's the lights hitting the white satin material or what, but she has a glow around her. She gazes at me all the way down, with a smile on her face and tears glistening in her eyes. I step forward and take her hand as Jill takes the bouquet of flowers from her hands.

I hold both of her hands in mine as Cassie begins. It seems as if we are standing here, eyes on each other, for hours, but really it was only about five minutes. Next thing I know, Cassie is pronouncing us man and wife and telling me to kiss my bride. I cup both of her cheeks and slowly draw her in, smelling her essence as I take her lips. I kiss her softly at first and then I crush her to me and really kiss her. Cheers go all around, and Cassie is introducing us as Mr. and Mrs. Taven Anderson.

For a moment I think I hear a scream coming from the Compound and there would only be one person who could scream like that and be heard. I look over at Miguel and I know that he heard it too. He smiles at me, but there is a little sadness in his eyes. He blames himself for bringing her here, but it isn't his fault, how could he have known.

I turn back to my gorgeous bride and take her in my arms to hold her close. Kai now has music playing and everyone breaks out the liquor. It's a good time, well spent with family and friends. Max brings out a wedding cake and once Liz is done smearing it in my face, Jack and Nate dig into theirs, but Nate thought it was funny watching his mother smash cake into my face and he does the same to Jack. Big brother doesn't find it as amusing as I did and now there is a full fledge food fight going on.

I turn to Liz, "Do you see what you started? You are such a bad influence!" She slaps me on the chest and chuckles.

"It's all harmless fun, it washes."

"Mm, maybe we should take some back to the playroom tonight." I nip at her neck and make her quiver.

"The playroom?"

"Oh yes! You have been a very good girl, not taking your pills and letting me fuck you. We want to reward you well."

"I didn't have much choice in the matter, but just to let you know a little secret, I had already decided to stop taking them." The devilish smile she gives me pretty much does it for me.

"I am going to take the boys into the Compound and tuck them in. Then I'm coming back here and kidnapping my bride, so I can take her home and do very bad, and very dirty things to her." I can smell her arousal and know that she is ready to start our wedding night as much as I am. I flash over to the boys and pick them up, each under one arm and flash to the Compound.

I shut the door to the boys' room and head down the hall towards the front door. I turn the corner and run right into a small body. I reach out quick to steady them and keep them from falling, when I realize that the person I've run into, is Beth.

"Oh, I'm sorry. I am in a hurry and wasn't paying attention." I explain and move to go around her.

"It's okay, I understand. You want to get back to the festivities." She bites down on her lower lip, and I think she is trying to seduce me with her look, but all I want to do is laugh. I can't believe I thought she was beautiful. She has nothing on my Liz.

"Actually, I want to get back to my "wife", Mary-Beth." I can't help but sound annoyed.

"Are you sure that she is your destined mate, Taven? I am only asking, because I was sure that you were mine."

"If I were your destined mate, Beth, there is no way that you would have been able to leave me like you did. You obviously know nothing about mates." I scowl.

"I was a new vampire myself and scared when I realized I drank too much from you! You were my first in everything Taven! My first kiss, my first fuck, and my first and only made vampire. I looked for you afterwards, but you were gone. I didn't mean to leave you like that." She was pleading with me to understand.

I sigh, "Okay, fine, so you didn't mean too. What's done is done and I now have a mate. What exactly do you want from me? Do you want forgiveness? Fine, I forgive you. Now go somewhere and be happy." I go to turn around, but her hand snakes out and grabs my arm.

"Taven, I have searched for you for centuries and you are just going to turn your back on me now? Turn your back on what we had?"

"YOU are the one that turned your back on me when I needed you the most! Besides, it's obvious that we weren't meant to be, since I have found my true mate."

"Just because she is a good fuck doesn't make her your true mate!"

I am now seeing red, "No it doesn't, but her carrying my child proves that we are destined!"

She gasps at this news, "No! It can't be yours, Taven. I am your mate!" Her voice is a higher pitch now and her hand is now squeezing my arm.

"Get your filthy hands off my husband, Vamp, before I rip it off and feed it to the wolves!" I whirl around to see Liz standing just inside the front door.

"Baby, stay back. I will handle this." I see her trembling with rage.

"I think it's time that you leave Mary-Beth… now! You are no longer welcome here."

"You are kicking me out? You loved me at one time, Taven. If I hadn't left, we would still be together!"

"No Beth, I was in love with the fact that you kept my demon at bay, but I know now that the only reason he never came forth with you was because you were not our mate." I grit my teeth, "I would have still found Liz even if we were still together and I would have left you. It will always be Liz for me. Liz and my family are everything to me and they will always come first! You mean nothing to me. You were put in my life to make me who I am today, so I could find the love of my life, the one person that I am destined to be with!"

Beth's lips tremble for a moment and then her whole demeanor changes and she is shooting daggers at me and then Liz. "You," she points to Liz, "You will pay for taking what is mine!" Before I can grab her, she flashes past me and then Liz, right out the front door.

I am practically knocked off my feet with the force of Liz throwing herself at me. I wrap her tightly in my arms, "She's gone, baby. It's okay."

"I don't know what came over me! I know I am no match for her, but when I saw her with her hands on you… something snapped, and I wanted to pounce on her and rip her eyes out!"

I grin at the thought of what that would look like, "That was your instinct as my mate, love. I have to be honest, you looked pretty hot standing up to her like that." I smile down at her.

"Of course, you would think that!" She chuckles.

"Yeah, well now, I'm thinking it's time to take my wife home and to bed." I wiggle my brows at her.

Liz pouts her lip out at me, "I thought you were taking me to the playroom. I'm not ready to go to bed yet. Besides, I'm sure the demon wants a piece of his bride as well."

My dick swells to an uncomfortable size with her last comment, "Oh, I see someone likes playing on the dark side. I think it's time that I take it a step further. After all, it is our wedding night and I still need to reward you." I can feel my demon on the surface, and I can hardly contain him any longer.

Liz stares at the key to the playroom in her hand, paying special attention to the keychain. I see her eyes widen with surprise when she notices the letter "L".

"What's this?" she asks grinning at me.

"What do you think? I designed this room with you in mind." My voice is a bit husky, "Now open the door, wife."

She bites her bottom lip, which drives me crazy with need, and turns the key, unlocking the door. I reach over her head and swing it wide open, "After you."

She hands me the key and goes straight to the middle of the room like a good girl.

"Strip." One word is all I need. I watch as she slowly pulls her dress up and over her head, letting it drop before she does the same with her strapless bra. She goes to the waist of her lacy thong, and I stop her, "Leave them for the moment." I walk over and cup her sex. She is soaked with her juices. I fall to my knees and demand that she spread her legs. I run my tongue over the wetness, tasting her essence. It would be a waste not to. I stand back up and tell her to resume.

She stands before me without a stitch of clothing on. I lead her over to where I already have the rope and cuffs ready, with a collar attached as well.

"Bend over and spread that delectable ass for me." I whisper in her ear, and she does so, spreading her legs further apart, so I can get a clear view from behind. Mm, I am salivating just looking at that pretty pink, wet pussy, all stretched open for me. Grabbing the cuffs that are dangling from rope, I take one wrist at a time, and restrain them behind her back. Next, I am placing the neck collar around her pretty neck and strapping it closed. I stand back to admire the beauty of my mate, bent over and restrained.

I come down to eye level and take hold of her chin, "You will remain in this position until I uncuff you. Do you understand?"

"Yes, Sir."

I stand up and rip my shirt over my head as I walk over to the dresser. I return with the vibrating anal plug and lube. She jerks as the cold gel runs down her ass crack, then again when I insert a finger to lube up her puckered bud.

"Don't move." My hand comes down across one cheek, and then the other. I squirt lube onto the plug and then slowing push it, working it into her waiting ass. I pick up the hand-held remote and turn it on. She whimpers, but quickly goes silent, "You can make all the noise you want, my little dirty girl. I want to hear every little moan, every whimper, and every scream. The two things that I forbid you to do is speak out of turn or come. No coming unless I say so, and then I expect you to do so on my command."

I move, so that fuckable mouth is lined up with my cock and I undo the front of my slacks, pulling them and my briefs down. My hard cock springs forward, slapping her in the face.

"You like that don't you?" I slap her with it again on each cheek, "Open up for Daddy." I thrust into her mouth as soon as it's wide enough, grabbing hold of her hair and pulling it just enough to make her moan with pleasure. I change the vibration to the plug, so it's now pulsing throughout her ass as her mouth takes a pounding. Her breathing begins to quicken as her climax builds, and just before I know she is about to come, I turn the plug off, but continue to pump my cock into that lovely mouth of hers.

"That's Daddy's girl, take me all in. Milk my cock, so I can come in that pretty little mouth of yours, that's it!" Her cheeks are hollowed as she sucks me off and drags her tongue around my girth. My balls ache for release and I thrust faster, hitting the back of her throat. A few more pumps and I turn the plug back on, causing her to moan and vibrate my dick. The explosion is fast, shooting hot seed all down her throat. "Fuck me, baby girl! That's a good girl, take it all!" I pull out and give myself a few more pumps, milking the last of my seed out and spilling it over her mouth and chin, "Damn, now that is fucking hot! Think I will be leaving it there until I am ready to clean it off." With my dick still hard as fuck and the anal plug still vibrating in her ass, I walk up behind her, driving my dick right up into her dripping wet pussy and wishing that we could stay like this forever.

SIXTEEN

LIZ

I feel so exposed, bent over and restrained like this, but it also gets me so hot. I would never have thought that this would be the kind of sex life that I would have. Taven has introduced me to so much. Some wouldn't understand it, some would think that it is a form of abuse, degradation, and just plain sick. Hell, I had my doubts about it at first, but the trust that I have in Taven and the love that he shows me while in this room, just ignites the passion in all of it. I love being his dirty girl or his little slut in this room. I can live out my dark sexual thoughts and dreams with him in here. Submitting to my vampire is the best thing that I have ever done. Call me sick, call me mental, but I call it love, because in this room, we are one with each other. He takes care of all my needs and in return, I take care of his needs, and so yes, I am bent over, restrained, collared, and out on display for the man I love, but I am panting in need, wanting more of what only Taven can give me. I feel free.

The vibration from the plug in my ass is hitting every sensitive spot and with Taven's cock pounding into me, I can feel my climax coming on, but know I can't let it go. It is pure blissful torture. I begin to whimper trying to hold it back.

"What's the matter, baby girl? Do you need to come? Do you want to cream all over my cock?"

"Yes, Sir...Please!" Just as I'm about to let go, the vibration stops, and Taven pulls out.

"Too bad. I'm not ready for you to come yet, baby girl." I feel a sting on my ass as he slaps it, but then rubs it away.

He leaves me for a moment and returns with some kind of chain. There are three separate chains that connect in the middle with what looks like clamps on each end. Taven kneels and bends under me, taking a nipple into his mouth and swirling his tongue around until my nipple is hard. He takes one of the chains and clamps my nipple before he moves on to the other one. The sensation of having my sensitive nipples clamped sends shivers throughout my body. All thoughts of the third clamp are gone until I feel him attach it to my clit. Oh, my god, my body is quivering with need, I want to come so bad.

"Ah, you love this attention, don't you? I knew you would, just like I knew I would love seeing you like this; restrained and at my mercy." Taven whispers seductively, "I knew the moment that I first saw you, that you were going to be mine. I knew you were meant to be my mate, but what I didn't know was how much of a dirty girl you were." He nips at the tips of my nipples before disappearing again.

"I am going to take that pussy of yours again, and I'm going to fill it up to the brim with my cum. You wait for my command and when I tell you to come, you better cream my cock really good! I want to see our cum mixed together as it drips from your pussy and runs down your thighs." He flicks his wrist and the flogger he now has in his hand hits me across my chest from below, sending tingles through me when it hits my clamped nipples. He does it again, only this time he teases my clit. I moan and whimper. I want to beg him for my release, but I can't speak out of turn.

"What do you want my little dirty slut? Tell me what you need." He nibbles my earlobe as he continues to use the flogger on my most sensitive parts.

"I need you to fuck me, Sir. I want to make you come, so I can come all over you. Please fuck me fast and hard, take me now..." I'm panting from all of his attention.

"That's what I love to hear, baby girl. I'm going to take that slutty pussy now." And he does, not gentle, mind you. No easing into it, just drives his cock right into my dripping pussy and continues slamming into me, taking my breath away each time. I love how he can be so rough, but also gentle when the time calls for it. This is not one of those times. He is fucking me just the way I want him too.

I feel the vibration again and my desire starts building to new heights. Taven is grunting with each thrust, "Daddy's going to fill you up now, baby girl, get ready!"

His cock pulses in me and it explodes within. Taven roars as he pumps vigorously into my pussy, filling me with load after load of his hot seed.

"Come for me, slut... come now!" He doesn't have to tell me twice, I release myself at his command, screaming his name over and over.

"Fuck Taven! It hurts so good! ARGH......!" Just as I'm on the down slide, there is a sting on my neck as he bites into me and I'm soaring up and over again, "OH MY GOD, I can't take it... it's too much!" It is too much, but I don't want it to end, and he knows this. He grabs my hair and pulls my head to the side. My legs want to collapse, but Taven has hold of me tight. I am screaming his name and almost every swear word I know, until he finally retracts his fangs, and I can start to come down from the orgasmic rollercoaster ride that he just took me on.

"That's it, baby girl. You did good...I am proud of you." He pulls his cock out and I can feel the sticky fluid running down both of my legs, "Ah, just what I wanted to see. You are picture perfect, baby." I see a flash of light and hear a snap. He walks around to the front of me and shows me the picture on his phone. I can't believe he took a picture, but as I look at it, it starts to turn me on. The way I look all trussed up and bent over. My wet pussy on display with our cum running down my legs... yeah, that's fucking hot!

Taven grabs my chin and slams his mouth into mine, shoving his tongue in and tangling it with mine. He pulls away just as quick, "I fucking love you, Liz!" His gaze and his words turn me on all over again.

He turns the plug off and pulls it out slowly before uncuffing my wrists and taking the collar off from around my neck. He carries me over to the bed and sits me down between his legs, rubbing the kinks out of my arms and shoulders, from being restrained. He is sprinkling kisses down my neck.

"Feel better?" He asks in a quiet loving voice.

"Yes, Sir."

"Good, because I am far from done with you." With that being said, he changes our positions as he lays down and has me straddling him. He reaches over to the nightstand and grabs the bottle of lube and a vibrator, a huge vibrator, "I'm going to take that delectable ass of yours now. I'm going to make you come over and over. I won't make you hold it; in fact, I demand that you cream all over this toy as I fuck you with it." He smiles as he squirts the lube all over his cock, "Rub it in, baby girl, rub it all over. I want to be able to slide right into that tight ass of yours."

Reaching behind me, I do as he commands, pleasure building up within me at his words. He lifts me up and lines his cock up with my hole he plans on penetrating. His tip pushes through my puckered ring and I moan, throwing my head back as he pushes in inch by inch until he is firmly planted within.

"Fuck, you are so tight back here! I want to lose my load already!" He leans me back and slides the vibrator into my pussy. I feel so full, and every nerve is on fire. He turns the vibration on, and I come right away, "Yes, that's it. Just what I want to see." He slides his cock out to the tip and then thrusts back into me. I bite my lip to keep from screaming. He begins a steady rhythm, pulling the toy out, but not all the way, as his cock slides in, and vice versa. Within minutes, he has me coming again.

"Damn, you are so beautiful! One of these times, I am going to video me fucking you like this, so you can see what I am seeing. I guarantee it will make you come just watching it!"

After a few more of my own orgasms, I can tell that he is close, so I start moving faster, up and down as I watch the emotions dance across his face. Need, want, desire, and love. They are all there, in the depths of his eyes, and I want to take him over the edge. He is grunting and groaning the faster I go, "Drink from me, baby. Feed our baby and take me into the abyss that only you can take me to." He pushes the vibrator all the way in and leaves it as he sits up and I sink my little fangs into him.

"ARGH... FUCK!" He screams and pumps into my ass faster. I feel his cock swell in my ass and then hot fluid shoots like a volcano. I can feel it seeping out of my ass as he continues giving me his load. Soon I'm right there with him as we tumble into the same abyss. Our screams are earth shattering, but nobody hears them but us. I retract my fangs and it is over, both collapsing on the bed, with me sprawled out on top.

After catching our breath, he pulls out of me, takes the toy out, and rolls to his side, bringing me with him, "Sleep baby, you made me so proud. I love you." He kisses me tenderly and then tightens his embrace.

"I love you too, Sir." I mumble as I slip into a deep, peaceful slumber.

When I wake, I am no longer in the playroom, but in our own bed. Taven is here, holding me tight. Tears spring to my eyes as I think about the events from the day before. All of my dreams came true yesterday. I may not know what the future holds, but I do know that I will never be alone. This man, this vampire, is my world and he has giving me the life that I have only dreamed and fantasized about.

I look up at the gorgeous man sleeping beside me. He looks so peaceful. His beautiful blue eyes hidden behind closed lids, I reach up and lightly run my fingers through the soft strands of his hair. He makes a small mewling sound in his sleep, making me smile. I love this beautiful man. Lowering my eyes, I run my fingers over his chest. A chest built from hard work and long ours at the gym. I run my lips over the slight sprinkle of hair, tickling them with his hair's softness.

"If you continue doing what you are doing, love, I will be forced to take you right here, right now." I gasp at the sound of his voice and look up. His eyes are still closed, but a smile plays across his lips.

"I am just admiring what is truly and completely mine." I whisper, "Besides, it wouldn't be a bad thing, taking me now. I am always hungry for you."

He opens his eyes slowly and there they are, his beautiful blues. His lips descend upon mine and he takes me with all the love and passion that he feels for me. It's not a hardcore, 'I want to fuck you now' kiss, but a tender 'I want to make slow passionate love to you' kiss. Things start to heat up, but then there is a knock on our door.

"Mom, Dad, are you awake yet?" Nate's little voice comes through the door.

Taven's smile reaches his eyes, "I love the sound of your boys calling me Dad."

I smile back at him, "They decided that on their own. They love you, Taven." Another knock comes, and I call out for him to come in. The door opens, and Nate runs and tries jumping on the bed, but Taven catches him in mid-air.

"Gotcha ya!" Taven laughs as Nate's little giggle slips out, "What do you need buddy?"

"I just wanted to see if you were awake. I didn't wake up in my own bed, it felt weird." He crinkles his eyebrows.

"Sorry honey, we thought it would be fun for you to have a sleep over at the Compound." I try to explain without telling him the real reason, but he looks at me confused.

"Mom, why are you naked in bed? You should be wearing a shirt, so dad doesn't see your private parts." I feel the heat rush to my face and hear Taven snicker.

"Yeah Mom, why are you naked?" Taven cocks a brow at me.

"Well, honey, moms and dads are allowed to see each other's private parts, because we are married now." I bite my lip, not really knowing how else to explain.

"That's just gross! When I get married, I'm telling the mom that she has to wear a shirt. I don't want to see that!"

Taven and I burst out laughing, then Taven speaks, "Yeah, I think it's gross too, but mom doesn't listen to me. What should I do about that, buddy?"

Nate puts a finger to his mouth as if he is thinking on it, "Well, I know that when I don't listen, I get punished and get put in time out. Maybe that's what you should do!"

Taven glances at me with a shitty grin on his face, "I think you are right little buddy! Mom, you are in time out. Do not leave this room until I say so!" Nate giggles at Taven's punishment for me.

"Dad, will you make me some pancakes while Mom is in time out? I'm starving, and I don't want to go back to the Compound right now."

"I sure can, little man! Why don't you go get everything out and I will be down in a minute."

"Okay!" Nate jumps down excitedly and runs from the room.

"And you," he turns to me, "are in time out. You stay here and think about what you did!" There is a twinkle in his eye and I giggle, shaking my head.

"You could have helped me out there, instead of influencing him!"

"How much fun is that?" He winks and kisses me quick before climbing out of bed, completely naked, by the way.

"Tell me, DAD, why am I the only one being punished when you are breaking the rules too?" I cock my brow at him.

"Because it's more fun dishing out the punishment to you! Now be a good girl and stay in this room." I throw a pillow at him, but he is already closing the door and it hits the door instead.

TAVEN

I'm sitting in my office, trying to get some much-needed work done, when there is a knock on my door, and I look up to see Miguel standing there.

"Come in, Miguel."

"Thank you, sorry for the intrusion."

"No problem at all. I can use a little break. Did you need something or is this just a social call?"

"I just wanted to say congratulations again and to apologize about Beth's behavior last night."

"Thank you and thanks for being there at the ceremony. It means a lot to me. As for Beth," I sigh heavily, "there is no need to apologize. None of that was your fault. Have you spoken to her this morning?"

"Briefly. She said she is going to disappear for a while… to think."

"She needs some serious help Miguel. She truly believes that we are destined mates, and she is very angry at Liz."

"Well, I will definitely help where I can, but I'm afraid she is no longer taking any of my calls or texts. Just give her time. Maybe she has come to terms with it and just needed to get far away." He looks at me, but I see the doubt in his eyes as he says the words.

"Maybe you are right. I'm not going to worry too much about it, but I will keep my eyes out for her. I didn't like the way she threatened Liz and she especially didn't like the news about Liz being pregnant."

"That's understandable, with her state of mind that is."

"Yeah, well, anyway, I am not starting off my marriage with this hanging over us. I have no time for Mary-Beth and will not waste a single brain cell on her unless I really have to. So, with that being said, if you need help with your research, let me know. If I am not able to help, I have a few men that can assist you." I smile at my old friend.

"Thank you. I will definitely take you up on your offer. I know you are a busy man, so if you would point me in the direction of those who can assist me, I will go brief them."

"I am thinking Kaid and Phoenix will be perfect for you. Aside from Kole, which is too valuable to give up here, those two have a talent in these types of situations. Now, Phoenix is one of my newer recruits, but he is also one of the best. Please let me know if there is anything else you may need."

"You have done quite a bit for me already and I appreciate whoever you send to help in my research. I will leave you be now, talk to you soon." He walks out, closing the door to my office.

I sit here and wonder what will come about with all this research. I haven't come out and asked him, but it makes me wonder what his plans are or if he just wants to keep tabs on them. Guess I will know once he is ready to tell me or maybe I will have a chat with Kaid and make sure he reports all of their findings to me. I am liking the latter better. If my men are out there working on it, then I should know what they are getting into. I trust my friend and mentor, but I also know how selfish he can be and that he always has a hidden agenda.

Liz and I have decided to hold off on our honeymoon for a while. With the boys still being new fledglings, Liz wants to make sure that they are well adjusted before we take off for a few weeks, and I can't blame her, so it is back to our daily lives and work details.

There is a new club that opened up on the outskirts of town, it's practically in the middle of nowhere. I think it's a little weird to open a club up that far away from the rest of the night life, so I want to check it out. I am riding with Xavier and Jagger, but Cooper and Axel are following in a separate vehicle. Because this is a new detail and we know nothing about this new club, I have Duncan, Jax, Dane, and Jayde on standby in case we need assistance. I don't think they will be needed, but it's protocol.

It's still early as we pull into a parking spot, but the parking lot is already practically full. We sit and watch the comings and goings of patrons… nothing out of the ordinary really. The building itself looks like a big two-level log cabin with a big lighted moon that blinks to each moon stage and stops at the full moon stage for about five seconds before starting the rotation again. The sign right below it reads Club Moon. From the outside, it looks to be a good-looking establishment, but we all know that looks can be deceiving sometimes. Hopefully, this isn't one of those times.

My men and I get out and walk up to the door where there is a roped area, I'm assuming for the crowds, but there is no crowd this early in the evening, so we just walk in. We enter a room with a counter off to the left side that has a gal taking coats to hang up. On the right side, and right before a set of double doors, there is another counter for admission. The woman standing there is tall and lean, with long dark hair and dressed in a green tight dress. She smiles at us as her eyes roam over each of us and she licks her lips.

"Well, hello there... welcome to Club Moon. Nice to see that there are some real men in the area!" She is practically salivating at the mouth. I used to love getting that kind of reaction from females, but since Liz, it's gotten to be irritating. My men, on the other hand, are lapping it up... well, except for Xavier. He is a quiet one and does not like the attention.

I ignore her flirtations and pay the cover fee for us all. Stepping through the double doors was like stepping outside a cabin in the woods. Aside from the blaring dance music, the club itself is a woodsy scene. Faux trees and plant life are everywhere. The floor is smooth glass with dirt, leaves and sticks underneath it, making it look like the ground within the woods. It is actually a pretty awesome scene if you ask me, very different from any other club that I have been to.

I look over at the others and see that their reactions reflect my own. Whoever the club owner is, did a smash up job in here. Tables are made up of tall tree stumps and the bar itself is made of real wood with a see-through glass top. We head over and wait for the bartender to finish with another customer.

The man behind the bar is built like us, which is surprising. He isn't a vampire, that I can sense, but he has a scent to him that I have never detected before. His dark hair hangs a little past his ears, but is trimmed nicely, and his eyes look to be a dark gray color. He eyes us warily before smiling and greeting us.

"Welcome, what can I get you fine gentlemen tonight?"

I smile back, "I'll take a Bud, thanks."

The guys place their drink orders, and we wait for the bartender to return. I pay for the drinks, and I smile at the guy, "This is a pretty nice place you have here. Is the owner around?" I like to meet the people that own the establishments that we detail. Unless I think they are shady, I introduce who we are, leaving out the vampire part, and let them know that we watch for the riff raff that may come snooping around.

"Thank you," the guy smiles, "We spent a lot of time designing it. I'm Gray, part owner. My partner and brother is over there," he nods towards another big dude with dark hair, who is making his rounds and greeting customers, "That's Ash. He likes to make our customers feel at home here."

"That's good for business. So, how long have you been open? We just got wind of this place yesterday."

"We opened last weekend. We have only been in the area a few months. Moved down here from up north... needed a change of scenery I guess."

"Well, Augusta is a good place to be. Welcome to the area." I reach over and shake Gray's hand, "I'm Taven, and these are some of my men. We are known as the Elite. We like to keep watch over the area, you know, take care of the troublemakers and all. Places like this can sometimes attract them and we hate to see fine businesses, such as this, get ruined by those people. For the most part we just drive by, but we may stop in every once in a while, and check inside."

Gray tenses up a little after I mention who we are, but I just continue on, acting as if I hadn't noticed.

"Well, we do have our own bouncers, so I don't think we really need the assistance, but I will happily take your contact information just in case we ever need it."

"Oh, I completely understand. I think you might have misunderstood what I was saying. I wasn't asking you for a job. This is what we do and as a new establishment in our territory, we will keep watch for any kind of trouble that may find its way here." I smile nicely at him. I can see that he isn't happy about it, but he nods his head anyway.

"We do appreciate it. I am sorry, but I have other customers. It was nice meeting you and feel free to stop back anytime." Gray walks away from us and starts filling other customer orders.

"Was it just me or did he seem a little tense?" I ask the others.

"Oh, he was tense for sure. Makes me wonder what kind of people they are. He had to have heard of us, because the second you told him who we are, he tensed." Xavier takes a big swig of his beer.

"Shit! We now have to keep a close eye on this place." Cooper mumbles.

"Maybe it's nothing. He may just think that we are going to chase away his customers. Let's hold off making assumptions right now. I will send in some men as customers for the next couple of weeks to watch the place first."

I can't really explain the feeling that I have about this place. It doesn't really seem like a bad feeling, but something in my gut is telling me that there is more to this place than just a regular night club. We finish our drinks and then head out, waving at Gray as we leave. He nods his head at me and gives me the strangest look… a look as if he is challenging me.

SEVENTEEN

LIZ

I am pacing back and forth by the door to the garage in the Compound, waiting for Taven and the others to get back from detail. The pains in my stomach are beginning to worsen and there are no more blood bags down in the medical ward. He must have forgotten to restock since he used up his stash during his rescue. I contacted him about an hour ago and he told me that they were wrapping things up and would be home soon. I didn't want to tell him why I was asking. If he said they would be home soon, then they will be home.

I don't know if the baby can sense it, but as soon as I hear the garage doors open, a pain rips through my gut. I can't wait any longer, I throw open the door and tackle Taven as he shuts the SUV door. He is laughing at something until I jump on him and plunge my fangs into his neck.

"Whoa, get a fucking room man!" Cooper chuckles.

I glare at him before turning my attention to Taven's neck and talk to him through our bond since my mouth is a little busy.

'What's this all about, baby?' He asks me concerned.

'The baby is starving, and I was in pain. I couldn't wait any longer, sorry. You haven't restocked your blood since you used the last of it or else, I would have drunk that.'

'Shit! Sorry baby. You should have told me you needed my blood. I would have come home sooner.'

'I didn't want to bother you while you are working.' I hear myself moaning and grinding a little against him.

"Seriously, guys. Go to your own place! We don't want to watch you guys get it on!" Cooper sounds irritated at this point and in return it must have pissed Taven off, because he roars at all of them.

"My wife is feeding our child! Get the fuck out! And go tell Kole to turn the cameras off in here until I tell him to turn them on!"

I giggle against his neck, because I know how turned on he is right now and the last thing he wants to do is have an audience. A little over a moment later, he is tearing my yoga pants off me, and not sure when he undid his own, but as soon as the last shred of material is off me, he slides his cock into me at the same time his fangs sink into my neck. Slamming into me while holding me up against the SUV, it is quick, but oh so good! We tumble over the edge together, screaming into each other's necks.

I retract my fangs first and then he follows, "Fuck Baby, you got to give a guy a warning first! I almost took you in front of them." He chuckles and nuzzles my neck, while he is still deep inside of me.

"My bad. I will try to refrain myself from jumping your bones again."

"Well, you don't have to refrain altogether, just give me a warning." He snickers, "In the meantime, I will stock up my blood again. I don't want my girl suffering." He kisses me deeply and then slides out of me.

"It's a good thing I'm headed home. Wouldn't want the warriors getting a show with my lady bits hanging out. All because you can't control yourself." I look down at myself and then look back to Taven and I see the desire in his eyes. God, he is insatiable… I love it! "Like what you see vamp?"

He grabs my crotch and runs his fingers through the mess we made together, "I fucking love it, and you know it!" Lifting his hand, he brings it to my mouth, and I suck on each finger, cleaning them off, "Round fucking two, baby!" He picks me up and flashes us to our house.

Honestly, who needs a honeymoon when every day is a honeymoon when you are married to the love of your life? It's been three weeks since we got married and not one day has gone by where we haven't had sex. He goes to his office and works while I tutor the boys during the day. We slip off together during our break times and then we will head to bed once the boys are asleep and be up well past midnight, exploring each other. This is my life now and I couldn't be happier.

It's the weekend and Ally has decided to come visit since Breck is away for a couple of days on some detail work. Us women decide that we are going to go out for a few drinks and some dancing tonight and the guys are home with the boys. Since prego here can't drink, I am the DD for the night. We have stopped in to one of the local clubs, but it's pretty dead, so I asked Siri where all the hot spots are, and she comes back with a list of all the night clubs. One sticks out, because I have never heard of it before.

"Hey, there is a new club in town called Club Moon. All the reviews are good, and they all give it five-star ratings. Maybe we should check it out, it looks pretty awesome." I hold the picture out to the girls, and we all agree to go check it out.

It's about ten o'clock and as we pull into the parking lot packed with cars, I whistle, "Well, no wonder the other club is dead; it looks like they are all here!"

"Now this is my kind of club!" Cassie is bouncing up and down with excitement.

"Calm down Case, you act as if you have never been to a packed club before." I laugh as I pull into a parking spot at the rear of the lot.

"It's just seems like it's been so long, and I just want to let loose and go wild!"

And she does, the moment we step through the double doors and see the interior. It's like we've stepped inside, just to step back outside. All of our mouths drop open at what looks like a beautiful, wooded area. Cassie squeals in delight, before rushing over to the bar. I go to find us a table while Jill and Ally join Cassie up at the bar. Luckily, there is an empty table in the back corner, so I quickly snatch it up. I look back at the girls and watch as they each take two shots before coming to search for me. I send them a quick text on where I'm at and a few seconds later they find me.

"Holy shit! Did you guys see that bartender? He is smoking hot!" Jill fans herself.

"I know right?" Cassie responds, "If I didn't have my own hotness at home, I'd be all over that one!"

I look towards the bar, but I don't have a clear view of the guy, "Well, since no one thought to grab me a water, I guess I'm going to have to go check him out myself!"

"Oh shit!" They all say in unison.

"I'm so sorry Liz! But hey, you have to go check him out… he is yummy!"

I make my way through the crowd and squeeze myself between two women who are trying to flirt with the bartender. The girls weren't lying, he is hot, but he has nothing on my man! He swings dark gray eyes my way and his face lights up. Ignoring the women beside me, he leans over on his elbows and shows me his pearly whites.

"What can I get you beautiful?"

I blush at the compliment, "Are you going to kick me out if I order a water?"

"Honey, you can order whatever you want. I wouldn't dream of kicking you out." He winks at me and then hands me an ice water.

"Thank you!" I yell over the music and leave him a tip before turning and heading back to our table.

"So, what do you think?" Cassie asks.

"He is pretty hot and a smooth talker as well, but I will stick with my hottie at home."

"Right? Nothing wrong with looking at eye candy when we aren't able to look at our men." Cassie throws her head back and laughs.

"So how many of you did he call beautiful while you were ordering?"

They looked at each other and then back at me, "He didn't call us anything. He smiled and asked what he could get us to drink." Jill replies.

"Huh, guess he didn't like your ugly mugs! He called me beautiful... so there!" I stick my tongue out at them and smile.

"That's only because you are glowing with this pregnancy." Cassie snickers, "You are beautiful."

"Awe, why thank you!"

"Okay, enough of this mushy shit... let's go dance!" Ally jumps out of her chair, almost knocking it over. Jill grabs my hand and pulls me out onto the dance floor.

About an hour in and our second time on the dance floor, a group of guys dance their way over to us. They are big guys; so big, that I think that maybe they might be vamps, but I can't be sure, my senses aren't as good as actual vampires. They start trying to dance behind us and we kindly ask them to stop.

"Ah, come on. Just trying to dance with some pretty ladies here!" One of them smiles at us.

"Hey jackass, what don't you understand? We said no!" Cassie stands there with her hands on her hips.

"Why don't you want to dance with us? Are you only into girls or what?"

"No... we just aren't into dipshits like you! And... we are not available!" Cassie and Jill both are getting into their fighting stances. Good Lord... this can't be good.

I grab their arms, "Come on, let's go take a breather and have a drink."

"Good idea, gorgeous! I'll buy the first round." This coming from a different guy.

I whirl around on him, "That was not an invitation for you to join us! Like my friend said, we are taken!"

"I don't see your men here, so they must not be too good of men, letting their women out alone."

Jill, being the only trained one here, hauls off and punches the guy in the face, but cries out at the impact, "FUCK!" I can already see her hand swelling. I look at the guy and he's wearing a smirk.

"I will let that one go, seeing as you already learned your lesson. That was a great punch by the way, if it would have been thrown at any of the regular men here."

I glare at him then turn back to Jill, "Go sit down. I will get you some ice." I make my way over to the bar and ask the bartender for a baggie with ice. He wrinkles his brows at me.

"Did one of your friends twist an ankle or something?"

"No, some creeps were hitting on us and became rude, so my friend punched him in the face. It was like she punched a brick wall. Her hand is swollen now."

His face clouded over for a second, but then he smiles as he hands me the bag of ice, "Are you beautiful ladies causing trouble in my club?"

"I'm sorry. We tried walking away, but they wouldn't leave us alone."

"Can you point them out?"

I turn and look over the crowd, but I don't see them any longer, "They must have taken off."

"Well, your friend must have scared them off then." He chuckles. He comes around the bar and walks over to the table with me, "Which one of you is rocky?"

Jill looks up at him sheepishly, "I'm sorry. I normally have better control of my temper. It won't happen again."

"Look, I don't like trouble in my club, but if you are being harassed, I'm not going to blame you. Let me know the next time you happen to see the assholes and I will take care of it."

"Okay, I will."

"Looks like you might have broken your hand. You may want to get to a hospital."

"Thank you...?" I look up at him, because I don't know his name.

"The name's Gray." He shows his pearly whites again.

"Well, thank you very much, Gray. We appreciate it." I turn to Ally, "Wanna come with me to get the car and pull it around?"

"Sure." She grabs her purse and follows me out the door.

Just as we reach my car, darkness shrouds me as something is placed over my head and I scream. I hear Ally scream as well and then I'm being lifted into a pair of arms before being thrown into a vehicle. I call out to Taven through our bond just as I feel an impact on the side of my head and everything goes dark.

TAVEN

I have been going through detail reports since I put Nate to bed three hours ago. It's now a little past eleven and I am almost caught up. I go and grab a beer from the fridge and head back to my home office. I take a swig and then all of a sudden Liz's frantic voice screams in my head, 'TAVEN…HELP M…!'

My lungs seize up as dread builds through my entire body.

'Liz, what's wrong?' I call out to her, but she doesn't answer. I try a few more times and then I grab my cell and speed dial her number, but it goes to voicemail. I then call Jax.

He answers on the second ring, "What's up buddy?"

"It's Liz, she's in trouble! She called out for help and then nothing and she isn't answering her cell. Try Cassie!"

"Okay, hold on a moment."

My gut is twisting as I wait for him to talk to Cassie through their bond. Something is wrong, I can feel it. I drop to my knees as I wait.

Jax finally speaks to me, "She said that Liz and Ally went out to pull the car around front like three minutes ago. Jill punched a guy, because he and his friends kept hitting on them and they think she broke it."

"It's been about two minutes since she called out for help! Shit! Get the guys together. I'm bringing the boys to the Compound and I'm going to have Raven and a couple of the recruits stay behind to watch the kids."

"Will do!" He hangs up and I flash upstairs to wake Jack up and to pick up Nate.

"You will never guess where our mates went tonight and where we are headed to!" Jax growls as soon as I storm through the armory door.

"Where?" I sneer.

"Club Moon."

I roar and punch a hole through the wall. I have been sending men in there for weeks now and nothing ugly has ever gone on. So why, why on the one night that I don't have my men go and our mates do, something happens?

"As soon as I got off the phone with you, I contacted Cassie again. She had Gray go out and check on them. He found both Liz and Ally's purses on the ground by Liz's car. I am sorry buddy. We will get her back, you know this."

"I do know this, but in what state?" I bellow. "That is my mate and my child that are missing!"

"Exactly! So, Lets go get them back! We will do whatever it takes!"

We are storming into the club within fifteen minutes, and I see Cassie and Jill, faces all puffy from crying, sitting at the bar with both Gray and Ash, the brother that I haven't met yet.

"What the fuck happened to my wife and Ally?" I demand to be answered.

Gray looks bewildered, "YOU are the blonde's husband? Fuck!"

"The blonde has a name, and her name is Liz! What kind of establishment are you running here? This is exactly why we do detail, so shit like this doesn't happen!"

Gray puffs up his chest and stands tall, is this fucker trying to intimidate me? His brother puts a hand on Gray's arm and tells him to calm down.

"Taven, is it?" Ash inquires.

"Yes, and you are Ash! Now let's stop with the niceties, so I can find my wife and child!" My voice booms throughout the club.

"Child?" Both brothers asked in unison.

Rolling my eyes, "Yes, my wife is pregnant!"

"Well, that explains her ordering water." Gray snickers.

I glare at him with murder on my mind.

"Uh, sorry."

Cassie and Jill explain what all had happened up until the time Liz and Ally had left to go get the car; Duncan is seething over his mates broken hand. Once they are done, Ash interrupts, "We do have video of the parking lot and you may want to see this, follow me."

I have Jax and Xavier follow us into a back room where a huge set up of monitors from all different angles are set up. Ash sits down in front of one and brings up the video from the front door.

"This is recording them leaving the building, and this one over here," He points to the screen right next to it, "shows them walking to the car. You see your wife going for her keys and then…"

There it is, two huge men in ski masks throwing a hood over both Liz and Ally's heads and picking them up while they thrash around. I am seeing red right now, I feel my fangs extend and then feel Jax's hand on my shoulder, silently warning me to calm down.

Ash continues, "I looked over at another video and see this van sitting here. That's the van they are thrown into, but it doesn't leave right away. I think they were waiting for the other two women to leave, so they could grab them as well. They finally take off when they see Gray come outside and walk towards your wife's car."

Gray pipes in, "There were a few vehicles leaving at that time, so I didn't pay attention to any specific one, but I do remember seeing this van pull out. It squealed it's tires a bit as it did."

"Can we zoom in on the license plate?" I ask as my whole body is shaking.

"Already did." Ash hands me a piece of paper, "I also called a buddy of mine to run the plates. I'm afraid the plates are stolen."

I grab the top of the chair in front of me when my legs want to collapse. Xavier and Jax both grab me. I slowly turn towards Jax, "She doesn't have much time."

"We will find her, Taven."

"No, you are not understanding… the baby!" Jax's eyes widen at the realization of what I'm saying.

"Fuck!"

"What the fuck is this?" We turn to Gray as he stares at a screen with live video. He zooms in and when he does, there is Liz, stumbling into the parking lot. I see Max and Kole running to her and I take off running myself.

"Liz!" I call out to her as I get outside. Max is carrying her and hands her to me as soon as I reach her, "Baby, talk to me! Are you hurt?" I can see a nasty bruise by her eye on her temple where it looks like she had been hit.

"Taven?"

"Yes, baby. I'm right here! How did you get away? Where is Ally?"

"I don't know. I remember us being thrown in the van with something over our heads and then I felt something hit me on the side of my head. I didn't come to, until just a few minutes ago. All I heard was, "We don't want no pregnant bitch", and then they threw me out of the vehicle… just down the street. They must still have Ally."

"She must have told them to be careful with you because you were pregnant. She saved you!" I hugged her to me tightly until I hear her hiss.

"Did you not hear the part where they threw me out of the vehicle? I meant literally."

"I am so sorry, baby!" I am going to kill whoever did this to her… to them!

"You have to find her… find Ally!"

"We will, baby, we will." I kiss her forehead and then she passes out.

As soon as we got back to the Compound, I contact the Sanford Compound and I'm told that Breck is still away on detail, but they give me his cell number. I'm sitting in a chair in the medical ward while Liz lays sleeping in a bed, hooked up to machines, so we can monitor the baby. After being pushed from a vehicle, we didn't know if there is any damage, so we called in Dr. Howard. All looks well with mother and child, but she wants to keep an eye on her for a little while longer.

I dial Breck's number, and he answers on the fourth ring, "Who is this? Where did you get this number?"

"Breck, it's Taven from Augusta."

"Oh, hey! What's up? Ally isn't annoying you already, is she?" He chuckles.

"Breck, I need you to get here as soon as possible. Something has happened."

I can tell that his hackles are up at this point, just by the sound of his voice, "What's wrong? Is Ally okay?"

"I don't know at this point, because she has been taken."

"What the fuck do you mean, she's been taken?"

"The women went out for drinks tonight. Liz and Ally were kidnapped when they walked out to the car to leave. I think the plan was for them to take all four, but Cassie and Jill stayed inside. We can talk about this when you get here, though."

"You seem pretty calm for your mate being kidnapped."

I sigh, "That's because they threw her out of the vehicle when they found out she was pregnant. I think Ally saved her by telling them that Liz is expecting."

"So, my mate is now alone with these sick fucks?" He roars through the phone.

"Breck! I understand what you are feeling right now, but getting pissed at me isn't going to help!"

"I left her in your care, Taven! Why did you not have detail on them while they were out?"

"There was no need for it at the time, everything has been back to normal here. This was just a bunch of horny guys pissed off at the women, because they wouldn't dance with them!" I realize the words I chose, were not the best ones to use.

"So, HORNY guys took my mate?! I swear if they touch her in any way, I will shred them to pieces!"

"That is your right, Breck! In fact, that's my plan. None of them will come out of this alive. That much I do promise! How soon can you be here?"

"I'm actually only twenty minutes away from you with the detail I'm on, so I will be there in ten minutes."

"Don't drive too reckless, we need you here, and so does Ally."

"Don't worry about me, I'll be there. You better be ready to rock out when I get there!" He hangs up before I can say anything else. We don't even know where to look!

I stand up and brush a kiss on Liz's forehead before I step out of the room. I call over to Club Moon and Gray answers.

"Gray, it's Taven."

"Hey, how is your wife doing?" He sounds concerned... more concerned than he should over another man's wife.

Emphasizing the word, "'My wife and child will be fine. I need a favor."

"Of course, what can I do?"

"You know where the women were sitting, right?" I had a pretty good notion that he knew Liz's every move and I grit my teeth at the thought.

"Yes, I do. I walked over to check Jill's hand when Liz came over for ice." Smart move, covering up how he knew where they were sitting.

"I need video coverage from when they were dancing. I'm hoping we can see the mother fuckers that were harassing them. Ally's ma... guy is on his way and will want more information than what we have. Can you send them over to me right away?"

"Yeah, I sure can. Hey, if you need any more help, let me know. We will help as much as we can."

"Yeah, thanks." I give him my email to send the video over and then hang up. I think they have helped enough! Running a club where anybody can be kidnapped, is not a person I need help from!

Five minutes later I receive multiple files of videos at different angles, along with a message from Gray telling me that he knows who the men are, and he can take us to them. BINGO, GOT YOU MOTHER FUCKERS!

EIGHTEEN

LIZ

I wake up to find myself alone in the medical ward, hooked up to monitors. I try to scoot myself up in the bed, but my body aches all over. Just as I'm about to give up, Dr. Howard comes into the room frowning.

"You should be taking it easy Liz. You haven't had any blood yet, because you have been out cold and anyone who gets tossed out of a car is bound to be sore all over… or worse."

"Is the baby okay? That's all that matters."

"Yes, the baby is fine, but it isn't all that matters! You need to take care of yourself, so you can take care of that baby."

"She is right, love." I turn at the sound of Taven's voice as he walks in.

I smile and reach my arms out to him as he sits on the edge of my bed.

"Are you able to take my blood, baby? Breck is on his way here and we are heading out to go get Ally. I want you to drink before I need to leave, otherwise I will fill a bag for you."

"I can drink, but I want to make sure the baby is okay before you leave. Doc, can you do another ultrasound before he leaves? Just to be sure."

The doctor smiles warmly at me, "Of course, Liz. I had planned on it anyway."

After squirting the gel on my belly, she rubs the wand over my stomach and a heartbeat thumps through the speaker. The doctor hits a few buttons and then turns to us smiling.

"Baby is doing very well. I didn't want to say anything before, because I wanted to show you at the same time." She is grinning at us.

"What is it? What did you want to show us?" Taven asks.

Dr. Howard points to a spot on the screen, "Do you see this right here? It looks like little lines... that is the sex of your baby."

Taven and I look at each other confused and then look back at the doctor, "What do you mean? I don't see anything." I say squinting my eyes at the area she is pointing to.

"That's exactly it. You don't see anything, because you are having a healthy baby girl!" Dr. Howard happily informs us.

My eyes widen and a smile spreads across my face. I look over at Taven and he still seems to be in shock. I grab his hand and squeeze, "It's a girl, babe!" Then something crosses my mind, "I'm sorry, you probably wanted a boy... a little warrior like yourself." The smile falls from my face.

Taven looks at me and then he smiles, "No, love. I was hoping for a little girl. I have two boys already." He kisses me on the lips and then pulls back.

"But they are not your biological kids. I would think you would want one from your bloodline."

"Sweetheart, we have eternity together and if you think we are stopping with our baby girl, you are sadly mistaken. We will have boys, but if you think about it, Jack and Nate are my bloodline now. I am their maker, they have my blood running through their veins, therefore, they are mine in every sense of the word."

I can't help the tears that course down my cheeks at his words. I wrap my arms around him as I look at the doctor, "Thank you Dr.

Howard. If there isn't anything else, can I have a few moments with my husband before he leaves?"

"Oh, of course!" She starts heading for the door, but then turns and looks at me. I am going to hang out until the guys get back, just in case you need anything." I nod at her and then she is gone.

Taven is already bringing my head down to his neck, "Drink sweetheart, feed our daughter." I get a glimpse of the unshed tears that glisten in his eyes as I lean into his neck and bite down. He moans as his desire starts to build by getting fed from, so I undo his jeans and pull out his magnificent cock. My hands start to slide up and down as his hips move back and forth and he groans next to my ear, "Fuck baby, you should be taking it easy."

I take his hand and move it up and under my hospital gown, directing it towards the wetness pooling between my thighs. He grunts and slowly slides a finger into the wet opening while he runs his thumb over my clit. As I begin to take larger pulls from his neck, his hips start to move faster, and I feel the pulse in his cock as it swells. He moves in closer just as the first stream of cum explodes and lands on my stomach. Feeling his seed spraying all over my skin excites me and I let go, coming all over his hand. I can feel my juices running out past his hand and down the crack of my ass.

Retracting my fangs, I sigh with content while Taven moves down between my legs and cleans me with his tongue.

"God, Liz. You make me so fucking hot! Especially seeing you with my cum all over your creamy flesh."

I smile up at him, "Well, just wait until I get out of here. I'll let you cover my whole body with it." I bite my bottom lip and gaze at him.

He growls and smashes his lips to mine, kissing me with a hunger that I can't describe. His phone buzzes and he swears, "Shit! Breck must be here. I have to go, love."

"It's okay. Just do me a favor?"

"Anything for you."

"Kill those pieces of shit for me... slowly!"

A smile creeps up on his face, "It will be my pleasure. Consider it done." One last passionate kiss from my warrior and he is gone, leaving me panting in his wake.

Shortly after I'm left alone, Cassie and Jill come to see me. I'm pretty much feeling like my old self again after drinking from Taven, but I have orders to stay in medical until Taven comes back.

"Hey, how are you feeling?" Jill inquires.

"Much better now that I have fed. How are you guys holding up?"

"Okay, I guess. We just feel really bad about the whole situation." Cassie can't look at me. Instead, she stares at my hand laying on the bed.

Grabbing her arm, I make her look at me, "None of this is any of our faults! Those assholes had their own agenda for us." I look between both Cassie and Jill, trying to get them to stop blaming themselves, "Besides, I was the one that found the club. I'm not even blaming the club. Gray and his brother have been a huge help in trying to find Ally."

Cassie grins when I finish talking, "Jax says that Taven is slightly jealous, because he thinks Gray likes you."

"What? Even if Gray does like me, why would he be jealous? He is mated and married to me. We are having a child! He already has me and I'm not going anywhere... he knows that."

"Oh, it's just a jealous mate thing. I find it amusing." Cassie snickers.

Cassie sits on the bed beside me and I chuckle, thinking about what just happened there less than a half hour ago.

"Um... you may not want to sit there."

She jumps up quick, "Why is that?"

"I just fed from Taven."

"Yeah, so?"

"I don't know what you do during that time, but I don't feed without taking care of my man at the same time."

"Oh gross! You are such a whore!" She is disgusted, but laughs.

"Oh please, like you don't do it too! Besides, I learned everything from hanging out with the two of you!"

"She has a point there, Case. You are our whore mentor." Jill playfully shoves Cassie.

"Well, at least I've accomplished one good thing in my lifetime." She winks at me.

"Oh, since I have you two here, I might as well tell you."

"What?" They both look at me and ask in unison.

"Taven and I are going to be proud and loving parents of a beautiful baby girl!"

"Oh, my God! That is awesome... another little girl!" Cassie claps, but then I look at Jill and my smile drops.

"I am so sorry Jill! I didn't even think!" I feel horrible. Forgetting for a moment that Jill lost her daughter to a miscarriage when she was carrying triplets. How could I be so thoughtless?!

"No, it's okay, really! I am so excited for you guys. Duncan and I will be trying again soon and even though no one can take her place, it will help a little.

"Did you ever give her a name?"

"Yes, but I haven't told anybody. It's been too difficult to bring it up."

"We totally understand. You will when you are ready." I give her a reassuring smile.

"Well, since we are already talking about it, I might as well tell you. I mean, you two are like sisters to me."

"Like sisters?" Cassie arches a brow at Jill, "You mean we ARE sisters."

"Oh, you know what I mean! Anyway, we named our little girl Caylin Jo McPherson."

I can see the unshed tears in her eyes, and I grab her hand. "That is such a beautiful name, Jill! I love it."

Unlike Jill, Cassie let her tears slide down her cheeks and hugs Jill, "Okay, okay!" Jill chuckles, "Let's move on to a different topic."

"So, what have you guys heard about the men going after Ally? I mean do they know where she is?"

"All I know is that after looking at the surveillance videos, Gray found the men and he knows who they are. He is taking the Elite to them now. Breck is beside himself and is blaming Taven for getting her into this situation." Jill bites her lip waiting for my reaction.

"WHAT?! Why is he blaming my husband?"

"Just calm down, Liz. Taven understands that Breck doesn't really blame him. Breck is just scared out of his mind."

"Well, as long as he gets that notion out of his head that this is Taven's fault, because he will not want to deal with me if he doesn't!"

"I think you should try and get some rest, Liz. You have been through a lot. I promise to come wake you the second we hear anything." Cassie pats my leg.

"Ugh, I am feeling exhausted, but you better not forget to wake me with any kind of news!"

"I promise, I will." After they say goodbye, I sink deeper into my bed and fall into a much-needed deep sleep.

TAVEN

Breck comes at me when I walk into the room, and I'm able to duck before his fist slams into my face. Xavier and Cooper grab him by the arms and haul him back.

"Calm the fuck down Breck or I will throw you in a cell! I may not be your boss, but I am still a superior and you will do well to remember that!"

"Fuck you, Taven! This is all your fault! If you would have done your job, then none of this would have happened!"

"I don't know how you men run your Compound, but we do not keep our women under lock and key here! They are free to come and go just like the rest of us, unless there is imminent danger. I had been watching that club for weeks and found that it is a legit business. This is just a freak thing. In case you have forgotten, my wife was taken too! It just happens that they didn't want to have anything to do with a pregnant woman."

I'm half tempted to tell him that if he were a real man… he would have his mate knocked up by now, but I figure it wouldn't do anything to calm him down.

"I can't lose her Taven!" Breck breaks down and drops to his knees.

"I know you can't, and we ARE going to get her back! You need to pull yourself together and be strong for her now. We don't know what we are walking into, and we don't know what their plans are. You need to be prepared for the worst, while hoping for the best."

"Promise you will not take my revenge from me, Taven. I need to take them out. Promise me!"

I put my hand on his shoulder, "I give you my word, Breck. You will not be stopped from doing what you need to do, and my men know this. Now let's get moving. We need to meet up with Gray and Ash at the club. They have more men coming with us and only they know where to find these mother fuckers."

Breck gets to his feet and holds his hand out for me to take, "I am sorry I tried jumping you like that. I'm just scared and needed to take it out on someone."

"You are forgiven, now let's go."

We stop by Club Moon to meet up with the brothers and then we are on our way, going in the opposite direction of Augusta. The brothers pull off to the side of the road after about ten minutes; it's secluded out here, woods all around.

I turn to Gray and Ash when we have all exited our vehicles, "How do you know these men?"

The brothers look at each other before looking back at me, "They are outcasts. We once considered them family, but they are the type that don't like to follow orders." Ash spoke up, "We gave them an ultimatum and they chose their own path. They take what they want, and they do not care who it hurts, as long as it pleases them."

Gray chimes in this time, "I need to warn you to be prepared. They are ruthless."

Breck has a guttural voice, "How ruthless?"

Gray looks at him gravely, "Like Ash said, they take what they want. Maybe we got here early enough, but you need to prepare yourself. I can guarantee you that she is still alive, but you may not like the state that we find her in. Some of the men in this camp work late hours, and since they share everything...." He pauses for a moment, "I can bet that they are keeping her alive at least until the others get their share."

"Breck, maybe you should wait here, so you don't have to see how we find her." I say softly, "We can come get you once we have them contained and you can finish them off."

He stands straight up, "No, I will be there when we find her. I will not let her think that I am abandoning her. I will be with her through it all."

I nod at him. I can't imagine being in his shoes and hearing what could possibly have happened to her. By the sounds of it, it isn't good.

"Let's go!" I go to walk up the path, but Ash grabs my arm.

"There is something else that you need to know."

"Well, out with it! We need to get in there now!"

"These men... they aren't normal people." He says as he stares into my eyes.

"Well, no shit! They are sick sons of bitches who need to be taken out!"

"No, you don't understand. They are not regular people, and they are not vampires like you and your men either."

How the fuck does he know what we are?! He must have seen my reaction, because he answers, "We have known what you are since you and your men first walked into our club. We know how to sense vampires, but apparently you don't know how to sense our kind... shifters."

I'm blown away! To hear Miguel talk about it is one thing, but to actually see them in the flesh is something else. No wonder they are big fuckers like us. I shake the shock off and look back at him, "So how do we kill the mother fuckers?"

"The same way you are able to be killed. The only difference between us is that we shift into wolves, and you don't... that's it. I just didn't want you to be unprepared in case they do shift... and I guarantee, they will."

I turn to my men, "You hear them. Prepare yourselves... don't let them surprise you! Arm yourselves well." I go back and grab my sword that I threw in the back just in case. I usually just use knives, but I'm not taking any chances.

We end up hiking uphill for about two miles, but luckily, we are able to use our speed, so we are there within a minute or so. We keep our distance and stay downwind, so they can't smell us coming. With their campfire, it helps even more with hiding our scent. We zone in on their site to take everything in and to see how many we are up against. We luck out when we see that there are two of us to each one of them, but what we don't know is when the rest will be back.

I move around to see if I can see where they are keeping Ally, but I don't see her. I assume that they have her in a tent, but then something catches my eye and I focus on a man that is part way behind a tree. What the fuck is he doing? The guy moves, and I am horrified by the sight before me! So much, that I want to lose the contents of my stomach.

There is Ally, chained to a tree by a fucking dog collar, completely naked and beaten. This filth is jacking off in front of her and then he is coming and spraying it all over her! It looks like he wasn't the only one to do it either! My heart aches for the girl. She has always been so warm and loving and now she looks broken. I don't know how anyone can get over something like this.

The vile dog is saying something, so I strain to hear.

"Why the fuck do we need to wait for the others to get back? Let's just take our turn with her now and they can have their turn when they get here!"

"Because asshole, this is what we all agreed to! You are lucky we are able to jack off to her!"

"Can't we at least shove our cocks in her mouth or make her jack us off?"

"Just be patient! Fuck Simon, you act as if you haven't had a woman for a while!"

"Hell, it's been two days since you let me fuck that sweet little redhead that you keep! That one there is a feisty one!"

"Yeah well, I don't want her worn out or too ruined. I like fucking her tight pussy and the more I let you fucks have her, the looser she gets!"

I can't listen to them anymore or else I'm going to lose my shit! I head back to the others and inform them of what I saw. Looking at Breck, "It isn't a pretty sight, but from what I gather, they haven't raped her... yet. They are waiting for all the men to return before they take turns. Also, we need to check every tent and building, because there is at least one other woman here, a redhead."

We all move forward as quiet as possible until I see their noses go up in the air and sniff. Then all hell breaks loose.

Shouts are heard alerting those who are not aware of our presence. There are growls and metal clashing as my men make it into the camp. I draw my sword and battle it out with a huge burly guy with glowing amber eyes. He snarls at me and then shifts, leaping at me with his fangs bared. I flash to the side and bring my sword down, taking his monstrous head clean off. I am knocked over as another huge dog jumps on me, ripping my side open with his claws. I let my fangs out and sink them into the side of his neck, tearing out a big chunk of flesh.

I get up and look around. I see Breck fighting off another big shifter and I run over to assist. I grab the brute around its chest and lift him up thinking Breck will stab him through the heart. Instead, he sends his fist flying into the shifters chest and yanks out its heart. I stare at the murderous look he has on his face.

"Go get your mate, Breck. She's chained to that tree over there." I point him in the direction of where I saw her, "We got this, buddy." He nods and runs towards his mate.

I look around again to see who else I can go after and my eyes land on Ash. He is fighting a shifter in human form until the guy shifts and Ash follows suit. I watch in amazement as Ash transforms into the biggest and blackest wolf I could ever imagine. His eyes are glowing amber as he tears through the other shifter with his fangs and claws.

I blink and come back to what is going on around me. There is no one else to fight and I see that Breck is having a hard time with the chains holding Ally, so I run over to help, grabbing a blanket off a clothesline in the process. I stop in front of her and cover her naked form up and then join Breck. The chain is too strong for us to break, even with our combined strength.

"Breck, I'm going to go look for a key. Why don't you find some soap and water and clean her up."

The poor guy is shaking with rage, but he nods his head and goes in search for supplies. I run from tent to tent and from cabin to cabin, grabbing any key I can find. When I get to the last cabin, I stop dead in my tracks. My eyes go to the big iron bed. There, curled up in the corner is a woman with red hair and big green eyes, a horrified look on her face as she stares at me. Like Ally, she is chained to the bed, a collar around her neck.

I hold up my hands, so I don't scare her, "It's going to be alright. We are here to save you. What is your name?" She doesn't answer. "My name is Taven. You are safe now. Do you know where the key is kept, so we can unlock that collar?"

She points to a cabinet in the corner. I open the drawers to it, but don't find anything. "Open the door." She finally speaks. I throw open the two doors and there is a row of six keys lined up. Grabbing all of them, I make my way over to her and I see her cringe.

"I promise I will not hurt you. I am kind of the police… I protect people like you." She continues to watch me closely but doesn't move away when I get closer. I grab a button-down shirt from a nearby chair and hand it to her to put on. That seems to calm her a little more.

I start trying each key in the lock and finally, with the fifth key, it unlocks, "Please don't run off. Stay close to me and I will make sure you get home safely, okay?"

Nodding her head first, she then speaks, "My name is Diana."

"It's nice to meet you, Diana. When we leave this cabin, it's not going to be pretty. We killed all of the men that were out there, but there are still a lot of people out there. They are with me, so you don't need to be scared."

"Okay. Thank you for coming for me. I didn't think anybody ever would." Her bottom lip trembled.

"To be honest, we came for one of my men's girlfriend. We didn't know you were here. Are there others?"

"I don't think so. I think only the leader is allowed to keep someone and I am the only one in here."

"Okay, are you ready?"

Shaking her head yes, I help her off the bed and she clings to me with a death grip. We step outside and I see Gray walking towards me, "There you are! Did you find any keys?" He stops dead in his tracks when Diana lifts her head to him.

"Actually yes. Can you see to Diana's well-being while I go assist Breck?" I watch as Gray nods his head while he has the strangest look on his face.

Diana clings to me and I have to peel her hands away from my chest, "It's okay Diana. This is Gray; he is the one that led us here. We wouldn't have found you if it weren't for him. He will keep you safe, I promise."

She looks back to him and then smiles, reaching out her hand to take his. Gray is looking at her in bewilderment and I can't help but wonder...

The same key worked in Ally's collar that I used for Diana's. Once she is free, Breck picks her up and takes her straight to a shower house, so she can really clean up. Once she is done, Breck and I leave to take her back to the Compound, leaving the rest of the men here to wait for the last of the vile beasts to come back, so they could be taken care of as well. Diana says that she is fine leaving with Gray and Ash, and they promise me that they will get her taken care of. I don't really like that idea, since I don't really know them well, but she insists on staying with them. Who am I to stop her, so I leave her in their care. Now I will always wonder if that was a wise choice.

Nineteen

LIZ

It's early morning when I feel soft lips moving down my neck. Masculine hands roaming over my thighs under the blankets, pushing my hospital gown up as they move further up. I begin to whimper as electrical sparks shoot throughout my body from my very core.

"Morning beautiful." Taven's husky voice whispers in my ear. I lift my arm and take hold of the back of his head, bringing it down to where my vein pulses in my neck. There is a pinch, and my body comes alive, throbbing with the desire that only this man can quench. A crescendo of pleasure builds with each pull from my neck and each stroke of his hand. My body is on fire, and when his fingers find my wetness, I jerk with the sensation it brings.

I hear him growl before he lifts my leg up and slides into my sheath in one smooth thrust, taking my breath away. His growl turns into a groan as he pulls out slowly, just to the tip and then drives his cock back into me. His fingers move to my sensitive bundle of nerves as he begins to move in and out.

As he fucks me ever so slowly, I feel his love crashing through me and it sends me tumbling. I cry out as pleasure crashes through every inch of my body, causing my toes to curl and making me unable to move, as wave after wave of my orgasm claims me. Once he retracts his fangs, my body finally becomes my own again and I can move, but Taven remains inside of me, still sliding in and out slowly.

He lifts my leg higher, and without pulling out, moves himself between my thighs. Moving my gown higher, and up past my breasts, he takes a nipple and swirls his tongue around it before moving to the other one, all the while staring at me intensely. I watch as the storm clouds swirl within his eyes every once in a while, and I know his demon needs me too.

"Take me to the room, Vamp, I need my demon."

"Not yet. I want… I need to make love to my wife and feed our child before I can let him have his way with you." With that being said, he takes my lips briefly and then pulls away, just to bring my head to his neck.

I feed… I feed fast and hard. Pull after pull of his delicious blood and I have him emptying his seed deep inside my womb, ripping another orgasm from me as well. Gripping my hips, he holds me down as he plunges in me one last time, roaring my name as he spills the last of his hot liquid within. I pull back, and sink into the bed, spent.

"Fuck me, baby! I love making sweet love to that hot little pussy of yours." He gasps.

"Good. Now take me to the playroom so you can fuck me the way your demon wants to fuck me."

He growls low, "It's a good thing that I am immortal, or else you would be the death of me!"

"Are you saying that you aren't ready for round two?" I smile sweetly at him.

"Oh no, sweetness. I am ready for round two, three, four, five, and six!"

I can feel the flush creep into my face. I usually don't blush anymore around him, but when he says these things while gazing at me with those smokey eyes, filled with lust, I can't help it.

"I suggest we get me dressed then, warrior, so you can take me home."

I notice a difference in the playroom as soon as I walk in. There, at the bottom corner of the bed, is a video camera on a tripod. Looking around the room, I see a camera in all four corners of the room. Tingles run through me at the thought of being videotaped. I would never have allowed this in the past, but with Taven... I know it is safe and I am so fucking turned on.

Taven takes in a big whiff, "I see you like the thought of watching as I fuck that gorgeous pussy and tight little ass of yours." His devilish grin makes me drip even more, "Why are you just standing there? You should be completely naked by now. This insubordination warrants punishment, baby girl."

I quickly undress and kneel, my hands behind my back in submission. My heart is thumping in anticipation of the punishment.

"First, you scare the shit out of me when you get yourself kidnapped, and now the insubordination," he tsked, "What shall I do about that?"

"Whatever you feel is necessary, Sir." I smile smugly.

He walks over to me and pulls my hair, so I am looking up at him, "Oh, you like it when I punish you? I would think twice about that. Do you want to know what I have in mind for you?"

"Yes, Sir."

"I think the best punishment will be not letting you come at all. What do you think?"

Fuck, is he serious? How can he do this to me? I have never had to use my safe word, but I am thinking I will be this time.

I whimper, "Please, Sir. That's too much."

"That's the point, my greedy little slut." He rubs his thumb lightly down my cheek to my lips. Pushing it into my mouth, I suck on it before he pulls it back out.

"Take my cock out." He commands, and I lift my hands to pull down his pants. His huge cock springs free and I lick my lips, desperate to get my lips around it.

"Ah, you think you are going to get this, do you? I think not... at least not yet. On your feet and put your hands in front." I do as he says, and he locks a set of cuffs around my wrists. "Come." He drags me to the bed by the cuffs and bends me over the edge, my head shoved down to the mattress. He turns my head so it's facing the foot of the bed and I watch as he goes to the video camera, and angles is down at me. "God, you are perfect."

Walking back over, he stands behind me and tells me to spread my legs. His fingers run through my folds, soaked with my arousal. Back and forth, they slide and then up my crack to my tight, puckered bud. My breath hitches and I whimper when he inserts it into my hole.

"I'm going to fuck this tight little ass of yours in a minute. Are you ready for it?"

"Yes, Sir."

"Tell me how much my dirty little girl wants me to fuck her ass." I can feel his cock now running through my folds, lubing it up with my juices.

I moan, "Please, Sir. I want you to fuck my ass with that big dick and fill me up with your cum. I want you to take me hard and fast."

"That's a good little slut. I'm going to give it to you just how you want it and then some, and you are going to take it all like a good girl." He dips the tip of his cock into my pussy just to lube it up more, teasing me when he pulls it back out.

He spreads my ass cheeks and starts to push through my bud until the tip breaches the ring. Groaning, he slides the rest of the way in.

"Fuck, baby. You are so damn tight back here. It makes me want to come right now!" He pulls out to the tip and then drives back into me over and over, picking up speed as he goes. I'm crying out with each thrust, feeling the climax building with every nerve that it touches.

His pace picks up and I feel his claws extend over my hips as he growls. I know if I were to look back, his eyes would be glowing. His vampire is the one fucking me and I don't know how, but I just got even wetter just thinking about.

I feel his cock swell in my ass and then he is marking me with his seed. Just when I don't think I can hold off coming, he pulls out and finishes all over my ass and lower back. I can feel the sticky fluid running down my ass.

"You almost came, you naughty little girl!" He runs his hand through his own mess before rubbing my pussy, smearing it all over and then bringing his fingers to my mouth. "Suck. Taste what you do to me my dirty little slut."

I moan as his cum smeared fingers enter my mouth, but he pulls them out once he sees how much I am enjoying the taste. He brings his hand back and I feel the sting as he slaps my ass. He plays with my clit while delivering five more slaps. One more slap and he would have tossed me over the edge, and I know that he knew that.

Lifting me up, he lays me down in the middle of the bed and stretches my arms over my head, connecting the cuffs to the rope that is attached to the headboard.

I looked down at my husband who now has my legs spread as wide as they will go and what I see almost has me creaming right here. In my husband's place is his demon… my demon and vampire all in one. His eyes glow, but they are also swirling with the demon's storm. His fangs are extended, and his claws are running up and down my legs, not lightly, but not roughly. Just enough to leave red claw marks in their wake.

The dominance in his stormy eyes has me panting with need. I look lower and… Holy Fuck! His cock is almost twice the girth than his normal gigantic size. It scares me, but also excites me at the same time. So much that without realizing what I am doing, my climax breaks free, and I ride it out, while only his claws are touching me. I smile when it's done and open my eyes. Hardened eyes are what I meet when I look at him.

"My dirty little slut just disobeyed me. Now it's time to pay!" My eyes widen as I think… OH FUCK!

Without a second thought, I yell out. "PURPLE!"

TAVEN

How I let my demon take over completely, I don't know. I am always in control of him when in this room, but something snapped and now I am struggling to get control again, because as much as my demon loves our mate, he really wants to punish her for disobeying! I can't let him do it. I enjoy the roughness of our time in this room and it helps keep the demon contained, but I am not into the really sick shit that it's into and I refuse to use Liz like that.

I can see that she knows she is in for it by the look on her face and I am trying to get back in control. Then I'm taken by complete surprise as she yells out her safe word. Thank fuck for that!

I snap out of it and feel myself get back in charge. Without saying a word, I uncuff her wrists, pick her up and carry her out the door. I lay her on our bed and I crawl in beside her and just hold her tight. Neither of us say anything for the longest time, but then Liz breaks the silence.

"Do you want to talk about it?"

"I don't know how to explain what happened. It's never happened like that before."

"What do you mean? What's never happened like that?"

"I have never not been in control of it before. I mean, my demon really wanted to punish you. I don't mean out of anger or anything, but to do things to you that you are not ready for and that I would never do to you regardless, because that is more sadistic than anything."

"Maybe it was just all the stress from the last twenty-four hours."

"Yeah…maybe. I just don't ever want to hurt you like that."

"Hey," she says leaning up on an elbow, "That's what the safe word is for isn't?"

"What if it wouldn't have gotten through to my other side?"

"I trust you Taven. I always have, and I always will! We will just stay clear of the room after stressful events. How's that?"

I pull her back down to me and hug her tight, "How did I ever deserve you, Liz?" I kiss the top of her head and let my lips linger there.

"Because you are one lucky son of a bitch!" She giggles, and that was it. I jump up and start tickling her until she is crying Uncle.

I meet with Miguel late this morning and enlighten him on the events from the previous night and wee morning hours. He is not thrilled that he missed out on the action but is delighted to know that he could add another known shifter pack to his list.

"Well, I am sure I can set up a meeting between you and the brothers if you would like to ask them anything… you know, for your research." I smile smugly at him.

"That would be great if you could do that for me!"

"Sure, but I may need to go with you, since they do not know you."

"I have no problem with that."

"Good, I will call today and set it up."

Once Miguel leaves my office, I dial Grays number. Another reason why I want to go is because I want to check on Diana. I wonder if she is safe at home or if she is still with the wolves?

Gray answers on the fourth ring, "Taven, what can I do for you?"

"Hey Gray, I just wanted to check on how things went with Diana. Did she get home safely?"

"Actually, she is still with us. She isn't ready to go home and face her family yet, so we are letting her stay with us until she is ready."

"I see. It is her decision? She hasn't been coerced into it?"

"What exactly are you asking, Taven? Do you think we are keeping her here against her will? We are not sick fuckers like the ones we took care of!"

"Sorry, I just had to ask. I still feel responsible for her somewhat since I was the one that found her."

"You have no need to worry. Just take care of your own mate and we will take care of Diana."

I find it funny the way he words that last phrase, just like I wondered about the look he gave her last night, "Fine, whatever. I do have a favor to ask of you though." I go on and explain about Miguel and his research.

"That is fine. He can ask a few questions as long as they are appropriate."

"Great, thanks. I will be coming along with him and if you don't mind, I would like to bring Liz. You know, give her a little girl time with Diana and maybe bring some clothes over for her."

"I think that would be okay. Meet us at the club later…let's say around four-ish?"

"Sounds good. See you then." I hang up and sit back in my chair. Hm, seems like Gray likes to keep their location hidden as well. I understand his thoughts on it, but one thing he doesn't realize is, I am the vampire law…and now shifter law around here. If I want to find him, I will find him.

Liz and I walk into the club and Miguel follows. I grab Liz's hand before going through the doors. Call it jealousy or whatever you want, but Liz is my mate and I saw how Gray talked about her the night before, regardless of my suspicions.

Gray and Ash are sitting at one of the tables and Diana is sitting between them with her back to us. Gray looks up and smiles at Liz.

"There she is! How are you feeling today?"

"Hey Gray! Nice seeing you. I'm actually doing really good, thank you." Liz smiles back, and I squeeze her hand… not really meaning to.

Ash stands up to shake my hand and then Liz's hand, "Nice to meet you. I am glad you are safe."

"So, I hear congratulations is in order!" Gray shows us his pearly whites and I roll my eyes.

"Yes!" Liz smiles up at me and then back to Gray, "We just found out we are having a little girl. I am so excited, we already have two boys at home, Jack and Nate, so…." Diana's head whips around at Liz's words.

"Oh my God, Liz Brady?" Diana squeals and jumps up. I look over at my wife and she is in utter shock.

"Diana?! Oh God... I didn't realize it was you!" Liz and Diana embrace and the rest of us are standing there wondering what the fuck is going on?

"Um... Liz? You mind telling us how you two know each other?" I chuckle.

"Oh gosh... sorry. Diana is my cousin. Diana, this is my husband, Taven Anderson."

"Well, isn't it a small world! The man who saved me is married to my favorite cousin!"

"So, what are you doing in the area anyway? I thought you were traveling with friends?" Liz inquires.

"I was, but I was starting to get home sick. I wanted to come see you and the boys."

"You just can't stay out of trouble, can you?" Liz snickers and then hugs her cousin again.

"I can't help it if trouble finds me every time! I try to stay clear of it."

I interrupt to ask Diana how she is holding up.

"Not too bad, I guess." She blushes, "I have bad dreams every time I go to sleep, but otherwise it's been okay." I watch both Ash and Gray rub her back at the same time, "These two have been so sweet and have made me feel at home."

"So, you are okay with staying with them? You are more than welcome to come stay with us, now that you are family and all." I ask.

"Yes! Please come stay with us Diana! The boys would love to see you!"

Both brothers face's cloud over at the mention of Diana coming with us. Huh? Not just one, but both? Or is Ash just acting out, because it's his brother?

"I think I am going to hold off and rest for a few days. If I remember right, your boys are full of energy, and I don't have it in me just yet. Is that okay?"

"Oh, of course it is honey! I will come visit you when I can in the meantime, how's that?"

"Yes, that would be great!" Diana hugs Liz again.

As the girls move off to catch up and go through the clothes that Liz brought for Diana, Miguel and I take a seat at the table with the brothers.

"Interesting turn of events, I'd say!" I shake my head.

"Yes, it is." Gray responds as he looks thoughtful.

I drop the topic and go on to introduce Miguel to Gray and Ash. I listen as Miguel shoots question after question to them both and they answer every single one. I didn't think any of the questions were out of line, so I start to relax.

Towards the end, Miguel start inquiring about the similarities between Vampire's and Shifters. He is right on most of the information that he had collected in the past. The one thing that he hadn't heard though is about the destined mates between a female and the Alpha family.

Seems as though in shifter packs, when there is more than one male in the Alpha family, they all share a destined mate. No matter how many males there are. My mind can't even wrap itself around this information. I could never share Liz with anybody! Just the thought of it turns my stomach.

I turn my attention back to Miguel's questioning.

"So, who is the Alpha male in your pack?" He cocks a brow looking back and forth between the two brothers.

Ash smiles, "I am."

"I see. Are there more than just you two brothers in the Alpha family?"

"Nope... we are it."

"And have you or any of your pack found your mates? I only ask, because we haven't found our mates in centuries, until now and it's only been three of us that have so far. Just wondering if it's easier for you."

"Actually, no. None of us have any mates... yet." Gray answers this last question, while gazing right at Diana.

"Well," Miguel holds his hand out to Ash and then to Gray, "That's all I have for now, but if I can think of anything else, would it be okay to ask?"

"Yes, of course. It was nice to meet you Miguel. It's always nice meeting the "so called" enemy and finding out they are actually good ones like us." Gray chuckles.

"You are right on that account." Miguel smiles back. He turns to me, "I am going to take myself back to the Compound and let you stay a bit. Looks like your mate is enjoying catching up." He nods towards Liz.

"If you are sure?"

"Yes, yes. I will see you later, Taven." And then he is gone.

I need to find out if my instincts are right or if I have it all wrong. With Diana being family now, it changes everything. I turn towards the brothers and just ask them outright.

"You think Diana is your mate, don't you?"

Ash sighs, but then nods his head yes.

Gray smiles smugly, "There is no thinking about it. We know she is our mate."

"Please tell me you haven't tried to force it on her or anything." I grit through my teeth.

"What kind of men do you think we are? We would never force a woman to do anything that she isn't ready for! Especially after what she just went through!" Ash's eyes start to glow.

"Calm down there, buddy! I just needed to hear it, since she is my wife's family and all." Ash blows out a breath and apologizes to me.

"Honestly, and don't get pissed at me Taven," Gray held his arms up in defense, "There was a slight pull last night when I met Liz for the first time." I clench my fists under the table. "BUT it wasn't a mating pull. It must have been because she is blood relation to our true mate."

I calm myself down and think about his logic, "That could be. So, I no longer have to watch you closely around my wife anymore?" I ask grinning.

"No, Taven. You don't have to hate me either. We are all on the same side here. I don't want your wife, she's all yours."

"Damn right she is!" I look over at the love of my life and she stares back at me, then winks and my arousal starts, "Hey, sweetheart, we better head out now. I can bring you by tomorrow if you would like."

"Okay, be right there."

I turn to Gray, "You may want to turn the cameras off in the south parking lot for a little bit."

"Why is that?" He wrinkles his brows together.

"Because I'm not waiting until I get home after the wink she just gave me." I growl and stomp over to my mate, throwing her over my shoulder as I walk out. I can hear the brothers hooting with laughter as I do so.

TWENTY

LIZ

It's been a month now that my cousin Diana has been living with the shifter pack. She seems to have come out of her ordeal pretty well. Of course, if what Taven has told me is true, she has not one, but two hunky men taking good care of her. I am not sure if she knows that they are shifters, she hasn't said anything to me as of yet, but she is my blood and I know she will be fine with the knowledge. I can barely handle one man, let alone two…whew! I'm not sure if I would love to be in her shoes right now!

It's my weekly visit with Diana and as I am walking into the club, like I do every week, I get this cold chill up my spine as if I am being watched. Taven is too busy to leave the Compound, so he had Xavier bring me. I look back at him after I get the chill, and he notices the apprehension on my face. Xavier gets out and walks around the SUV towards me.

"What's up Liz?"

"I am not sure. I just have this feeling that I am being watched." I whisper, "Don't look around. Just get back into the vehicle and act as if you are leaving. Then come back and check the area out, if you would."

"No problem boss lady."

"Please don't call me that. How many times have I told you men this?"

"Whatever you say, boss lady." Xavier gives me a cheesy smile and winks.

I just shake my head and grin, thinking on how lucky his mate will be when he finds her. Xavier is a very good-looking man and once you get past his brooding looks and attitude, he is a big ole teddy bear. I would never call him that to his face though.

I open the door and run right into Gray, "Oh shit! I am so sorry."

He grins at me, "No problem beautiful… it was completely my fault!"

"You better not let my hubby hear you call me that." I wink at him.

"I'm not scared. I am just giving a compliment where a compliment is due. Besides, he knows damn well where my interests lie."

His comment makes me think of my earlier thoughts, "Hey Gray? Can I ask you something?"

"Sure… shoot."

I look around to make sure my cousin isn't around, "Does Diana know what you and Ash are?"

He looks at me, all joking aside, "Not yet. I mean, I think she gets the feeling that we are more than what she thinks we are, but no. We have not told her anything. We want to make sure she is completely over her ordeal from last month. She is getting there, but we feel she isn't ready to hear it yet."

"Hmm… a little advice?"

"Sure." He lifts a brow at me.

"Don't wait too long. Diana does not like being left in the dark. She may be a little skittish at first, but she will come around. It will also help if you two hotties make your move." I give him a knowing smile, "Make her fall in love with you first. She will not be able to walk away, no matter what."

I don't wait for a response. I just turn and walk through the double doors and into the club. I see Diana sitting at our regular booth looking through her phone. The brothers spoil her terribly. After a few days of being with them, they gave her a phone and a spending allowance. If that doesn't tell you something, I don't know what does!

"Hey bitch, what are you up to?" I ask as I slide in across from her.

"Oh, just a little online shopping. I am tired of wearing the same things over."

I snatch her phone, "What are you shopping for?" I look and my eyes bulge before I am grinning from ear to ear, "Hm, why would you be shopping for lingerie? Are you planning on slutting around during your little stay?" I giggle as I hand her back her phone.

"Will you keep it down, asshat! Ash is in the other room doing inventory! I don't need him hearing you say that!"

I lean in and whisper, "So, are you?"

"Why do you assume I am buying these for anyone particular?" Diana quirks her brow at me.

"Come on! You mean to tell me that you are living with two hot ass guys, and you haven't thought about them in that way?" I take a drink of my water to hide my smirk.

She leans in further, "Of course, I have! I just can't choose between them. I really like them both!"

"So, why choose? Go with both." I shrug my shoulders and take another drink of water, which was probably a bad idea, because I choke on it when I see her horrified look, "Don't look at me like that, Diana! It's two thousand and eighteen, threesomes are the norm for some people."

"I don't think I could ever do that!" Her eyes are about to pop out of her head.

"Why not? I think it would be so hot! Wish I would have had a chance to try it, before meeting my husband, but our sex life is perfect, and I wouldn't change a thing."

"You would have seriously done two guys at once?"

"If they looked like those two, hell yes! Don't knock it till you try it. Sometimes you need to let your slut out to see exactly what it is you are needing and wanting when it comes to your sex life."

"I don't know about that. I mean, I know I like to get wild, but with two men? How would I even approach them with it?"

"I am pretty sure you won't have to. Those two guys have a thing for you... I can see it. Let them approach you. You just need to give them the signal that you are ready and willing." I smile deviously at her. She blushes and smiles back.

The rest of our visit is just mainly talk about family and my pregnancy, but the two hours seems to go by so fast and next thing I know, Taven is walking into the club to pick me up.

"I thought you were busy and Xavier was going to bring me home?" I smile as he dips his head and kisses me lightly on the lips.

"I decided that I needed to see my gorgeous wife and couldn't wait any longer, so I came. Is that okay, or did you want alone time with Xavier?" He kids.

Punching him in the arm, "You are such an ass!" I laugh.

"Mm, I am what I eat!" He nuzzles my neck while Diana starts making gagging noises.

"That is so fucking gross!"

I chuckle and look over at my cousin, "Remember what I said earlier... don't knock it until you try it!" I wink at her as she stands up shaking her head.

"I think I will go see if Ash needs any help. You two are too much!" Diana eyes me incredulously.

"Don't forget what we talked about earlier... let it happen." I call after her. She raises her hand in response.

Turning back to Taven, "So, you are what you eat, huh? Not only are you an ass, you're also a pussy!" I grin.

"And that would make you, my love, a dick!" He claims my lips quick and then before I know what's going on, he is throwing me over his shoulder and stomping out of the club.

We don't even make it out of the parking lot before Taven is pulling the SUV into a secluded corner of Club Moon's parking lot. Putting the vehicle in park, he slides his seat back, unbuckles his pants, and pulls his girthy cock out, "Suck." It's the only word that comes out of his mouth and the dominant way he says it has my panties already wet.

I don't argue. I can't take my eyes off the slab of meat standing erect right in front of my face.

I lean over and slide my lips over just the tip, swirling my tongue around and smearing the pre-cum that leaks out. Taking more of him in my mouth, I moan at how soft and silky he is, but at the same time, he is hard as a rock. I begin to suck him up and down, hollowing out my mouth for just the right kind of suction. One hand is at the base using the same rhythm as my mouth, while my other hand wraps around his balls and begins their massage.

Taven is groaning and thrusting his hips, fucking my mouth the best he can in the little space available. He grabs the back of my head, tangling his fingers in my hair and starts moving my head up and down faster. It doesn't hurt, but it does turn me the fuck on and I start sucking even faster, moving my tongue around his cock as I go.

I feel his cock pulse, swelling as it does, and I know that any moment he will be filling my mouth with his hot stickiness. He doesn't disappoint. Slamming himself to the back of my throat, he holds my head still as he releases load after load down my throat. I try swallowing as fast as I can, but there is just too much and soon, it starts seeping out of my mouth. After a few more pumps, he pulls me up and there is a soft pop as my mouth releases his still hard cock. I swipe the cum that is dripping down my chin off and lick it off my finger.

"God you are so fucking beautiful. I need you to take your pants off now, because I want to fuck that delectable pussy of yours!" Taven's smoky eyes bare down on me.

"What... here? Someone will see us!" I gasp amusingly, but the very thought sends tingles throughout my body.

"Let them see! Let them see what they cannot have. I love the idea of fucking you and having someone watch and know that they will never get a piece of you!"

Hypnotized by his words and the seriousness of his facial expression, I find myself sliding my pants off, and I go further by pulling my shirt over my head and throwing that to the floor as well.

Moving over to his place behind the wheel, I throw my right leg over him and straddle his legs. His cock twitches in anticipation. Very slowly, I move up and position his cock at my wet entrance. I feel the head break through my opening and then I take my time, taking him in one inch at a time until finally his cock is sheathed completely, my pussy walls clamped around him. I lean in and take his lips and think, this right here... this is home.

TAVEN

God, the things that this woman does to me! I watch as she slowly takes my cock into her wet pussy. Her walls are clenching all around me, almost making me lose it right there. Once she has my cock completely tucked away, she brings her face down to mine for a gentle kiss.

"Are you ready, baby?" I ask, my voice low and husky.

She nods her head yes and I grab hold of her hips, lifting her up, and then I start fucking her fast and hard. Her tits are bouncing in my face and I grab hold of one of her nipples with my mouth, sucking and nipping as slam my cock into her. She cries out my name, which only makes me take her harder. I can feel the SUV rocking as I take her, but I don't care. Like I said, let them see.

I bring a hand between our bodies and start rubbing her clit. I can feel the pressure building within me as my balls ache for release, but I want her to come first. Just as I am about to explode, I pinch her sensitive bundle and she screams as her orgasm hits her so powerfully that she is crying out, "It hurts Taven, it hurts so good!"

I lose myself and my load right then and there. She continues bouncing up and down until she milks every last drop out of me. I sink my fangs into her and she is riding the orgasmic rollercoaster all over again.

"FUCK, BABY! You are so fucking wet!" I say once I've retracted my fangs.

"This is what you do to me, babe." She is still panting from her orgasms.

"I love hearing you say that. Tell me how you love it when I fuck you good." I demand.

"Your cock is so good; I could never be satisfied with another. I love how you stretch me and you know how to fuck me. Your cock is the only one my pussy ever wants!" Liz licks her lips as she gazes into my eyes.

"Good, because this pussy is mine... it belongs to me," I grab her ass with both hands and squeeze, "same goes for this fine piece of ass!"

She brings her head down and smashes her lips to mine. We both come away panting and gasping for air.

"Let's go home, warrior." Liz whispers as she slips off my shaft and settles back into her seat.

"Do not get dressed." I tell her, "I want you to remain naked. I am going to take you again when we get home." I can tell she is turned on at my statement, but also a little nervous of the fact that anyone that we drive by will see her nakedness. She doesn't realize that it turns me the fuck on, knowing that anyone can see her like this, but it's me and me only that gets to touch and take her.

I leave Liz sleeping peacefully in our bed and make my way over to the Compound. There are a few things I need to take care of right away, one being Mary-Beth. After Liz told him that she felt like she was being watched, Xavier left and then circled back around to the club by foot. Sure enough, he found Beth slinking around the perimeter. She was so in-tuned with Liz that she never saw Xavier sneak up on her. He brought her back to the Compound and threw her in a cell.

I am now standing in front of that cell glaring daggers at her, "What the fuck were you planning to do to my wife Beth?"

"Whatever do you mean Taven?" She asks all innocently, as if I am stupid.

"You know damn well what I mean... cut the bullshit, Beth!"

She casually strolls over to the glass, so we are only a foot apart. She devours me with her eyes as she bites her bottom lip. At one time, that look might have stirred something in me, but now, all it does is turn my stomach. She is still as beautiful as she was when we first met, but she has nothing on my mate.

"I am just trying to protect what is mine. I am your maker, Taven. You will do well to remember that." She looks me straight in the eye and cocks a brow at me as she crosses her arms at her chest.

"Yes, you made me into who I am today, but that is all. I despised you for centuries because of what you did, but that ended when I met Liz… my mate! I would have never met her if it weren't for you." I respond with a sneer, "But that doesn't mean that I have to like you."

"I don't care what you say, Taven. We were in love and I made a mistake, but now I am back, and I am claiming what is rightfully mine!"

"I am not yours, Beth. When are you going to get that through your head? We only have one true mate, and as you can clearly see, since Liz is pregnant with MY child, she is it for me!"

"Oh please! How do you know it's even your child? She could have slept with any regular person to get pregnant." She spat.

I am seeing red at this moment and she is damn lucky that there is this glass wall between us.

"Watch yourself, bitch! That is my mate and I do not like what you are insinuating about her!"

Something flashes in her eyes, "Does she keep the demon at bay like I did?" She asks.

"My demon stayed hidden when you were around, because it knew you weren't our mate. It revels in the knowledge that we now have our true mate and Liz embraces both of us!" I smile deviously at her, "Get it through that fucking head of yours… Liz is my mate, not you! The sooner you understand that and except it, the sooner we can all move on!"

"I will never except it Taven!"

"Fine, then you will be stuck in this cell for eternity, because I will not let you harm a hair on my wife's body!" I spin and walk away, turning all the lights out and leaving her in the dark, where she belongs.

No sooner had I gotten back to my office, my phone starts to buzz like crazy. I sigh deeply and reach in my pocket to retrieve it. Coco's name is lit up and I swipe to answer it.

"Hey Coco, what's up?"

She starts by telling me that they have been having issues at a local biker bar with biker members from opposing clubs starting shit with each other.

"At first, we thought it was regular people that were starting it, but then I answered a call and realized that it isn't just people, but vamps as well." She states hesitantly, "It's a never-ending battle, isn't it?"

"Yes, it is." I agree. Once I hang up with her, I call a meeting with my Warriors and let them in on what's all going on.

"I know we are all busy with detail work, but we will have to put that aside until we get this biker shit under control. I will be splitting up shifts into three and there will be five of you to each shift. Max, you and Raven will be part of it as well. I want as many of you out there as possible. Kole will be handling the technical stuff as always, but he will also help when needed, as will I." I look around the room before continuing, "I want reports on my desk after each shift. Xavier, Duncan, and Max will head each shift and if anyone has a problem with that, you can come see me."

I see them all lift their shoulders and shrug, letting me know that there are no issues. I was worried that Jax might have had one, seeing as he is one of my best Warriors, but he is also the newest, aside from the recruits, so it wouldn't be fair to Max. Besides, Max doesn't get much field work since he is also the Compound's chef and I want to remedy that. Liz has made it clear that she would love to help relieve Max with some of his duties, so I am taking her up on it. Pretty sure Max is thankful too.

I go with Xavier and his crew that night for the first shift, so I can see first-hand what we may be up against. It makes for a long boring evening, when I could be home getting laid by a beautiful woman. I'm sitting here thinking about how Liz looks when she has her lips wrapped around my cock and when I'm sliding into her wet tight pussy. My dick hardens with these thoughts, and I try to push them aside and keep my mind on the matter at hand.

"Boss… earth to Taven!" I shake my head at the sound of Xavier calling my name.

"Sorry, my head was somewhere else. What's up?"

"I was saying that it looks like things are starting to get a little rowdy. Maybe we should head in for a closer look."

I glance towards the bar, and sure enough, there are a few bikers outside, getting into each other's faces.

"Dammit, you're right…let's go."

Three of us head in for the time being, leaving Jagger and Dane watching from the SUV. We walk up casually, keeping our eyes on the growing crowd, and our ears open.

"I told you that your kind isn't welcome here! Are you deaf or just dumb?" One of the bikers from a group who wear all black leather and a patch across the back with the name Sons of the Devil on it, is up in another biker's face. The other biker is wearing a blue jean vest with their Biker Club name on the back… Dirt Hogs.

"Like I told you before, this bar is not affiliated to any specific club, so we have as much right to be here as you do!" The one in the jean vest fires back.

I sense right away that the Sons of the Devil are not your ordinary Biker gang. They are vampires.

Just as the one in black leather steps closer to the other guy, I speak up, "Is there a problem here?" I use my authoritative voice, hoping to calm the situation. These guys don't know me from Adam though, so they both sneer at me.

"Just keep walking. This has nothing to do with you!" The one in black tries to command.

"Yeah... unless you want issues... you need to walk." Jean vest guy pipes in.

"Well, I'm afraid I can't do that. You see, my team and I have been called in to deal with a bunch of rowdy fuckers and by the looks of it... that would be you guys!"

Jean vest guy snickers, "What? Are you the police?"

Xavier and Axel chuckle at his question. I smile at him, "We are better than the police. We are the Elite, and we like to keep order in this town. So, you can either back down... or we can take you in. It's your choice!"

I see that the members in the black leathers know exactly who we are, and they all take a step back. They are smart. As for the jean vest members... not so much. Of course, they wouldn't. They don't know who we are and what we are capable of, unlike the Sons of the Devil.

I ask the jean vest loudmouth to step the fuck down and he dares to step closer, trying to get in my face, even though he can't be much taller than five-foot-nine to my seven feet. I give him a crooked smile as six more of his crew try to circle around the three of us. I look up to the black leather guy and his smile matches my own, knowing full well the damage we can do.

Looking down at the jean vest guy, my arms crossed over my chest, I shake my head, "Don't be stupid, just walk away." I hear a motorcycle pull up behind me, but I don't turn.

Just as this short shit is about to make a move, I hear a female voice call out, "Johnny, you need to stop this! Why are you always looking for trouble?"

"Stay out of this Amanda! Go back to the club, now!" Jean vest guy yells back.

This tiny, slip of a girl comes and stands in front of me and Xavier, hands on her hips and her legs spread apart, taking her stance, "You don't have to follow in his footsteps Johnny... you are better than him!"

All of a sudden, this Johnny guys hauls off and back hands the young girl, who can't be much older than twenty, causing her head to whip to the side and loose her balance. Luckily, I am standing right here, and I catch her.

Xavier seems to lose his shit and picks the biker up by his neck, up over his head. He is squeezing the fuck out of the guy's neck, and I have to stop him before he crushes the asshole's windpipe.

"Xavier, put him down before you kill him." I sigh heavily. Xavier lets go and the douchebag drops to the ground like a sack of potatoes.

"Looks like you pissed off my warrior. Haven't you ever been taught not to lay a hand on a female?"

Johnny takes in a lung full of air, "She's my sister!" He sneers, as if it is totally okay to hit her.

"So, it's okay to hit your sister?" I ask incredulously.

"I need to keep her in line somehow!"

Xavier growls, and I put my hand on his shoulder to calm him. This is very unlike him, but I can't think on it too much right now.

"Get your ass over here, Amanda. Get away from them!" Johnny goes to grab his sister's arm, but Xavier gets to her first and quickly, but gently shoves her behind his massive body.

"What the fuck? That's my sister... get your hands off her!"

I look back at this Amanda girl, "Do you feel safe going home?"

She nods, "I'll be okay."

As gently as possible, I move her and nod towards her bike, "Get going then. We won't let him get into any more trouble tonight."

She looks between her brother and us. Her eyes widen as she looks up at Xavier and slowly backs up. Giving her brother one last look, she gets on her motorcycle and takes off. Leaving a cloud of dust behind her.

Turning back to this Johnny clown, "Now, I will say this one more time... either you can walk away, or we will have to take you in."

Johnny spits at the ground by my feet before turning around and walking to his own motorcycle. He looks at the Sons of the Devil, "This isn't over!" He revs his bike up and then takes off, his crew following him.

I sigh with relief. That guy was giving me a headache. I look over at the other group, "Mind telling me what's going on? I really don't want any of you getting exposed and I will not hesitate by taking any of you out, you know that."

The one that was arguing with Johnny steps forward and extends his hand, "I'm Wes, and this is some of my crew. We are not here to make trouble, but that motherfucker is a piece of shit! He comes in here, ordering everyone around. His father was so much worse, but he went and got himself killed, so now the son has taken over. He thinks he needs to fill his father's shoes. He has become worse over the last few weeks. Starting fights, abusing women… you name it. We just finally had enough of his bullshit and decided to do something about it."

"Well, thank you for letting us know. My men will be hanging around 24/7 from now on. We can handle it from here."

I go to turn away, but Wes stops me, "That Amanda girl, his sister… she isn't as safe as she thinks she is."

"What do you mean?" Xavier takes a step towards Wes, who in turn, takes a defensive step back.

"All I'm saying is that I've heard conversations about her. Her brother is trying to sell her virginity to the highest bidder within their club. I overheard him telling them that as soon as her virginity is taken, he will let her be passed around to the others." Wes's eyes look troubled, "I've talked to her a few times, and she is a very sweet girl. Kind, smart, and doesn't belong there. She has said how she wants to leave it all behind, but she doesn't want to leave her brother. He is all she has left, but he is damaged goods. Their father saw to that."

"Well, thanks again. We will definitely keep watch on her as well. Try and stay out of trouble in the future, okay?"

"Can't make any promises." Wes gives me a cheesy smile and I shake my head. Nodding at Xavier and Axel to follow, we head back to the SUV to finish off our shift.

Xavier's fists are clenched tight, and I see rage in his eyes. I have seen that look before… hell, I have had that look before. I blow out a breath and smile to myself, this ought to be fun!

TWENTY-ONE

LIZ

It's my morning to cook breakfast, since Max just got off his detail at the biker bar. Even though I am taking over some of the duties, he still leaves a menu on what he wants served. I see the said menu hanging on the fridge and I shake my head with a smile, "He is such a shithead." I mumble to myself and then jump as I feel arms come around me, "Oh, my fucking God!"

"Did I scare you?" Taven's deep voice whispers in my ear.

"Do you have to sneak up on me like that?" I try to be stern with him, but when he spins me around and I look into those beautiful light blue eyes, I smile.

"I honestly didn't mean to, sweetheart, forgive me?" He nuzzles my neck knowing it makes me melt.

"Always." I wrap my arms around his neck, but I pull away quickly when I feel his arousal. "Taven! Did you not get enough last night?" I laugh.

"I never get enough of you, baby."

"Well, I have work to do, so it will have to wait."

"What were you mumbling about when I came in?" He asks me.

"Oh, it's nothing. Max leaves a menu for me when it's my shift. I think I'm going to rebel and make my own thing though. Just for shits and giggles."

"You are playing with fire, woman." Taven chuckles.

"Hm, I love living dangerously!"

Taven laughs and then slaps my ass, "I will leave you be then. Just wanted to stop by to say I love you. See you soon."

"Awe, I love you too, babe. Muah…" I blow him a kiss as he walks out. He pretends to catch it, making me giggle, "Big bad vampire my ass!" I say to myself out loud.

"I heard that!" I hear Taven yell from down the hallway.

I've just finished cleaning up and I am now making a tray up to take to Mary-Beth when my boys come bounding into the kitchen.

"Hey you two! Do you need any breakfast, or did you already eat at the house?"

"We had cereal at home." Jack replies, "What are you doing now?"

"I need to take this to a prisoner down in the cells."

"Oh, can we come with you?" Jack asks.

"Yeah…I want to go!" Nate jumps up and down.

"Oh, alright, but you need to behave!"

We make our way downstairs and Stone is the only one in the guard room at the moment.

"Hey Stone, I have Beth's breakfast. Can you unlock her cell for me?"

"Sure can, boss lady!"

"Ugh! Stop calling me that! My name is Liz… L.I.Z.…. got it?"

"Yep, sure do, boss lady!"

I roll my eyes at his shit-eating grin and then follow him to the cell. Beth looks like she is still in bed sleeping as Stone unlocks the door. His cell phone buzzes, and he looks down, "It's the boss."

"That's okay, she is sleeping, and I will be in and out."

He nods his head as he turns and takes a few steps away. I walk over and place the tray on the bedside table and turn to leave, but Beth is standing right in my way. There is a sadistic smile on her face as she leers at me.

"Step away Beth." I command her, but she doesn't move.

"Oh, nobody here to protect you now, is there?"

"You won't dare try anything, because Taven will kill you if you do!" I move my hands over my stomach to protect my baby.

She takes a few more steps towards me and my legs hit the back of the nightstand, "Let me through Beth!"

"Taven is mine, whore! He was mine first and he will always be mine! You and your brats need to leave him alone!" She spits at me when she speaks, and I feel it hit my face.

Wiping my face, I straighten up and glare right at her, "I am Taven's mate, and I will never give him up, he's mine!"

Beth gives me a murderous look just before she jumps at me and latches on to my neck. It stuns me for a moment, but then I watch as both of my boys jump on her back and each bite down on both sides of her neck. I scream and then Beth screams as my boys tear out a piece of her neck. She flings them off her as she is still drinking from me. My body is on fire, like I am burning from the inside.

Beth is snatched from me, tearing some flesh on my neck. I watch as Stone lifts her up over his head and brings her down over his knee, breaking her back. Taven flashes in just in time to see Stone's handy work. Taven looks at me and the damage to my neck. Fury like I've never seen emits from him. He spins back to Beth and picks her up, jarring her broken back and causing her to scream.

"I told you to never to touch my mate! You will pay, bitch!" He clenches his teeth together as he takes her head and twists, then pulls until she is completely decapitated.

I bring my hand up to my mouth and then look over at my boys who are now staring in awe at Taven. I look back at my husband and he is shaking as he makes his way over to me. He drops to his knees and pulls me into his arms.

"I am so sorry, baby. She will never hurt you again!" I throw my arms around him, but I am feeling so weak that I can't hug him tightly. He looks down at me and his eyes go wide before he is biting into his wrist and letting his blood pour into my mouth, "Drink it, baby!"

I start to swallow, but it's a struggle. Finally, after what seems to be longer than a few minutes, I am starting to feel better. By the time I pull away, the flesh on my neck has already knitted itself back together. I sit up straighter, and my boys throw themselves at me.

"Thank you, boys. You pretty much saved your mama!" I look at the both of them, "You did good, she was a bad person." I can't believe how my two precious boys jumped to my rescue; it was a natural instinct to them. Maybe I should be horrified, but I'm not. This is who they are now, and they are going to grow up to be fine young men... or vampires... however you want to look at it.

I look up at Stone, "Thank you for getting her when you did."

"I just wish I had pulled her off a little more gently. She wouldn't have torn your neck if I had. I just became crazy when I saw her feeding from you."

"No, Stone. You did fine, I'm okay." I smile up at him.

Taven picks me up and carries me out and to our house. I can feel his heart pounding a mile a minute and I reach up to cup his cheek.

"It's okay. I am fine, you can calm down now. Your heart is beating a mile a minute, babe."

"I can't help it! I heard you scream, and I flashed right over, thinking I was going to find you and our daughter dead." He places his forehead against mine.

"I am fine now, and you took care of her. You and our boys... and Stone."

We are at the house now and he is making his way up to our bedroom. The boys come running in as Taven lays me down.

"Mom, we cleaned ourselves up. Can we go play now?" I look shockingly at them. They just tore the neck out of a vampire, and they are acting as if it's just another day. I shake my head yes and turn back to Taven.

"I think you may be a bad influence on the boys." I chuckle.

"Nah, they just knew that they needed to protect you. Their instincts kicked in. Now they are themselves again." He shrugs, "Why don't you get some rest, love."

I'm really not in the mood to rest, so I play with him for a moment, "Can you help me undress? I want to get out of these clothes."

"Of course." He helps lift the shirt over my head and then slides my pants all the way off.

"Underwear too, please." I ask.

He pulls my panties and bra off and I can see his eyes smoldering while he looks down at me. He leans over and kisses my forehead, before he goes to leave. I call out to him once he reaches the door and he turns to find that I am spread open and rubbing my clit, while playing with a nipple with the other hand. He moans.

"Liz, you need to rest!" He is saying this as he slowly makes his way back to the bed.

"No, what I need is you. I need you to shove your face into my pussy and get me really wet, so you can fuck me good!" I don't break eye contact with him the whole time I am telling him my needs.

He growls and begins to rip his clothes off, "If you put it that way, how can I refuse?"

He comes at me like a tiger stalking its prey and I spread my legs wider for him to feast. Lifting my legs up and over his shoulders, he lightly licks from the bottom of my lips to the top, swirling his tongue around my clit before doing it all over again. I grab his head and grind my hips, shoving his face up against my sex. His tongue enters and fucks me as his fingers tease my sensitive nub. I'm moaning and grinding because it feels so fucking good, but it doesn't seem to be enough. He senses this through our bond and inserts two fingers into my slit, spreading them like scissors as he pumps them in and out. I feel the pleasure building within and start moving my hips faster and he keeps up with my tempo. He takes my clit into his mouth and gives it a deep suck and I let go, wrapping my thighs around his head tightly.

Once it subsides, I'm left panting, but he isn't done with me yet. He flips me over and pulls my hips up, so my ass is in the air. I can feel my juices flowing down my thighs and he dips down to lick each side, not wanting to waste any of my nectar.

"God, you taste so good! I can never get enough of you!" He then plunges his cock into me and doesn't let up. I am begging for my release. I feel him insert just the tip of his thumb into my tight puckered ring and I shatter, screaming with the intense orgasm ripping through me. "That's it, cream all over my cock, baby." I hear Taven, but I can't focus on his words, he has me completely out of it.

I collapse with him still inside, taking him down with me. He places soft kisses along my back and then moves some hair away from my face and whispers, "Get up. I'm not done with you yet."

My limbs are like jelly as I try to do as he says, but eventually, I am able to sit up. He lays down with his back propped up with pillows and crooks his finger at me, telling me to come over.

"I will give you a little reprieve, but you will suck my cock while you recoup." He smiles at me, and I give him one in return. He would never let me rest before, just keep going until he was satisfied as well. He knows that the bigger I get with his child, the more I do need to rest, and he is considerate. Just like he will not take me to the playroom again until after the baby comes, because he doesn't want to do anything that may hurt her.

I crawl up and between his legs, taking his big cock with both my hands. It's slick with my cum and my hands glide up and down easily, but Taven doesn't want a hand job. He takes hold of the back of my head and guides my face down to his waiting erection. I gently lick the tip before I give it a nice quick suck and then advance down, taking as much of it as I can in. I love his cock. It's so big and the thought of it hitting every pleasurable spot inside of me turns me on instantly. I start pumping faster, hollowing out my cheeks for the kind of suction that I know he loves.

Taven is groaning with every stroke my mouth gives as he fucks my mouth hard and fast. I can feel him swelling and I go even faster, swirling my tongue around his shaft, but he pulls me off of him with a grunt. I am not disappointed for long, though. Lifting me up, he brings me down, so I am straddling him. I land right on his cock, and he slides right in, holding me there but for a moment.

"Ride me, baby. Take all of me inside of that perfect pussy of yours and don't stop until we are both coming!" He leans in and claims my lips as I start moving back and forth. I start off slow at first, but then he is pinching and squeezing my very sensitive nipples and I start fucking him like never before. He releases my lips and stares down at where our sexes meet.

"Oh yeah, just like that. Fuck my cock good, my dirty little girl!" He nips at my nipples, and I throw my head back, crying out because it hurts so good. I feel his fangs pierce my tit right above my nipple and I come... hard! The best orgasm is when he is drinking from me. It feels like I am flying and then tumbling into space. My body is trembling with all the sensations that his bite gives me and just when my climax peaks, fireworks explode all through my body and I continue to tumble.

"FUCK ME, TAVEN! Don't stop...please don't stop!" I am screaming for more even though the climax is too much. It borders on painful, but it's a pleasurable pain.

He releases my tit and stops pumping, but grinds his cock into me, extending the orgasm that is tearing my body apart, "Yes baby, keep going. Give it all to me!"

Finally, I start falling back down to earth. Breathing so hard, trying to catch my breath. I open my eyes and see the love shining through Taven's as he smiles at me. Without saying a word, I bite down on his neck and his body jerks.

"God damn, baby! That feels so good... suck harder. That's it, drink..." He holds my head to his neck as he begins trusting up into me.

I meet his thrusts as I take big pulls from his neck. He his groaning and calling my name the closer he gets to exploding. With one last pull, he roars and fills me up to the brim.

TAVEN

Fuck, I can't take anymore! Liz takes one more big pull and I explode like dynamite, filling her pussy up with so much cum that it's running out and soaking the bed. I roar out her name as I give her my load, pretty sure they can hear me from the Compound.

Liz pulls away from my neck and I love the way she looks with my blood around her lips. Just as much as when she has my cum seeping out of her mouth. My cock is still jerking inside of her pussy as I continue to empty inside of her. Leaning back, I and gaze into her eyes as I rub her belly and my unborn child. This woman is everything to me and she has given me everything. I don't know how to ever repay her, except to love and cherish her always.

Now that my cock has finally quieted down and is bone dry, I lean back into Liz and lick the blood from around her lips before claiming them completely, "God, I love you, Liz!" I mumble against the softness of her lips.

"I love you too, warrior." She sighs.

We reposition ourselves, so I have her cradled in my arms with her head laying on my chest. I stroke her side up and down, causing goosebumps to appear all over her body, making he giggle.

"I think this might have been the best sex yet!" She says, snuggling deeper into my side.

"Sweetheart, sex with you is always the best! Just think, we get to do this for eternity." I hug her tighter to me, never wanting to let go.

Liz and I shower after a quick little nap and then go our separate ways. Her going to find the boys to get some lessons in and me, to my office to look over reports.

Max knocks on my door just as I sit down and smiles at me when I wave him in. Not sure what he has to be smiling about, unlike me, who has just been fucked thoroughly.

"What's up, Max?"

"I put my report on your desk, but I wanted to talk to you personally about a message I am supposed to give you." He is still smiling and it's starting to become unnerving.

"For Christ's sake, what is up with the shit-eating grin you have going on?" I growl. My good mood is starting to dissipate the more Max stands there.

"Oh, nothing at all. Like I said, I have a message for you, and it is kind of urgent."

"Well, why have you waited this long to give it to me?" I am now very annoyed.

"Hm, maybe because I knew how busy you have been all morning, I didn't want to interrupt. Besides, I was trying to keep Jack and Nate from running to their mother's aid again when they heard the two of you screaming!" Max now has a twinkle in his eye, and I finally catch on as to why he is acting strange. I can't help but smile myself.

"Yeah, it was pretty intense. Sorry for jumping down your throat."

"Please rephrase that last sentence," Max laughs, "I don't think Liz would like that too much." He winks at me.

"Fuck you, you sicko! You are not my type." I roll my eyes at him. "Anyway, what's this message?"

"Oh yeah, so this vamp came walking up to the SUV and handed me this piece of paper to give to you. I don't know what it's all about. He just said that he needed to speak to you as soon as possible, then he walked away."

I open the piece of paper and all that was scribbled on it was a cell phone number and it was signed by Wes. I quickly explained to Max who Wes is and then I dial the number right away. Wes picked up on the second ring.

"Talk to me." He answers.

"Wes, it's me, Taven with the Elite. I had a message to call you?"

"Oh yes. Listen, I know you guys mainly handle vamp stuff, but I thought you would like to know that I think something is wrong with Amanda. The sister of that asshole, Johnny."

"Why do you think that?"

"Well, she usually comes into the bar every day at the same time and shoots pool. I haven't seen her in here since that night. I am not sure if you want to check into it but seeing as how protective you and your man was of her that night, figured I had better tell you."

Shit! This is the last thing I need. I can't just let this go, especially if what I am thinking is true.

"Thanks Wes. Now that you have my number, keep me informed of everything you think I need to know about."

"Sure thing. I hope you find her and that she is okay."

"Me too, Wes... me too." I hang up and sigh heavily.

"What's up, boss?" Max is still standing there with a questioning look on his face. I relay the conversation to him, "I will round the men up in the meeting room."

"Thanks. Oh, and don't mention what the meeting is about, especially to Xavier. I want to be there when he hears it."

Max gives me a strange look, but nods and walks out of my office.

All my Warriors are in the Conference room when I get there. I go over my conversation with Wes, my eyes always coming back to land on Xavier, waiting for what I knew would come. Once I am finished, I can see the rage in his eyes, but the explosion never comes. He is the first to leave the room and as I am sitting here thinking maybe my feeling is wrong, we all heard a loud bang and the Compound shakes. At first, I think it is an actual explosion, but as I run out to the hallway, I see a huge hole in the cement wall of the hallway and Xavier stomping away.

Fuck! I knew this wouldn't be good.

EPILOGUE

TAVEN

I am sitting here with my men staking out the place that the Dirt Hogs call home. It is almost like a Compound, something like one of our old ones. It has taken us over a month to locate this place. We still have no word on Amanda. We don't know if she is safe or if the worst has happened to her. The members have been stirring up shit all over town, thinking they own it. Even the local police force has been working on this case.

Xavier has been in the foulest mood since the news of Amanda's disappearance, and he will not talk to me about it. He just keeps telling me that he is fine. I know better. I also know the look of a vampire trying to fight fate. I should know, I was the same way. I really don't know too much of Xavier's past. He isn't one to share too much of his private life, but he is a damn good warrior, so I let it be.

Our plan of action tonight is to just do a basic check of the member's homes, which means sneaking onto their property and become peeping toms. I know, why not just go in with guns blazing, but we still need to do this by the book since they are regular people and not vamps or shifters.

We each take a building on the property and scurry undetected. It isn't looking good at all. These are some sick motherfuckers. Half-naked women, some completely naked, run around laughing and giggling while men chase after them. Couples having sex in the same room as others eating their dinner or watching television. Kids running around playing while all this is going on. What the fuck is this shit?

With my stomach turning, I leave to head back to the waiting vehicles. Everyone's reports are the same as mine. Sick, twisted, and demented things going on, but no sign of Amanda.

As we start loading back into the vehicles, I place my hand on Xavier's shoulder, "We will find her, I promise."

Xavier shrugs my hand away angrily and stomps off. I sigh and climb into the SUV. I feel for him, I really do, and I won't stop until we find her. I just hope that it doesn't destroy my warrior before we do.

I get back to the Compound and see Dr. Howard's car parked in front. That's weird, I don't remember Liz telling me that the Doc was coming. I come into panic-mode and hurry into the Compound. Just as I walk through the door, I hear Liz through our bond.

'It's time Taven. Our little girl is on her way.'

'I'm here! I just walked in…I'm coming.'

Panic turns into excitement as I flash over to medical and see Liz already prepared to give birth. Cassie and Jill are on each side of her helping her through her contractions. As I move closer, Jill moves over to Cassie's side, so I can be by my mate. I take her hand in mine and bring it to my lips.

"How are you doing, baby?"

"It's not too bad right now, but we just started the epidural, so the pain is already going away." She beams up at me.

Doc is between Liz's legs checking her, "We have a little bit yet. Just try to relax for now." She smiles at Liz and then steps out of the room.

"Do you want us to leave, Liz?" Cassie asks.

Before Liz can answer, I am shouting, "NO! Honestly, I am scared shitless and don't know what to do. I would appreciate both your help." I chuckle nervously, "That is, if it's alright with you, sweetheart?" I say to Liz.

Smiling, she squeezes my hand, "I was going to say the exact same thing. I mean, I'm not nervous, I've already done this twice before, but I am worried about you."

Relief floods through me. Yeah, big bad vampire… I know! Liz's mumbling from the other day echoes through my head.

As the hours pass, I start to think that something is wrong, but Dr. Howard promises me that everything looks good. Then, out of the blue, she is urging Liz to push. Cassie and I are holding her hands as Jill rubs her back.

"You need to push, Liz. That's right…just like that. You are doing good! Okay, relax for a moment." Doc instructs Liz.

Liz falls back to the bed and smiles up at me. I kiss her forehead and smile back, "You are doing so good, baby!"

"You are too, warrior." She smirks and winks at me.

I can't help but to stare at this gorgeous woman that I get to call my mate, my wife, and the mother of my children. Love for her floods my entire being.

I hear the doctor telling Liz to push and I turn my focus back to the delivery.

"Keep pushing, honey, the head is coming!" Doc is telling Liz, "That's it…just a little more. Okay, relax… the head is out!"

I look down and see a head full of blonde hair and tears spring to my eyes.

"Now Liz, when I tell you to push again, I need you to just push a little. We need to get her shoulders out and I don't want you tearing yourself. Do you understand?"

"Yes." Liz is panting heavily.

"Okay… push."

Less than five minutes later, our little girl is out and screaming her lungs out; music to my ears!

"Okay Dad, come cut the cord." Doc is holding out a strange looking pair of scissors towards me and I take them as she instructs me on where to cut. The emotion that runs through me at the very moment that I separate child from mother is so overwhelming. My face is soaked with tears, but I don't care, let them all see! Doc's assistant takes my daughter over to another table, so she can check her out and get measurements before wrapping her up and placing her in my arms.

I walk over to Liz and hand her over, even though I don't want to let go. She opens her eyes and the bluest eyes that I have ever seen stare back at us. They look to be a mixture of Liz's color and my own. I've never seen the likes; just beautiful.

Everyone congratulates us and then quietly leaves the room, leaving just the three of us together. I kiss Liz on the lips and smile down at her.

"I thought the day you became my mate would be the happiest day, then our wedding day came, and I thought the same thing. Now you have given me a daughter and that tops it all. I feel like I am slacking in the department of gifting you with the treasures that you have been gifting me with." I don't hold the emotion back but let it all pour out.

Liz's eyes fill up with tears, "Taven, don't you know that everything you say I have given you is the same exact as what you have given me. We complete each other in every way."

I have never thought about it that way. I bend down and take her lips with mine. I pull away just as a head pokes in the door… it's Jack.

"Can we come in?"

"You sure can, buddy. Come meet your baby sister!" I chuckle as both Jack and Nate run in the room.

"What's her name?" Nate asks.

"I think we should all agree on a name for her. What do you think, Mom?" I ask my wife.

"I think that it a great idea." She smiles at the three of us.

A couple hours later Dr. Howard steps in to check on mom and baby. Seeing that everything looks good, she makes an appointment for us to come in a couple weeks for another check-up.

"The gang is all out there waiting to see…how did they put it? Oh yes… the boss child." She giggles and shakes her head, "That is a strange bunch out there."

"You have no idea!" Liz rolls her eyes and laughs, "You can send them in, thank you."

Doc wasn't kidding. Every single warrior, along with Cassie, Jill, and Jennifer come hauling ass in, trying to get to the baby first. It was a sight, let me tell you.

They are all cooing and ah-ing over our daughter.

"So? What is the princess's name?" Cassie rubs her hands together.

"What does it matter? All these barbarians are going to call her "Boss child" anyway!" The room erupts in laughter.

"No, seriously," Jax speaks up, "What's her name?"

"Well, we and the boys came up with it together." I say, "Meet Mina Elizabeth Anderson!" I smile proudly.

They all love the name. Handshakes and hugs go all around and then they slowly start filing out of the room. It's just the five of us left in the room… our little family. I stand here and think back to before I met Liz. My life was a little desolate. Yeah, I had my warriors… my brothers, but I wanted more… needed more. Then this unbelievable woman walks into my life with her kids, and I fell in love. It wasn't just our bond. I truly believe that if we would have met before I turned into a vampire, our lives would have turned out the same, but hey, who knows for sure.

This woman broke down my walls, accepted the demon inside of me, and gave us all her love. Instead of being destroyed by my demon, I finally embraced it and with her by my side, I know I can handle all the demons in the world. Liz is not only my mate, my wife, and the mother of our children… she is what I have always looked for and everything that I have always needed. She is my Salvation!

www.ingramcontent.com/pod-product-compliance
Lightning Source LLC
LaVergne TN
LVHW041659060526
838201LV00043B/494